WHEN THE RECKONING COMES

ALSO BY LATANYA MCQUEEN

And It Begins Like This

WHEN THE
RECKONING
COMES

A Novel

LaTanya McQueen

HARPER ● PERENNIAL

NEW YORK ● LONDON ● TORONTO ● SYDNEY ● NEW DELHI ● AUCKLAND

HARPER ● PERENNIAL

HarperCollins books may be purchased for educational, business, or sales promotional use. For information please email the Special Markets Department at SPsales@harpercollins.com.

FIRST EDITION

Designed by Jen Overstreet

Library of Congress Cataloging-in-Publication Data has been applied for.

ISBN 978-0-06-303504-1

21 22 23 24 25   BR   10 9 8 7 6 5 4 3 2 1

For those who have yet to see.

What will you do on the day of reckoning,
when disaster comes?
To whom will you run for help? Where
will you leave your riches?

—ISAIAH 10:3

WHEN THE RECKONING COMES

They are coming. In life, heavy was the crown of chains meant to keep their bodies down, but their spirits soon will rise. They are coming with their shackles, wearing them like armor, fuel that reminds them of their purpose. They bring the chains made from wrought iron, used across the wrists and ankles as they were stolen onto ships. They bring the iron collar, placed on as punishment, its four prongs sticking out to keep them still. They bring the leg irons, two horseshoe-shaped rings cuffed around the ankles with a bar between. The metal once rubbed against their skin, causing it to bruise and break. They are coming with the branding irons shaped with the initials of the men who seared their flesh, forever marking them with their names. Their own names were taken, erased, but they have them back now. The iron is hot from the burning flame. The skin will flush red after, the dermis deep enough to easily slough off. What remains will be the mark of the men and women who once owned them. They come bringing tools to slaughter and maim. One holds a gelding knife. His hand tightens around the handle, ready to take.

They are coming with the whip with its nine knotted lashes. Their hands carry glass jars of what will be rubbed in after. Turpentine. Lime juice. Hot brine. Piss. Whatever will make flesh sting. Virtue, you preached, came from being beaten. Redemption from blood. With the knotted whip raised high you delivered your sermon. The strike of the lash cracking the skin. In return the faltering pulse. Nearby, they watched in the fields as you then held your sons' hands, teaching your boys to practice the whip on the trees' flesh. Aim for the middle, you taught, imagine the trunk is the space between the shoulder blades, the safest spot to do the most harm.

They come wearing the clothes they died in. Clothes worn day in and day out when they were alive. See the house servants with their castoffs. They are barefoot, subjecting themselves to blisters and cuts rather than suffer wearing anything that would make them hotter. They wear quantiers. Softened oxhide cut to the shape of a foot and tied together with string. They wear the shoes bought by their masters. Children in calico slacks. Men tipping their straw hats to the women as they move further along. Women in their Christmas clothes, a few with ribbons tied in their hair.

How long, did you think, after all of this, it would be before their souls finally came for you in the night? These men and women remember. They remember the sight of their husbands and sons hanged from the trees they worked under. They remember the feel of the cold metal on their ankles. They remember the taste of it as the iron bit was forced in their mouths. They remember the taste of their own blood mixing with their saliva as it dripped down their faces, soaking what rags of clothes they wore.

It is too late to speak of such stories now, for they are coming—ready to sneak into your rooms, tiptoe through the familiar hallways, to find you and your loved ones in their beds, and maybe some of you will sense a shift in the air, something unfamiliar in the room, and maybe you'll open your eyes to see, catch a glimpse, but it will not be long, for make no mistake—they will not flinch, they will not hesitate, they have come for you, they have come, and as you open your eyes the last thing you'll see is the ax as the blade strikes down.

Do you see them hovering in the shadows? They are out there hiding in the thicket and behind the darkness of the trees. Hush and you can hear. It's been said that on a quiet day in the woods a sound can carry for miles, although trees can absorb it and there's also the thrush of branches against the wind, stifling what noise can be heard. In the summer, the sudden bursts of rain pound against the earth. Nature's inhabitants— the birds perched on branches or the frogs with their mating calls—fill the woods with their croak and thrum, their whistle and pitter. During locust season, everywhere, you can hear their high-pitched hum, making the air feel electric and alive. Late at night there is the sound of dogs on a scent, followed by their last, yelping howl.

Hush though, and listen. If you're quiet, you can hear their whispers in the water calling to those left behind. Hush and you can hear them lurking, waiting for the day they can make their return.

I.

AFTER, PEOPLE HAD asked Mira what she saw. After the arrest, followed by his release, for months afterward, people would ask, classmates at school, strangers even, whenever she found herself alone, they'd come up and want to know another truth—what happened out in those woods? At the house? Were there others like they say? Ghosts, we've heard. Spirits. Demons. We've heard the rumors and want to know. There must be more than you're telling. Has to be. What'd you see?

It took leaving to make the questions stop, but after having been gone for more than a decade, she was returning to Kipsen. Mira was driving home for the wedding of her childhood friend Celine, someone she now could say she barely knew.

Since Mira left, Celine had managed to make a life for herself. She'd gotten a cosmetology license and worked at the hair salon downtown. She had a series of regulars who tipped her well and she had managed to earn up enough to afford a semblance of a middle-class life, or at least play the part, enough so that when Phillip met her for the first time he didn't see what the rest of the town used to—a poor trash girl who'd once lived in the black part of town.

Celine had called her a couple months ago out of the blue. Mira was sitting at her desk grading when she saw the flashing light from her desk phone. School had let out for the day, and while she could have gone home, she preferred to finish her work in the classroom, to not bring any remnants of the job with her when she left. She hesitated in picking up to take the call, worried it was her principal wanting to talk further about the incident with one of her students, but soon relented, fearing if he did want to talk it was better to get it over with.

When she answered, she found that it wasn't the principal or anyone from the school calling, but Celine, and she was calling to say how she'd met the love of her life and was getting married. She wanted Mira to be there for her.

"It took me forever to find you. What kind of person isn't on social media? You've done a good job of disappearing. Almost, anyway. Your school has this number listed on its directory and it came up when I searched for your name. Thank goodness I thought to do that. Oh, Mira, just say yes and I'll send out the invitation. Look, I know we haven't really talked in forever, but it's my wedding."

Mira sat back in her chair, overwhelmed by Celine's exuberance and in how quickly she fell into an easy, unearned familiarity, as if it had always been this way between them, as if it was yesterday since they last talked and not years. Celine's giggly and energetic voice ushered in Mira a slight pang of nostalgia for their shared past. "His name's Phillip Hunnicutt. He's from Kipsen, or at least his mother is. She married into the Hunnicut family and moved back after their divorce. Aldridge is her name."

"Doesn't ring a bell."

"Not surprising, I guess. I don't remember anyone named Aldridge either, but the Hunnicuts? Of Honey Leaf Tobacco? Everyone knows that name. I think I smoked some of their cigarettes when we were kids. He's the grandson or something but he didn't want anything to do with the company so he owns a dentist practice. It's a little dull if you ask me though."

"How'd you meet a guy like that?"

"What are you trying to say?"

"Just that I wouldn't have imagined he'd want to live in Kipsen, and if he did, he'd be keeping to himself," Mira stumbled out, having picked up on the tension in Celine's response. Celine's emphasis on *trying*—what are you *trying* to say? The implication being Mira had meant more and had somehow failed to say it. A subtle yet targeted insult to distract from her own defensiveness.

"Well, you're right. I'd been trying to meet him since he moved here but couldn't figure out a good way to do it. The practice has been booked for months and months. Then Janice, one of my clients, said that she'd known his mother. That's why he came back—his mother was sick, ovarian cancer, and she didn't want to leave Kipsen, so he returned to be with her. Janice was throwing a small gathering at her house and invited me along. He took one look at me and that was that."

"That was that," Mira repeated. Of course. That's how it'd always been with Celine. Men looked at her and wanted her for her beauty but despite being beautiful, she was never able to hide her insecurities and after all these years she hadn't gotten any better. Underneath her pretense was the simmer of resentment for a poor childhood. While they'd all been poor—Mira, Celine, and especially Jesse, Celine dealt with her circumstances differently, harboring a bitterness for what she felt life owed her. Jesse used to tell Mira it was because Celine was white. "She thinks she shouldn't be struggling like the rest of us."

"That's not true," Mira would say, much to Jesse's irritation.

"You're always defending her."

"She's my friend. I thought she was yours too."

"I can be her friend and still criticize her sometimes."

Mira often felt like the glue between Jesse and Celine, sensing if not for her they would have ended their friendship a long time ago. As they'd gotten older, he'd become more suspicious of Celine, judging her because she was a white girl who chose to be friends with two black kids in segregated Kipsen. He'd often judged Mira too for siding with Celine instead of him when he made comments like these.

This divide hadn't always existed. Somehow, over the years of their friendship, Jesse forgot how they'd all become friends, but Mira remembered. It was early January of her first year of middle school, the air hovering above freezing, and Mira blew on her hands to keep them warm, watching as Celine approached her. Strands of her blond hair bunched at the top of the puffer jacket she wore. The jacket had a hole near the bottom and Mira could see bits of the interior peeking out. The jacket was a faded pink, the color of the Pepto Bismol Mira's mother used to make her choke down. Celine raised a hand and Mira noticed that Celine wore two mismatched mittens—one black, the other pink, the color of her coat.

Mira thought better than to comment on it when Celine introduced herself, and instead listened as she explained how they'd just moved into one of the houses up for rent.

"Which one?" Mira asked, curious.

"It's blue. Three eighteen Milson Road? Do you know it?"

Mira didn't, but only because so many houses went up for sale only to be foreclosed months later, the owners gutting the insides of anything of value to make up a fraction of what they lost. On her block Mira knew of at least four houses like these. Families moved into them because the rent was cheap but often left shortly after—because they couldn't make the payments, because they were in search of a better dream, because in the end, they couldn't bring themselves to live in this part of Kipsen. Whatever the reason, there was enough transition in the neighborhood that it didn't matter which house it was Celine had moved into. She probably wouldn't be staying in it for long.

Soon after, their bus came. Mira climbed its steps, found a seat, and sat near the window. She was surprised when Celine sat next to her, but there weren't many white students on the bus, since most had their parents to drive them or they carpooled with others. Celine also seemed like the type to need to be around people, or at least attention, and wouldn't have wanted to sit alone. She wouldn't stop talking and she filled the minutes of the ride with offerings about her life. Mira continued to listen as she rambled on about nothing in particular—television shows she'd watched the night before, her favorite subjects in school, a crush she had on the member of a boy band Mira had never heard of.

"You're so quiet. I've been talking so much. You got nothing to say?"

Behind them, the sound of snickering turned to a roar of laughter. A cluster of black students sat in the rear of the bus. Mira knew the students were making fun of them. Before Celine had entered the picture, they would tease Mira for preferring to sit up front near the exit. She didn't realize they viewed her action as a kind of denial. As the bus continued on its route, it picked up more students, and the dynamics sharpened. White faces crowded around her. To the black kids it looked like she chose to be with them.

Sitting with Celine had made the situation worse, but since Celine ignored what was going on Mira chose to ignore it too. One kid named Marcus was the worst. "Don't she look like one of those snowballs? Those cake things?" he yelled, commenting not just because of her jacket but because it was a play on snow-flake, a name he gave to any white person he saw.

The rest of Marcus's friends howled with laughter, and they all joined in the jeering.

Mira lifted her head to look back at Marcus, who made no attempt to hide his insults. Celine continued to ignore him, but Mira couldn't concentrate on anything except Marcus and his group sitting behind them.

The insults got louder. Soon, the whole bus was laughing at the two of them. Mira lowered in her seat a little, but when she saw Celine was unfazed she straightened up again and forced herself to listen to Celine continue her conversation.

"Quit it, Marcus. It's getting tired," someone finally yelled in response, and Mira looked to see a lanky boy with a reddish-tinted Afro of curls. He caught Mira's gaze before shifting to the window.

"Don't tell me what to do," Marcus snapped. "Hey, snowball, will you let me taste your cream?" Marcus yelled, laughing.

With that, Jesse got up from his seat and moved toward the front of the bus. He found the seat across from Mira and Celine and sat down. He didn't say anything but gave a simple nod, a subtle affirmation to let them know they were not alone. Marcus hollered for him to come back, but Jesse ignored him.

Marcus and his friends quieted soon after. It was clear to them Jesse had made a choice, and the insult of his decision silenced them. Jesse didn't ask to join Celine and Mira's conversation. He opened the flap of his bookbag and took out a photography book, one of portraiture, and flipped through the images. Throughout the rest of the ride, he concerned himself with the book and nothing else.

"Well," Celine huffed when they hopped off the bus, grabbing his arm and pulling him to her. "If you're going to do all that, we might as well at least know your name." Celine wrapped her other arm around Mira as they huddled along the sidewalk to the school building.

After that, they were always together. Despite whatever disagreements between them, they stood by each other because in a way they were all each other had. All through middle school and into high school they remained friends, until that day in the woods when everything fell apart and Mira moved away.

Celine was getting married. They hadn't needed to keep in touch for Mira to know how much this wedding meant. As teenagers, Celine filled their spare conversations with talk of gowns and decorations, flavors of cake and themes. Mira entertained the fantasy with her. They had so little in their lives that the dream of a wedding felt extravagant. They'd linger in the magazine aisle of the supermarket, flipping through the bridal pages as they scanned the dresses. Sheath or A-line, mermaid or ball gown. Sequins. Lace. Celine searched for the perfect one, always thinking she found it to later find another. They were all beautiful, Mira told her, they were all already perfect, but for Celine it was about more than the dress. The wedding was a chance for her to be seen as someone worthy, as beautiful, as deserving of the attention spent.

Still, they weren't teenagers anymore, and it had been a decade since she'd seen Celine, almost as long as the heyday of their friendship. They hadn't been friends for a long time, but Mira wondered about all of those years in the beginning. How long did the sense of obligation to someone last? Did she owe it to Celine to come to her wedding if they'd once been friends?

"Oh, I don't know what I'll do if you're not there," Celine continued on the phone, and the knot of guilt wrangled inside of her. Celine told her the wedding would be during the height of summer. Mira mentally mapped out the logistics of the trip, allowing herself to entertain the possibility. Of course she'd have to find something in her closet to wear, buy a dress on sale if she couldn't. A summer wedding meant she wouldn't have to take off from teaching. It was not a long drive from Winston-Salem; it would take a couple hours if she didn't hit any traffic, a half day at most. If she left early enough it wouldn't be so bad. A new dress, the cost of gas, and the expense of a hotel for a night or two. She could afford all that, so it wasn't a question of if she could or couldn't go. The real question was if she wanted to, and she couldn't say she did, not with any real sense of authority. "If it's the money, don't worry about it. I'll pay for your room. I can send you money for your travel too. Anything you need, Mira. Just let me know. All you have to do is come."

Mira bristled. Was this another insult hiding underneath? She couldn't be sure. "You don't have to pay for my travel. I can afford it."

"Oh, I didn't mean—I know you can afford it, but free is always better, isn't it? What about your room? It's the least I can do. They've made these suite-sized cottages on the property. I'm sure you'll love it."

"Wait," Mira said. It hadn't occurred to her to ask where the wedding would be. She'd assumed it'd be at the country club right on the border of the town, near the golf course and the old-moneyed homes, but the mention of cottages threw her off. "Where are you having this?"

"This millionaire bought and renovated the old Woodsman property. It's become a pretty popular touristy place since it opened. We're going to be the first to have our wedding there, which is a little exciting when you think about it."

"Celine, you can't be serious," Mira blurted, refusing to hide her disapproval. "You can't possibly be having your wedding at that plantation."

"You wouldn't even recognize it now," Celine responded, missing Mira's point. "The property's been completely redone."

Celine should have known it wasn't about what the place looked like, but then Celine hadn't been with them that day, only heard the story afterward like everyone else. Mira and Jesse were the ones who'd snuck off, and in the time since, who knew what it had become? The history rewritten, erased, having become something entirely new. This was what Celine was trying to convince Mira of as she pressed the phone against her cheek and thought back to a past she'd hoped to forget, to the girl she'd been, and to the friend she'd loved.

"Celine, what about Jesse? Did you invite him too?"

"Of course I invited him, and yes, he's coming. He's fine with the whole thing. We've spent a lot of time together since he found out about the wedding. He's been really supportive. When I worried over the expense he convinced me I was being foolish, and he's helped me decide on decorations and all the stuff Phillip couldn't be bothered with. I didn't think Jesse would be interested in this sort of thing, but maybe he's just lonely. I never see him talk to too many people around here. He keeps mostly to himself."

It was as if the wind had been knocked out of her. Mira leaned against the counter, breathing hard. It not only surprised her that Jesse would want to be involved, but that, at least from Celine's perspective, they'd become friends again, whereas Mira couldn't remember the last time she'd heard from him. She didn't know what to make of any of this. She'd spent years trying not to think about Jesse, about what had happened between them. Hearing Celine talk about Jesse made her ache with longing and regret. When she'd left Kipsen she'd also left him, thereby creating a resoluteness to the possibility of what could have been.

"What did you say when you invited him?" Mira asked Celine. "How did he respond?"

"I told him where it was and asked if he'd be okay attending. He said that it was all so long ago. He didn't care about what happened back then. I asked him if he was sure and he shrugged it off. He's really okay with it, Mira. In fact, he seemed a little excited about it, if you could believe that."

Mira didn't believe it, but what else was there to say if she was telling the truth?

"You can think of it all as a sort of vacation if you want. If that will make you say yes."

"A vacation." Mira held in her laugh as she considered the proposition. Nothing about someone else's wedding could seem like a vacation to the ones not getting married, but she decided not to give Celine an answer on the spot, instead asked her for a little more time to think about it. She figured maybe if enough time passed—she would just not pick up the phone if Celine called, ignore any emails sent—the decision would be made for her. After the wedding she could play it off as if she had forgotten to respond, that she'd become too preoccupied with the end of the school year. She'd make sure a few weeks later to send a nice gift.

Something from Neiman's, a gift she couldn't afford but would buy for her childhood friend anyway.

Mira had made up her mind, or she thought she had, but a few days after her conversation with Celine, she received another call. An unrecognizable number on her cell. Mira had missed it but saw the voicemail. She hit play and listened.

"Hi. Mira? Celine gave me your number. I hope it's all right," a man's voice began, followed by a pause, and she knew in that instant who it was. He forced out a slight laugh before giving a deep-throated cough, an attempt at buying time while figuring out what else to say. "It's been a long time, I know. I just wanted to call and—I don't know. I—" He started again, and Mira wished she could know what thoughts lay in the space between his words. Whatever came next would be a revision, only a fraction of the truth. "I—I've missed you," he said, and the message ended.

Mira called Jesse back immediately but the phone rang and rang. Flustered by the beep of his voicemail and not knowing what to say, she ended the call and didn't try again.

Listening to the message, she could picture him—scrawny and tall, ashy knees and elbows. His freckled golden skin and the Afro of curls the sun had tinted a reddish-brown. As he talked, she imagined him rubbing his hand over his mouth, an attempt at masking the small cleft on his upper lip. He was always self-conscious about the way it looked, and she imagined the mustache he'd tried to grow when they were younger had now fully come into being.

After Mira couldn't get hold of Jesse, she'd called Celine back. "Yes, I'll go to the wedding," she said as she circled the date on her wall calendar. "Yes, yes," she repeated, reassuring Celine but also in a way herself. She'll be there. She'd come.

Jesse's message had been brief, but hearing it eased an ache she'd never soothed. Throughout their friendship they'd always been on the cusp of becoming something more, and the yearning for what she'd missed out on had lingered over every relationship she'd had since. Each a short-lived affair, and each with a man who'd left her longing. Maybe, she wondered, it was because her heart still pined for him.

Now, alone in her car, she felt foolish in this admittance. Ten years was a long time. A whole new life could have been created in the ten years since she'd last seen him. He could be seeing someone. He could be married. And if neither of those were true, there were no guarantees he could be interested, not after all this time. She wondered if he thought about her.

A person moved through the world with no knowledge and no assurances, only hope and faith to guide them through the belief they were making the right decisions. Who could say now that returning wouldn't lead to the greatest heartbreak of her life? She didn't know, as no one could know, but hearing his voice on the phone was all the urging she had needed. Hearing his voice on the phone saying how much he missed her.

Mira pressed harder on the gas. She'd left the interstate long ago, pulling off to take this two-lane road that would eventually lead her home, or what used to be her home. The closer she got the more unrecognizable it felt. As she drove, Mira passed abandoned cars, their tires stripped, the metal exterior rusted, their glass windows shattered. She could guess what had happened—the car running out of gas, or breaking down, and the owner leaving it, not realizing there were thieves waiting to strip it and sell it for parts. Mira should have been worried, but she still had a half tank of gas and she knew the way, knew where this road would take her, and if she was patient enough, she'd get there.

It could have been whispers, the way the wind blew through the cracks of her car windows as she drove east on Highway 158 toward Kipsen. The sound unsettled her in its vague familiarity as she got closer, enough that she shook the feeling away and turned the windows up, putting the air conditioner on full blast.

Mira hadn't mentioned it to Celine, but she'd heard about the Woodsman house being bought. Her mother had told her shortly after it happened. A few years after Mira left for college, a man named Alden Jones came to Kipsen saying he was interested in buying all the land around the Woodsman property. Roman Woodsman had been a nineteenth-century plantation owner, mostly of tobacco, and his house once sat on over a thousand acres, one of the largest plantations in North Carolina. After Roman died, the family sold off plots of his land to white farmers, but over the decades afterward, whites fled the area and migrated north, closer to the downtown square, hoping to get as far away from the river as they could go. Those who left blamed it on not wanting to be near blacks who were buying up the properties instead, but sometimes after loosening with drinks they'd tell another story—at night they heard whispers beckoning them, and sometimes the whispers told them strange things, unconscionable things they'd never dare repeat in the daylight. A few went further, saying they saw visions they couldn't explain. "What kind of visions?" others would ask, and they'd only stare back, unwilling to go further.

Black families bought up the cheapened houses the white ones had left behind. By the time Mira's mother came along, people called the area Nigger Field. Whites relished in the slur as they warned others about the part of town they never visited.

Mira's mother hated the name, cursing under her breath every time she heard it, but a house there was the only one a loan would let her afford. When a man offered to buy not just the Woodsman place but all the surrounding land including hers, she accepted the deal with barely a breath of a hesitation. She took this white man's money and escaped to a beach town near the coast. His money was her deliverance and she never wanted to return. "Too much poverty and history," she'd told Mira, and never again wanted to be reminded of either.

"I don't understand why you're going back," her mother had said when Mira told her she was returning to Kipsen. "Nothing's left for you there."

"It's for Celine's wedding," Mira had answered. "She's willing to throw a whole bunch of money to get me to come, so who am I to say no? We were childhood friends and that seems to still mean something to her. You remember her, right?"

"What about the boy?"

Mira flinched at the question and she wondered if in her brief hesitation her mother caught her vulnerability. "Jesse? I don't know. I imagine he'll be there, so I'll see him."

"I always felt bad for what happened to him, but he should have known better."

"It wasn't his fault. It was my idea in the first place."

"He should have left all that alone," her mother interrupted. She paused, considering Mira's response, before adding, "Both of you should have just left that house alone."

Maybe Mira might have, but once, driving home, her mother had taken a back road, what she'd hoped was a shortcut, and they'd found the house hidden deep among the trees.

"Christ almighty," her mother had said, gasping at the sight. "There it is. I knew this plantation was nearby, but I didn't realize how close."

Mira was a young girl then. She sat in the back of the car, fiddling with a coloring book, when her mother told her to look out the window. "Do you see?" her mother asked urgently. She caught Mira's reflection in the rearview mirror and asked her again.

"See what?"

"Child, *look*."

Mira glanced out the window and gasped. Three stories tall, with several prominent Greek Revival columns, it was the largest house she'd ever seen. There it loomed, this relic of a distant era, a forgotten past. Hundred-year-old maples lined the path, their twisted branches framed the entrance. It was the trees that made Mira's mother slow her car, almost stopping, her breath held for just a moment. Mira saw those maple trees and wanted to turn away, but her mother made her hold her gaze, hoping it would be enough to sear the image into Mira's memory.

"We come from there, that's what my grandfather used to say. All our ancestors are buried out on that land, both white and black alike," her mother said.

Mira asked what she meant and her mother told her what she knew—that their line had descended from a woman named Marceline, a slave of the Woodsman family, but beyond that, she didn't know much else.

"Why don't you know more? You never asked your grandfather? You didn't have questions about Marceline or any of the Woodsmans?"

"I guess I thought what good is knowing about the past when it can't help me now?"

Mira sulked in her seat, annoyed at her mother for not providing more information about their family. Why tell her about any of it if she didn't know the whole story? She probably hadn't expected Mira's interest, but still her mother's revelation bothered her. Her mother seemed to sense this too and attempted to soothe the situation. "None of that matters, hon. We've got to move on."

Mira listened to her mother because at the time she thought her to be right. She ignored the questions she had over Marceline, deciding there wasn't much point in thinking about them. No one was left in the family for her to ask anyway except for her mother, and she'd made it clear she'd told Mira everything she knew.

Yet, every now and again the desire crept back. She'd hear another rumor about the Woodsman house, its mythos growing within Kipsen, and she'd be reminded again of her own connection to the place. Maybe this was why Mira had followed Jesse into those woods that day when he offered to take her to the house, and when she had seen—well, what exactly was it that Mira had seen? Even recalling it now caused the same tightness in her chest from remembering, and she once again told herself it'd been nothing. She'd forced herself to believe this was true. *Nothing* was what she'd told Jesse when he asked her what she saw. Nothing, nothing, nothing. She hadn't known how to tell him the truth, because she wasn't sure if he'd believe it. Nothing, she'd told him, deciding to disavow it all, and over the years, denying had given her comfort, and every day gone she'd worked to put distance between her and the burden of the past. The longer she was gone the less guilt she had for leaving. She thought if she moved far enough away and buried it deep, the truth about that day would never surface. What had taken Mira a long time to realize was that it was always there, hidden but never lost.

Mira fiddled with the radio. She was getting near the end of her drive and it made her antsy. She needed a distraction for this last leg. If only she hadn't forgotten to buy one of those cords that would enable her to play music from her phone. Most of the trip she'd listened to the same Billboard chart songs, but she was tired of that now. Her hand shook a little as she slowly turned the dial, searching through the static for the right song to occupy her mind. She wished she could remember the good stations as she passed another country song and two more pop ones. Finally, she came to an old blues song.

She relaxed in her seat, hoping the rhythm of the music would ease her tension, but a chain gang appeared up ahead. Chained together in five-man groups, they cleaned the ditch under the afternoon sun. They worked in their groups, picking up the trash thrown from cars flying too fast down the road. They all wore the same black-and-white-striped uniform. She'd seen images like this before, of men, even women, stripped of their identity, nothing more than anonymous blurs working their forced labor. The image was not new to her, especially in North Carolina, a state whose newly appointed prison commissioner believed in deterrence. "If a man is humiliated enough maybe he'll think a little harder about what he's done and choose not to do it again," he was heard saying, a quote taken from the commissioner in Louisiana, who was also known for his hard stance. Following in Louisiana's footsteps, he'd ordered that these inmates be dressed in old-fashioned striped uniforms and forced outside to work.

What was new were the shackles. Mira could see the glinting metal wrapped around the men's ankles. Immediately, the image conjured another—at the school where Mira worked, the administration recommended that at the first sign of trouble in the classroom teachers call the police and let them handle it. She'd never done it, but other teachers had, and typically they'd come and escort the student out of school. Sometimes they were back the next day but often times they were not. Mira never asked where they went.

A few weeks ago, a social studies teacher at her school, fed up with a student not doing the assignments and talking back in class, asked him to leave and go to the principal. The student refused. The teacher, Mr. Billings, a man who should have retired long ago, called the police. This was the story she'd heard, but the viral video a classmate had circulated afterward told the truth of what happened. She'd watched in horror as two policemen took hold of the student, yanked him from his desk, and drop-kicked him to the ground, pulling both his arms behind his back and cuffing him.

Mira recognized the student in the video. Javion. He was the kind of kid who forced himself to be invisible. Last to class, he'd slump down in his seat. Expressionless, no matter what she did or said. Other students at least attempted to laugh at her awkward jokes or feigned enthusiasm when she sarcastically chastised them for not being excited enough over the lesson.

Here she was, a black teacher, one of the few who remained at the school, the rest quitting after a year, moving on to one of the better-funded districts if they lucked out into a position, or they quit the field altogether. She'd stayed, and each day she tried again at connecting with her students, believing she could help them a little along the brutal path of their lives. Javion should be appreciative, but he never said anything, looked bored half the time, and his passiveness pissed her off—the way he made a mockery of her and the work she put into her classroom planning. Every day she'd dreaded seeing him a little bit more, seeing him judge her while putting in such minimal effort himself.

Finally, having had enough, one day she told him to hold back after class. The school had instituted a new policy that students couldn't carry their bookbags around, so he stood in front of her holding the mess of his binder and textbook, papers sticking out of both.

"I got to go to my next class. If I'm late I'll get detention and—"

"It's okay, I'll write you a note," she interrupted. "Look, Javion—" She stopped, and took a minute to think about what she wanted to say, how best to say it. "You've got to participate more. I'm trying and I need you to try too."

He'd shrugged her off. Even after she was trying to reach out and help. He kept looking over her shoulder toward the door, shifting his feet, impatient for her to get this talk over with. "Is that it? Because, lady, I hafta go."

Lady. His casual disrespect made her want to scream. "*Have to* go," she corrected. "We just had a lesson on this. You don't remember?"

Javion ignored her question. He was waiting her out, hoping she'd get through with what she wanted to say and then he'd be free. He was treating her as if she was someone meant to suffer through and not the other way around. "And no, that's not it," she'd snapped. She hadn't meant to, but there was something about him—it wasn't like he was the first apathetic student she'd ever had, but he unnerved her more than the others. Javion met her eyes and she thought the corner of his mouth upturned a little, into a slight smirk, but she couldn't be sure.

"Don't you want to be better than this? Do you care at all? Because from what I see it looks like you don't. I want to teach students who give a shit about their education."

"Whatever," he said, and that was it. Nothing else. She didn't know what else to do, what else to say, so she sighed and wrote him a note for his next class and told herself to forget it.

A few days later Mr. Billings called the police and she learned that Javion's brother had been killed at the start of the year. That shouldn't have mattered, but people needed the reason anyway. *Couldn't you see something was wrong?* they asked. *Why didn't you see?*

"How was I supposed to know?" Mr. Billings responded to them all, as if his ignorance was enough for his absolution, but the entire school ran on disavowal. During her first year, he'd pulled her aside. "Look, you're doing too much. You'll burn out," he told her. "You can't help all of these kids, especially the ones who don't even want it. My advice is to wait it out. You'll be left with the good ones, the ones you can help. Focus on who you know you can change. Education triage."

She'd scoffed at his advice, offended and horrified, but the years kept on, and with them budget cuts. Soon twenty-five students a class became thirty, then thirty-three, thirty-four, thirty-five. *Thirty-five.* Larger every year, and every year less money than before. Nothing she could do about any of it—not about the splotches of black mold growing on the bathroom ceilings, their textbooks ripped and outdated and never enough, winters with the heating system broken, students shaking from cold, from hunger, from fear of what awaited outside their brick walls, and every week came her colleague Mrs. Whither with her collection envelope asking for donations to pay off student lunch debt. Like clockwork she paused at each of the classrooms, searching for those who'd yet to turn their backs and lock their doors.

More dropped out. Mira learned their names and promptly never saw them again, replaced with new faces to remember, and each one gone, her failure. She sometimes saw the lost ones in the alleys near the school, lurking, avoiding eye contact before running down their neverland streets.

She should have known better than to say what she did to Javion, but this job, this work, was too much sometimes. She'd tried to ignore the way it was breaking her, but with every student absence, with every shrug and smirk, she harkened back to what Mr. Billings had told her. The administration conducted a formal review but he went back to teaching shortly after. Javion was suspended for a week but never came back. He was old enough to drop out if he wanted, and Mira assumed that he did.

Mira wanted to look away from the gang but couldn't. Any other day she might have kept going, a quick glance before focusing her attention back to the road. She wondered what made her pause. What made her look this time, stare even, to notice what she'd before ignored?

Many were young, barely adults, working toward their oblivion. They were shackled together under the noonday sun. Sweat darkened their clothes, dripped down into the crevices of their thin bodies. The burn it would make as their sweat mixed with broken skin, because the iron must chafe at their ankles, must by now have caused blisters and sores. They were invisible men. Numbers and not names. They had lost the privilege of being seen, existing on the periphery from the rest of the world, lost and forgotten.

This image of them in chains would never leave her. She could go far from here, put her foot on the gas and floor it, driving as far as she could, using the distance to erase her memory, but it would return. A day would come when she would find herself mouthing off to another kid, telling him he should be better, if he could just act differently, maybe care a little more, and later, much later, she'd realize that she said what she said in a desperate attempt to fight this potentiality.

"This was a mistake," Mira muttered to herself as she passed them by, thinking briefly she should turn the car around. Several pieces of a tire were spread across the road. Instinct kicked in as she gripped the wheel, forcing the car to veer. She braked, hard, and managed in the last instant to keep the car from careening into a ditch.

"Fuck," she yelled after it was over, her car still on the shoulder.

Mira waited for the sudden rush to fade. She turned the radio off and listened to the silence. She glanced out the rear window, searching for other cars, but this was a lonely road, like most of her drive to Kipsen had been, and she wasn't surprised to see she was alone. Alone except for the chain gang of prisoners now far on down. From this distance, the men were almost indistinguishable, only figures moving along. They crouched low in the ditch, searching for the discarded among the grass—cigarette butts, plastic grocery bags, fast-food wrappers. Their faces pointed down. A few periodically glanced ahead, looking to see how much farther they had left to go. They continued their repetitive movements. Their grab and throw. Step, step. Lean, grab, throw again. Step. Their gloved hands picked the trash from the dirt and threw it in the large plastic bags they carried alongside before continuing on the path.

One of the men stopped working. He lifted his head up to the sky, the sun, as if somewhere up above was the answer to a long-unanswered question. He wiped the sweat from his forehead and looked out toward the road, to her car, to her. She wanted to let him know he was not alone. A small gesture, perhaps meaningless, but she raised her hand in the air anyway in the hope he would see, but by then he'd already moved away, disappearing back to his work with the other men.

II.

When Mira thought back, the trouble had started with Celine's question, followed with Jesse's smirk that said he didn't believe her. "Don't you know it's the ghosts of slaves that roam that land?" Celine had asked them both. "Anyone at school will tell you. All that land is haunted."

A Sunday afternoon with the three of them sitting outside on Mira's front stoop eating lunch—dry Ramen, their fingers breaking the hard chunks, sprinkling the seasoning, popping pieces in their mouths; they finished off the hard crunch by licking their fingers clean, a salty lip smack. For dessert Fla-Vor-Ice freezer pops. Jesse had chosen strawberry, the ice pop leaving the rim of his mouth stained a delicious red. He brought the plastic opening to his lips and sucked the remaining juice. Mira bit chunks off her orange pop to let dissolve in her mouth.

"That all's going to melt if you're not quick enough," Celine scolded. She'd finished hers first, gulping the sweet coldness down. She watched as Mira and Jesse finished theirs while fanning herself with a ripped page from a fashion magazine.

"I'll just get another one," Mira answered, and Celine shrugged.

The afternoon sun bore down. They'd been outside only a few minutes and were already sweating, their clothes damp from it, but the cold of the freezer pops helped to temporarily temper the heat.

"It's so hot today. Maybe we should go back in," Celine whined.

"It's hot inside too," Jesse muttered. "At least outside maybe a breeze will come around. I checked the weather earlier and it's supposed to cool off soon. Maybe even rain."

Without their families they had the entire stretch of the day before them. Both Jesse's uncle and Mira's mother wouldn't be home until late, and Celine's father was never around much to begin with. She'd only met him a few times but they had been enough. Mira hated him, mostly for how she felt he treated Celine. He was a leering sort of man who held the swagger of someone who'd once been seen as being something, but he was nothing now. His looks had long since gone. Sloe-eyed, with a body bloated and heaving from the alcohol that had ruined him, he was a single parent filled with anger over his wife having left him to raise Celine alone. Being a diabetic meant a disability check every month to pay the bills. One would think his illness would have kept him from drinking, but every weekend meant he'd be sitting at Murphy's bar until it closed, followed by a rough-and-tumble trek home where, if they were lucky, he'd pass out on the couch.

While the day wasn't close to over, Mira already felt a sort of nostalgia for its end. She couldn't remember the last time they'd spent an afternoon like this. Not that long ago it seemed like they were always together, but that was before Celine got beautiful. Her dirt-colored freckles faded. She'd grown out her hair and bought a box of Clairol to lighten it blonder. During long afternoons she sauntered the aisles of their local Walmart, searching through the bins for discounted tubes of mascara or lipstick. Because she was beautiful, the white boys at school didn't mind she was poor, and because they liked her, the girls forced themselves to like her too.

Celine soon occupied herself with the older boys at school,

boys she believed were her ticket out of this town, and so she let them flirt with her if they wanted, let their eyes linger on the parts of her body she used to want unseen—the gap in her loosely buttoned shirt, the curve of her hips, her bare legs in cutoff jeans. She let the boys buy her beer or smokes that she'd later share with Mira and Jesse. They bought her gifts with their parents' money she'd hawk for cash, saving the bills in a little tin cookie box underneath the bed. She'd saved hundreds of dollars, not much, but she'd make it be because she was getting out of Kipsen. At eighteen she was going to take what she had and go and never look back.

Jesse said it was his photography that kept him busy. While Celine obsessed over men, Jesse turned to his camera, taking photographs whenever he found a chance. He hoped to get a scholarship to an art school and needed to work on his portfolio. From the broken swings down at the neighborhood park to a stranger's slow smile leaving the grocery, every shot was practice, worth it later in the viewing, and with each one he got better in his vision. Even now, his camera sat in the messenger bag hanging across his back. An Olympus panoramic camera he'd saved for months to buy. Also tucked inside was a list of future supplies.

Print easel
Darkroom enlarger
Filters
Safelight

Today they'd managed to come together. The school year was picking up and who knew what would happen after the year was over? They had today, and as Mira watched Celine and Jesse, she was grateful for the moment she knew would soon end.

"You want another freezer pop?" Mira asked Jesse after he'd finally slurped the rest down.

Jesse wiped his mouth with the back of his hand and dried it on his jean shorts. He fiddled with the plastic wrapping before throwing it on the grass. "Nah. Not right now, anyway."

"Hey, don't do that! Mom will yell if she sees any trash."

Mira's mother had both a flower and a vegetable garden where the rest of the houses in the neighborhood had neither. She paid a fortune for Zoysia grass, wanting the feel of a lush lawn. On weekends, her mother got up early to drag the mower out, pulling on the chain until the engine roared to life. Her house was an anomaly. Around them, houses stood in disrepair, their lawns full of patchy spots of dead grass or weeds. Mildew covered the sides of the homes where the sun wouldn't go. Her neighbors' houses had peeling paint and roofs with missing shingles, exposing the molding plywood underneath. Tenants hung blankets instead of curtains to cover the windows. Mira's mother often said they should be ashamed of the way it looked. White people would notice and it would confirm all the worst thoughts about who they were. Her mother believed it mattered what they thought, and it mattered what they saw, and so she put as much effort and expense as she could into the appearance of her home, as if to say—*See, I am not like the others around me, I am not what you think me to be.*

"Your mother cares too much about making herself seem better than the rest of us," Jesse said, not trying to hide his disdain.

It was no secret Mira's mother didn't care for Jesse. While she didn't think much of Celine either, the mere mention of Jesse's name put her in a fit. In Jesse she saw the image of every man who'd hurt her, exemplified by Mira's father. Both of them in their forties when they met, she'd believed he was serious about a relationship, but pregnancy showed her how wrong she'd been in her assumption. When she decided she wanted to keep it he decided he didn't want her. After he was gone, she convinced herself another man wouldn't want her, a single black woman with a young baby, and she soon gave up on finding anyone else.

Jesse was a black boy who'd grow up to become a black man, and since it was a black man who'd hurt her, she figured Jesse would hurt Mira too. "That boy, Lord, that boy," she'd say whenever Mira talked about him. "Why can't you stay away from him? At least with Celine, she's a girl, but Jesse? God, with all the work I do—I'm trying to get you somewhere, don't you see that? I'm trying to get you to a life worth more than this."

For her mother, this had meant Mira living a life of constrained, dictated action. It meant straightening her hair, sitting on the hard floor between her mother's thighs as she parted and greased her scalp before taking the flat comb to its kink, and later, when she'd finally gotten tired of the soreness of her arms from dealing with it, it meant relaxers, Mira suffering through the burn of her scalp as the cream tamed her hair. It meant boxy-shaped clothes that hid her figure. It meant clean, trimmed fingernails, never biting them, maybe painted with a pastel color on Sundays. It meant jewelry but no gold hoops or statement necklaces, no makeup until she was sixteen, and even then, no red lipstick. Lord, no red. Mira's mother hated the women she saw during church service, their lips stained red—*nigger red*. "You will not be like that," her mother would tell her, "if it's one thing I do in this life, it's going to be to make sure you'll not be like them." Mira knew what her mother meant, as if that was all it would take to alter her life's trajectory, as if as long as she did these things— lived a life of *yes* and *no ma'am* pleasantries, of never speaking beyond the answer to a question, of being watchful of her tone, even when upset, of never asking, never challenging, of being polite, *respectable*—somehow, in some way, she would be saved.

"He's going to be trouble, I know it. He'll drag you down. Black boys like that always do."

Black boys like that. Boys who didn't live with their parents. Boys who idled around parks with nothing to do, looking for trouble. Boys who should be spending time on schoolwork or a job. But what she didn't know was that Jesse lived with his uncle because his mother had died and his uncle, not wanting him to go to foster care, offered to raise him. His grades were as good, if not better, than Celine's or Mira's, and he considered photography his job, and he worked on it whenever he could.

Mira always shrugged off her mother's criticisms, choosing to ignore them rather than get into an argument, but she'd be lying if they never came to the forefront whenever she hung out with him, especially when he did something she knew would get her in trouble. Jesse caught Mira's look and apologized for the litter. He went to pick up the plastic wrapper and throw it in his bag. He took out his camera and began snapping shots of Celine and Mira. Celine played it up for the camera—puckering her pink lips and leaning toward him. She pulled on the edge of her T-shirt, showing her tanned shoulder in an attempt to be provocative, but Jesse just laughed.

"Take one of me and Mira this time."

"Oh, no, that's all right," Mira said, a rush of sudden embarrassment overwhelming her. She put a hand to her face in an attempt to hide from the shot, but Celine kept insisting.

"Mira, come on. I want one of both of us."

"Yeah, Mira, get in the frame."

At Jesse's prompting, Mira straightened. Unlike Celine, Mira wasn't good at having people look at her, so used to tamping down how she was seen. Whereas Celine showed off, baring more of her body for the camera, Mira engaged in a futile attempt at covering what skin showed. Being reminded of her mother's judgments about modesty, about respectability, made her pull and tug, but nothing else could be done about her clothes. She fussed a minute over her hair, her sweat and the heat of the day having frizzed up her press-out, but Celine quickly put her arm across Mira's shoulders and pulled her close. She fixed her smile brightly at Jesse. Mira forced her own smile toward the camera, but instantly wanted to stop, afraid of having this photo document the way she looked. She resisted the urge to pull away and turned her head straight at the viewfinder. Celine shouted at Jesse to say when he was ready and he nodded back. Mira watched him as he focused the lens, shy and embarrassed, but with the camera hiding his face she was able to meet his gaze. This felt safer. He was careful and patient, willing to hold the camera as long as he could, as long as it would take, if it meant getting the shot he wanted.

Jesse continued to wait. A forever existed with the two of them sitting side by side, Celine's arm feeling heavy and hot against Mira's skin. The longer Jesse waited, the more uncomfortable Celine seemed; she shifted her body around. Mira loosened, enjoying the moment a little. She stared at the camera, knowing the longer she stared the longer Jesse was looking back at her. Soon she stopped noticing Celine. She wasn't there at all. It was just the two of them. It gave her a small thrill.

Celine and Mira sat underneath the blazing sun and waited for Jesse to take the photo. Finally, when even Mira was about to say forget it, he hit the shutter.

"I wasn't looking!" Celine whined.

"Trust me, it's a good picture," he said as he tucked the camera back in his bag. "You two could be sisters."

"That's because we are," Celine retorted, giving a snicker as she pulled Mira close. Celine grabbed Mira's arm and held it against her own. Because it was summer, Celine's skin had tanned a light brown. "See?"

Celine was joking, but when Mira was younger she didn't understand the categories, why Celine was considered white and Mira and Jesse not. All three of them could be a mixture of anything, especially seeing them clustered together on her mother's porch. Who was to say what any of them were? When Mira looked at their skin, especially now during the heat of summer, the differences felt slight. Still, they were there, and come the early part of fall Celine's skin would pale, while Mira's and Jesse's stayed mostly the same. This was the true marker between them.

A breeze blew, cooling their damp skin, and the surprise of it caused them all to stop. The leaves made a rustling from the wind, calling their attention to the woods that bordered the periphery of their neighborhood. Jesse took a sideways glance toward the cluster of trees. The midday sun blinded him and he squinted to shield his eyes from the light. "That Woodsman Plantation is out in those woods you know," Jesse remarked. "Why haven't we ever gone to find it?"

Celine at first paid the question no mind, seeming to think he wasn't serious, but when she saw he was, she shifted in her seat. "It's because of all the stories about it."

"Other kids at school have gone. I've heard them talk of it."

"Yeah, *talk*," Celine emphasized. "You really think they'd tell the truth? Who cares anyway if they have? You don't have to be like them."

"You're one to talk."

A look of surprised hurt flashed across Celine's face and Mira knew she needed to do something before the two of them got into it and ruined the rest of the day. "Do you want to try and find it?" Mira asked Jesse.

Jesse quickly turned around to face her. His eyes lit up. "Do you?"

"No," Mira told Jesse, but changed her mind. "Well, I don't know. Maybe. I don't know where it is."

"I could find it, I bet. It wouldn't be hard. We should go."

"What's gotten into both of you?" Celine interrupted.

Mira ignored Celine, instead gazing at Jesse, wondering how serious he'd been, but he was fixed in the direction of the woods.

"Nothing's gotten into me," Mira said, shrugging off Celine's judgment in an attempt at hiding her interest. "I'm bored, I guess. What else is there to do?"

"It's a thousand degrees today. You really want to go traipsing through the woods to look at some derelict house? We can do that without going anywhere. Look around."

"We should go," Jesse agreed. "It's not like we're doing anything else. I'm kind of curious if all those stories are true."

Everyone in Kipsen had their own story about the Woodsman Plantation, each one different depending on who you asked. Black people focused on the revolt. One of Roman's slaves, Jeffrey, led a failed insurrection that happened a few years before the start of the Civil War. Jeffrey had planned to gather the slaves at Roman's plantation as well as two others—the Murrell and Kingsley—and take them over. No one knew exactly why it had failed. Some said it was because the slaves all debated on where to go first. Others believed the group had fractured, with a majority wanting to chance escaping to the river. Jeffrey knew they'd never make it through the night, not without killing their owners, but by the time he realized his followers had other plans it was too late.

Another story was that one of the slaves had betrayed Jeffrey and warned Roman about the attack. The question of who had betrayed him and the reasons why was often gossip fodder for the white people of the town, with many wondering which slave had been the good one, the one to be trusted, the one who had helped keep their ancestors alive.

The white members of the town told their own stories about the Roman family. Stories of horror that grew more macabre with each retelling. They described contraptions he used to torture disobedient slaves. He cut off body parts as punishment and kept the pieces in sealed jars as tokens. They told of slave corpses being sold to medical schools. They told stories of slave concubines, of torture rooms that would stretch limbs and break bones.

The most well-known story, the one everyone agreed on, was the belief that the Woodsman property was haunted. Here, again, people disputed the specifics. Some believed it was of the slaves who'd escaped to the river, making it to the swamps where they waited for their loved ones who never came. Their ghosts roamed the land now in search of their families. Others believed it was

Jeffrey himself, and the others from the revolt, who haunted the grounds, still vengeful for their reckoning. Then, there were those who believed that it was haunted by the bodies of all the slaves Roman had killed and secretly disposed of.

"They say that land is haunted," Celine responded. "The slaves from a failed revolt."

"I've heard those stories too," Mira agreed. "They say people have died up on that land."

"I heard Keisha Parker say that the spirit of the slaves that died come out at night, every one of them searching for who put their bodies in the ground in the first place. She said that's what happened to that white family up in the West End."

"What family? What happened?" Mira asked.

"They had a kid our age. A boy. He told his parents he was going camping but he snuck onto the Woodsmans property instead. I think it was a dare. That's what they found out after he'd gone missing a few days. Then they found his body hanging from a tree."

"You're saying he killed himself."

"Keisha says the ghosts drove him to it."

"Keisha says all kinds of shit," Jesse interrupted. He walked toward the woods. He turned back to them and smirked. "You'll believe anything people tell you."

"It's the truth," Celine affirmed.

"Fine, let's go, then. It'll be fun. I can bring my camera and take some pictures, and I'll prove to both of you nothing's haunted about that place. They're just stories."

"No way you'll even be able to find it," Celine said.

Jesse pointed off in the distance. "Like I said earlier, it shouldn't be that hard. We'll go that way, past those houses and into the woods. All we have to do is go toward the river. I know that much at least."

Faced with the real possibility that they were going out searching, Mira suddenly hesitated, regretting asking the question that had sparked all this in the first place. What if they got lost out in the middle of nowhere? Wild animals lurked in the woods. Maybe not ghosts, but real threats just the same. Snakes hiding unseen in the thicket. Bears or coyotes or maybe rabid dogs. And what if they got caught sneaking into a place that wasn't their own? They shouldn't go, but the idea of it lingered in her mind. She wanted to go, despite the perceived danger, despite everything. She wanted to go out and wanted Jesse to take her.

"Like Mira said—it's not like we have much else to do," Jesse continued.

"I'm not going," Celine blurted. She stood up and shook her head. "No way. I'm not doing it. Not today. It's too hot to be running around outside."

"You're scared." Jesse laughed, teasing, but it was clear Celine was afraid. This made Mira reconsider. Celine and Jesse were always the ones to do what made Mira hesitate. Their lives were full of dares. Celine always the first, urging Jesse to follow, and he always did. Celine and Jesse breaking into the high school and dancing barefoot along the buffed floors. Celine stealing Chiclets from the gas station, smiling to the clerk as she walked out unafraid. Jesse doing it too, although hesitating before jamming the packages of candy in his pockets, a small recognition of fear of being caught, knowing deep down the repercussions wouldn't be the same for him, and yet—Celine had done it and she'd been okay. For all his judgment toward her they were similar in this way, because he could not stand the idea of someone else getting away with something he couldn't. Every day the world reminded him, both directly and subtly, that because he was black his life held different rules, and Jesse behaved the way he did in defiance of this reality.

For once in Mira's life she wanted to do the same. How many times had she condemned Jesse for his behavior? *Stop being reckless. Stop being so stupid,* she'd scold. *We have to be better than that.* Jesse always said he didn't care, and he seemed to do what he did to prove this point, not realizing it proved the opposite. He cared, even if he pretended otherwise.

Seeing Celine's resistance stirred something inside Mira. She wanted to not care. This was a moment where she could be different from the person she'd always been, had been taught to be. She could do what even Celine refused to do. This was her chance, and she wanted to grab it out of fear of there never being another.

"I can't believe it," Jesse said, continuing to laugh. "Scaredy-cat Celine. Afraid of going in some old abandoned house. I thought you weren't scared of anything."

"I'm not scared."

"You are."

"Well," Celine huffed. "You'd be too if all the stories were about ghosts killing black people."

"I'll go. Maybe it'll be fun," Mira interrupted, standing up. Celine raised her eyes at them both. Celine had tried to hide it, but Mira saw her bewilderment at this turn of events and she secretly delighted in it. Celine said she was tired anyway and wanted to go home and finish her magazine. They watched her leave, and when Celine was gone, Jesse grabbed her hand. It was instinctive, as if he knew all along she would say yes, that together they would go, with her following him not just into the woods but anywhere he asked. She clutched her fingers around his, the heat of his palm warming hers, and before she could say another word they were off running toward the woods—running, running across the grass, through the brush, running until they were both breathless and sweating with Mira dragging on his arm in the hope he'd stop. They ran, with Jesse leading the way, and as Mira followed she tried to focus on her breathing, keeping a steady hum as she continued propelling her body forward.

"We're almost there," she heard Jesse call, and Mira gulped in another mouthful of air and pushed herself onward. She followed

Jesse, believing he knew the fastest way, and she gripped his hand as they went deeper, until the branches of trees blocked the sky and the light grew dark. A breeze hit her face, a slight relief, and once she had it she knew she had to have more. "Okay, I can't run anymore," she finally yelled out to Jesse, this time meaning it. She let go of his hand and stopped.

Jesse wiped his brow. "Hey, you see that?" He pointed to a structure in the distance and Mira's eyes followed. "It looks like a barn."

"It is. An old tobacco barn."

When they got close, Jesse stopped and reached out his hand for her. "Be careful of snakes," he said, and Mira nodded.

Inside, the barn was larger than it first appeared. Mira half expected it to be full of dried tobacco leaves. She imagined the smell of the cured tobacco, like a fresh cigar not yet touched by a flame, as she breathed in the stagnant air.

"A barn like this was used to hang leaves to dry," Jesse said. "There were these laths full of the tobacco plants and you'd hang them in rows going all the way to the top of the shed. I know because my grandparents farmed. Tobacco used to be the lifeblood of families around here. Everyone had a farm. If you went back far enough on the family line, you'd just about find a connection to tobacco in some way or another with at least half the town."

"You see that moving up there?" Mira interrupted, pointing to the rafters. Jesse kneeled down and picked up a rock and threw it. The sound ricocheted as a raccoon scuttled down.

"This barn means we're close," Jesse said after the animal was gone. "The house can't be too much farther."

When they came upon the Woodsman house the air grew cool and the rain clouds Jesse had promised earlier darkened the sky. The house was not how she'd remembered it. The property hadn't been kept up well. The exterior paint was peeling off, revealing the grayish brown of the wood underneath. The Greek Revival columns looked as if they would soon collapse and the whole structure would come crashing down. Bushes grew all around the front of the house. Weeds scratched against her legs as they made their way.

"I don't like this." Mira shuddered, unsettled. Yet an undeniable pull guided her toward knowing what lurked behind the plantation's doors; this unwilling, unexpected desire she couldn't control scared her more than anything.

Jesse, determined, ignored Mira and kept going. He took tender-footed steps, testing each to make sure they'd hold before attempting another.

"The door's locked."

"We could try around back. Maybe there's another entrance—"

"You think if the front's locked the back won't be? Nah, I'm not going around back. Neither are you. We're going to walk through this door right here."

Jesse punched the nearby window, shattering the glass, and climbed through, but he cut his hand in the process. A shard of the glass got stuck. He pulled it out in one quick stroke. Through the edges of the glass that was left, Mira watched the blood trickle down the side of his arm.

"Are you all right? You're bleeding everywhere. Maybe we should forget this and go."

From the other side of the window, Jesse said, "No, it's not that bad. Just looks it. The bleeding will stop soon. Besides, we're here now. We can't leave." Jesse ripped his shirt to use the fabric as a bandage. After he'd tied up his hand, he walked to the door and opened it for her. "Come on, I'll protect you," he said, half teasing. He ushered for her to follow, and she went, careful to avoid the blood drips on the floor.

Neither of them dared to speak as they walked through the foyer of the house, at least not at first, but they soon found it was better to talk. Mira took note of the surroundings. Glass from a shattered chandelier sprinkled one corner. Bug carcasses blanketed the floor. Mira tried to ignore the crackling sound of Jesse's feet flattening them as he walked around, while she shushed her feet along.

"There's furniture," Mira said, commenting on the white tapestries covering the antique furniture in the parlor. She stifled a cough as dust floated in the air.

"Abandoned, I guess," Jesse said.

They went from room to room as they explored inside the house. The floorboards creaked each time her foot pressed down; it sounded like a wailing. She took a breath and continued.

Jesse moved swiftly, as if he was searching for something. Some of the rooms appeared to recently have been lived in. Mira found a mattress in one, musty with the remains of mice nests.

"Looks like we missed the party." Jesse pointed to a bottle of Mad Dog on the fireplace. Mira was beginning to ease up when she heard a sound. It was a low, guttural hissing that filled up the room. Mira looked around but didn't see anything. The hissing made her stop and listen.

"Do you hear that?" Mira whispered. Jesse lifted his hand in the air to caution her from going any farther. He took a few steps toward the entryway of the next room and that's when he saw it. A buzzard walking across the wood floor. When it saw him, it made another louder hiss and raised its wings in the air. Jesse stepped back defensively.

"I think we found the culprit," he said, his voice sounding relieved. "He doesn't seem to like us."

They watched as the buzzard moved away from them, disappearing into the dark. Confident enough to keep going now that they were alone again, Jesse shifted his attention to what else in the house awaited them.

After the hissing had subsided, Jesse slid off his bag and unzipped it. He lifted his camera from his bag and straightened up. He peered through the viewfinder and slowly began to scan through the room, taking shots every few seconds. He did this for a few minutes, snapping photos of the broken chandelier, of the covered antiques that he mocked and said could be ghosts.

"I don't like this place. It feels creepy."

"You know, Mira, sometimes you can be such a child," he muttered.

Jesse's remark smarted even though she pretended otherwise. She could be as bold as him. He had to know this. She'd come, hadn't she? That should count for something. Celine hadn't come and was probably having a better time than either of them. Mira wished she'd stayed behind too, but she was here, full of naive hope that maybe Jesse would see her differently, but right now it seemed like he barely noticed her at all.

Mira's face burned. Jesse continued to snap more photos, too consumed to notice she was upset. He headed for the staircase, but Mira stopped him from going farther. Shouted for him not to go.

"What? Why?" he asked. "You see there's nothing. I'll be a few more minutes and then we'll leave. I want to see what's up-stairs. Go up and take some pictures. You don't want to come?"

Mira didn't answer and glanced at the staircase. She stepped toward Jesse, thinking she could do it, but stopped, fearing it was a mistake to continue. They needed to leave, but why? What was there to be scared of? Jesse took another step. He fiddled with his camera, snapping shot after shot.

When Mira wouldn't follow him, he lowered his camera. "You believe the stories, don't you?" he asked, and Mira nodded, feeling a blush of shame in the confession.

Mira braced herself for Jesse's teasing. "I wish I could be more like you," she said, sputtering out the words. Her eyes watered, further confirming a humiliating truth about who she was. "I wish I could, but I'm not. You were right about what you said earlier. I am a child."

Jesse didn't laugh like she'd expected him to. His whole demeanor changed, softening, opening himself up to her in an unexpected way. "Hey, no, I didn't mean that. I shouldn't have said it. I'm sorry. I don't know what I was thinking. Truth is, maybe I am scared a little," he whispered, and the kindness of his gesture pained her with her own yearning. Gone was his usual smirking expression, his bluster, and she was able to catch a glimpse of what he hid, a vulnerability he fought against, and she was grateful he allowed her to see.

"You go on outside and I'll meet you in a few minutes. I promise—a few more pictures and I'm done. We'll leave and we don't ever have to set foot inside this place again. Okay?"

"Okay," she repeated, feeling better as she wiped the wetness from her cheeks. She calmed herself and she turned away, but Jesse called out. The flash of the camera blinded her as she looked back at him. A quick unexpected shot.

"Got you. I knew I would eventually." Jesse's grin kept her from yelling. Anyone else and it would have been an intrusion, but not with him. "I'm sorry, but you know I wouldn't have gotten it any other way," he said when he saw her flustered face. "Don't worry, no one else will ever see it. This one—this one's just for me."

The summer's heat made her dizzy, the magnolia air thick and choking. Alone, listening to the wood thrushes give their back-and-forth trills, she allowed herself a possibility she hadn't before dared—he could feel the same. If he wanted, they could be together. In a slip of a moment she let herself believe this to be true, but just as quickly she dismissed the thought. She must have been mistaken, because how could he care for her? A knobby-kneed girl who barely even knew herself?

He'd waited before snapping the photo. That was the piece of it she couldn't shake. Snapping the photo when she'd let down her guard. Who was the girl he'd seen? she wondered. One who'd stopped being what others always asked of her. A girl laid bare, and it had been enough. More than. The girl he'd seen in the view-finder had been what he'd hoped to keep.

Mosquito bites on her arms swelled, making her itch. She resisted the compulsion to scratch the plumps. The longer she waited the more she fought the urge to run. Running was the impulse she had whenever she was afraid, but she didn't want to leave Jesse. He should be done soon, she thought, playing a waiting game to distract her body into stillness. "One more minute," she whispered. One more minute and he'd be done and they'd be on their way.

A noise came from inside the house. A crash came next and Mira looked in the window hoping for Jesse, to see him wave and let her know he was okay, but instead of Jesse she saw someone else—another figure, large and looming in the dark of the room. This man walked toward the broken window frame, toward her, stepping closer to the light. He moved until she could see him fully through the window, and what she saw was blood, blood covering his face, blood fresh and dripping down the front of his clothes, blood staining his hands; he was wiping off its smear but it was everywhere, darkening every part of him, and it was all she could see.

Her heart leaped in her chest and she screamed, a shrieking that echoed through the woods. She sprinted away from the Woodsman house, running across the thicket and through the trees until she was deep in the woods. Stopped, she remembered Jesse and called his name between chokes of air.

Silence greeted her. Without Jesse she had to decide what to do. She couldn't go back to the house, not after what she'd seen, but she couldn't stay out in the woods either. Not alone like this. Calling his name again, she hoped in the seconds after she'd hear him respond. She waited a few minutes more and, relenting, ran in the direction of home.

By the time she got back to her house Jesse was already waiting for her. He stood hunched over the grass as he tried to catch his breath.

"Shit, Jesse, I thought I'd lost you," Mira said when she caught up with him, the curse startling them both. Jesse saw her face and laughed. It was a release of tension, and Mira joined in his laughter, feeling okay for the first time since they'd left, but she soon noticed the cut on his arm. "Hey, you're bleeding again. Are you going to be okay?"

"Yeah, I think so," Jesse told her, glancing at the cut.

Jesse shifted his feet and turned toward the direction from which they'd come. "You left me, Mira. I heard you scream and I came for you but you were gone. What happened?" Jesse asked, hesitantly.

"We shouldn't have gone," Mira answered.

"But you said you wanted to find it. You said—"

"No, you were the one. You brought it up first. Why? What made you think of it?" Jesse's silence fueled her anger and she kept going, turning her questions to accusations. "You heard someone talking about going at school, didn't you? You always want to do what those white kids are doing. You heard one of them broke in and you thought you could do it too. That's the reason. It's your fault we went, and I—I—"

Mira couldn't finish. She kept picturing the image of the man in the window, and her heart pounded. His face obscured—scarred? She tried to focus, but when she remembered she saw the blood again. There had been so much of it. He'd been covered in it. His clothes, his face—his face. If she could sit down, take a moment, maybe she could finish, maybe tell him about what she saw, but she kept picturing his face and the same tension filled her chest and she was unable to speak.

"You what, Mira?" Jesse coaxed. Hearing him say her name, it sounded like a purr almost, and she calmed. Jesse said her name again, this time softer, and waited for her to finish.

"Nothing," Mira said, feeling guilty for lying. She bit her lip to keep from saying more.

Jesse rubbed the back of his head and glanced again in the direction of the woods. "I did see something, I think. When I was inside the house, but I don't know. Maybe I just wanted something to be there. Earlier you and Celine were trying to convince me otherwise. Come on, you must have seen something. Why else would you have run?"

"I told you I didn't see anything," Mira shot back. "Shadows from the trees maybe. You were right. Nothing was out there. You were right all along."

"Why won't you tell me the truth?"

Jesse remained a moment longer, stalling in the hope Mira would change her mind, but when Mira wouldn't, he shrugged and said he was going to head back home.

The afternoon sky was stained the color of a bruise, its darkness like a harkening shadow that made them hush, waiting for the thunder. The air held the pungent smell of rain about to fall. Mira pointed to the clouds and said maybe it'd be better if he waited inside until it passed, but Jesse told her no.

"I made some lemonade earlier. Let's go inside and we can forget that we even went. I could find my old card deck and we could play gin rummy like old times."

If he followed her inside and accepted her offer to forget, the day could still be saved. It wasn't too late to start over, he only had to choose. If something were to ever bloom between them, it would begin with this—with her asking, in the only way she could, if he would choose her too.

"Nah, I'm good. I better go."

Mira shook her head and watched him as he gave up, waved goodbye, and left.

A few days after, the police found pieces of a body less than a half mile away from the Woodsman Plantation, washed up against the riverbank. Fish had eaten bits of the flesh. A large abrasion marked the right side of his forehead, possibly from a strike against a rock as he was carried downstream.

Mira said nothing when the body was found, believing if she kept quiet maybe she could convince herself that they hadn't been out in the woods that day, but then Celine told someone where they'd gone, one of her newly made friends, a girl named Cassie she'd been trying to impress, and Cassie told her group of friends, and they told their other friends, and before anyone knew it the whole school had heard. Like a game of telephone, the story got changed with the retelling. *Jesse went out to the Woodsman. Jesse broke into the Woodsman place. Jesse's been sneaking out onto the Woodsman property. I heard he's been squatting in that Woodsman house, probably vandalizing it too. You know that's what they all do, destroy other people's property. Doing whatever the hell they want. Can't even take care of their own. Go out to where he lives and you'll see. No wonder he goes to the Woodsmans'. If you saw that dump part of town you wouldn't want to stay there either.*

"I didn't realize it'd be a big deal," Celine confessed to Mira, and that could have been the end of it, except the police found a path made from the river through the woods back to the Woodsman house. Except they found the blood—Jesse's, from when he'd cut himself. Except they found a bloodied scrap of fabric hanging from a branch. Except they found fingerprints on the window, and handprints smudged all along the front door. The police believed Jesse had been caught breaking in and ran. There was a scuffle at the river and the man was killed, his body dumped in the water in the hope it would disappear. Before Mira knew it, they'd arrested Jesse.

For days Mira waited for the nightmare to be over. He'd be released and they all could go back to how it was, or how it could be, but when rumors continued on she was left examining that last day they'd been together. She hadn't understood then, hadn't realized how he'd hoped she would confirm his fear of what they'd witnessed. Instead she'd lied and told him she didn't know what he meant, and when he'd pushed her, something permanent had shifted between them. Jesse must have recognized her lie and viewed it as a form of betrayal. A nauseating dread rose up within her at the awareness of what she'd done. With a trust broken, the possibility of whoever they could have been together was ruined. She'd thought the choice was his, not realizing that with her lie she'd been the one to make the decision, and it became clear there was no way to take any of it back.

III.

Not long after, the nightmares started. Always a menagerie of faces wearing masks, the masks painted black and outlined in white. The slits for their eyes were dark pools. The faces circled around her until she was surrounded, and then a spark flashed. Fire, and she watched as they all burned in flames.

She feared going to sleep because inevitably, she'd shock herself awake and spend the rest of the night wrapped up in the covers of her bed, waiting for dawn to tell her she was safe.

After a week of this she went to her mother in near tears and said she could no longer contain the truth. In a rush she let it out as best she could, telling her she'd seen someone else at the Woodsman house, that it hadn't been just her and Jesse, and all the while her mother sat quiet and steady, taking it in. Lips pinched, arms folded across her chest, the way she always got when she caught Mira in a lie.

"Quit trying to save that boy. I told you he would drag you down and look at you now, sitting here lying to your own mother. Didn't I say this would happen? He should have never taken you to that place. I should have never let you hang out with him. He's nothing but a hood like his father. Breaking into property not his own. Doing damage, and dragging you in with his mess. Lord, what are we going to do now?"

Her mother shushed her back to bed, saying that would be the end of it, but Mira couldn't let it go, not that night or the night after, and so when the morning came she snuck out of the house and boarded three buses to get downtown to the police station. It took her a half hour to muster the nerve to go inside, circling around the block, walking slowly, hoping when she got to the entrance she'd be ready. She repeated the story in her head, each time hearing her mother's scolding. "No one believes women like us," she'd said. "We're women and we're black, you think anyone's going to listen to you? You think anyone's gonna hear? We've always been nothing. We're never gonna be seen."

Her mother was right. Black girls like her had always been invisible. All Mira had to do was think about the stories of black girls gone, decades of the daughters of their neighbors, daughters of her mother's friends, having disappeared from their own streets as they made their way home from school, from work, from their friends' houses. Their cases were ignored by police and so the family members who cared took it upon themselves to try—plastering photographs on the trunks of neighborhood trees, cluttering the walls of the post office and the grocery store with *Missing!* signs. Girls, barely teenagers, were here and then they weren't, disappeared into oblivion with no one knowing where they could have gone. For black girls, terrors lurked everywhere. Up in New Bern three black women were found chained in a basement. There for almost a decade until one of them escaped. Neighbors saw her as she ran down their neighborhood streets, half-naked, what clothes she wore were rags. They saw her crying out and closed their blinds and locked their doors, and out of their own fear they ignored her as she ran for help until finally, someone with the sense to ask what was wrong found her and called the police. The house she'd escaped from wasn't far from where she'd lived. A few blocks difference between her and home.

Mira walked slowly inside the station. The lady at the front desk gave her a quick glance-over before ignoring her, shifting her attention back to her desk. Mira forced herself to speak up, to enunciate her words, lest they think, she could hear her mother saying, lest they think you belong here.

"Excuse me," she started. "Can I— I'd like to speak to someone about the Loomis case."

The woman gave Mira a hard look this time. "You'll be wanting Sheriff Brody," she said, and pointed down the hall.

Sheriff Brody was a stocky man with meaty arms that stretched his shirt taut. His arms flexed as he leaned across the desk. "Start from the beginning," he said when she'd told him she had information about Mr. Loomis. He smiled, showing teeth, and his eyes held a sort of glimmer. He was playing with her. A game where her answers would determine Jesse's life. Mira relayed her story as best she could, careful with her words, every sentence muttered with the fearful hesitation that this would be what would sound the alarm and be what would make him turn his back on her and her effort to help Jesse.

Because she was afraid, she did not tell the whole truth, only pieces. She'd been with Jesse and she'd seen a man. Someone else was with them in that house besides Jesse. Someone else was on the property. Someone else hurt Mr. Loomis, not him.

"Someone else, huh? Sweetie, you going to have to give me a little more to work with. What did he look like? Can you tell me that?"

Mira opened her mouth but realized she couldn't answer his question. She stumbled out an answer as best she could. "No, I—I can't."

Sheriff Brody leaned back and waited for her to continue. Mira rubbed her hands together, the only movement of her body she'd allow.

"You can't?" he repeated, and as the seconds passed, his demeanor began to shift to one of irritation. "Was he white?"

"Yes," she answered. "No, he was—"

"Well, which is it?"

"White. He was white, but—"

Mira stopped, trying to think, to get her answer right. She recognized that she had to give him something more. She had to keep this going, make him believe, and to do that she had to offer an element of the truth. "His face was bloody. It was covered in blood."

Brody stared at her, clearly unsatisfied. He got up from his chair and told her he had to speak with someone else. "Mira, you said? You got a last name?"

She told him and he left, the door clicking shut behind her.

He made her wait a long time. Long enough that her back ached from her posture. She began to slouch in the seat but straightened up, fearful he'd come back at the moment she'd begun to relax in this space that wasn't her own. She wondered if Jesse had been here, had sat in the same seat. If he'd been afraid. He wouldn't have shown it if he had. He would have tried to look bored. Drummed his fingers against the shine of the desk. He would have slouched.

Brody returned and sat down, and this time he didn't hide his annoyance. "Here's the thing," he said brusquely. His breathing was heavy, strained from even this simple movement, and he smelled like the earthy sweetness of the chew tobacco he kept hidden behind his cheek. "We didn't find evidence of anybody in the house except for him. Not even you. So, if someone else was there like you say, who was it? How come we can't find them?"

"I don't know," Mira whispered. He was intent on her confirming whatever story he'd fashioned together in his mind. She frowned, looked at the dirty floor below her, and waited for this to be over.

"How long have you two known each other? You and Jesse?" he asked, refusing to move away. "Have you known each other for long?"

"We've been friends since we were little," Mira answered.

"A long time."

"Yes," Mira muttered, agreeing.

The sheriff sucked air through his teeth and sat back in his chair. It squeaked from his weight. "Good friends, you'd say, yes?"

"Yes," Mira repeated.

"Good friends. Maybe more than friends?"

"No, I— He—"

"What? He what?"

"We're not."

"But you like him, no? Maybe want to be more than friends?"

"I don't understand what this has to do with anything."

"This is how I see it. I see a girl who can't seem to answer any of my questions with any sort of specifics. A girl who is maybe trying to concoct some sort of story to help her friend. Maybe it's because she likes him. Maybe it's because she wants him to like her back. That's what I'm seeing from the looks of things."

"No, we were both there! You can ask Celine!"

"Oh, we will."

At that moment the door opened and Mira's mother appeared, yelling loud enough that Mira jumped. "Come on, Mira, we're leaving. Get up, let's go. Whatever this is, it's over."

"Sure is," the sheriff uttered. He waved his hand in the air. "Go on, get your kid out of here. Wasting my time with her stories. You know lying to a police officer is a crime."

"I wasn't lying," Mira yelled.

"Hush, Mira."

"I wasn't," she told them both.

Mira's mother yanked her from the chair, her grip strong enough it bruised. She pulled her through the musty hallways, hurrying along with a force of a hurricane. Everywhere bodies crammed together, leaving the air smelling of their sweat and stench from the day's heat. Salvation was outside these walls and they needed to find it. "Don't look at them. Don't look." Mira followed her mother, keeping her eyes down, which meant not seeing the anguished faces of men and women who looked like her, who she could have been with a slight shift in circumstance.

They left the police station and got in the car. Her mother almost hit the curb as she pulled onto the road. She drove for a few minutes but then made a turn into the nearest parking lot to a Big Lots. At this time of day, the lot was mostly empty, a few straggling cars scattered close to the entrance. Mira's mother pulled into a spot and shifted the gear into park and turned to her daughter. "What were you thinking? God, Mira, after everything I've tried to teach you. Do you see now? They're never going to care about what you say. You get it? I don't want you to have to learn this lesson twice."

"Yes," Mira had said, and her mother, seeing the pain her daughter was in, pulled back onto the road to home.

Perhaps she should have tried harder. She could have chosen not to listen to her mother, trying again and again until someone heard, but what Mira learned that day was how easy it was to let someone convince you of their truth instead of believing in your own. She could not stop hearing the sheriff's words and his reasons for her story. He would never believe her, no matter what she said, and no one else would either.

But Jesse was let go. Celine confirmed what Jesse and Mira had insisted was true. One look at her was all Brody needed, and so the police accepted Jesse's alibi, even though they didn't fully believe it.

To believe, one must care, and who's to say anyone ever cared? That's what her mother had tried to tell her. That's what she'd tried to make her see. Who was to say anyone ever cared—for Jesse, for her, for any of the black kids like them? Who's to say anyone ever cared at all?

Once, they stole away. They'd heard the sorrow song's call, heard its meaning within, and as the sun descended, they lumbered their way home for the last time. Moonrise, they gathered across the grounds they'd always known, moving toward the churchyard, toward beyond, tender-footed as they stepped across the bones of their brethren buried below.

They moved through the underbrush, scratched the sores that formed from the insects that bit their skin. Ever cautious of rattlesnakes hidden in the grass. Down to the river they went, seeing the sprawling willow tree with its broken bough pointing to their deliverance. They followed the trail to the forest. Soon it would clear, showing a path into the water. They were told the water would save them. It would wash away their sins, cleanse their souls, and they waded into the water, waiting for their brothers and sisters who would steal them away to their new home.

Their lives were destined for a different fate, and they would face it believing it was better than what they had known. To suffer infection. Heat exhaustion. Thirst. To hear the knotting of one's stomach for weeks on end as the body slowly starved. Better to crawl for miles in the dirt and grass, the body low enough to smell the deep, fragrant earth as they inched toward another life. Better to be shot at as they jumped fences to escape, climbed trees, disappeared into the fields. Better not to be caught because yes, they were hunted, found, and dragged back, forced to return to their owners, or if not claimed sold at public auction. Yes, many never made it to the freedom they sought, but still they tried, and would try time and again.

They chose this, always this, because they knew it was better to drown in the rivers and swamps. To meet the sanctuary of wild animals who would tear their flesh to bits. Choosing to end themselves rather than go back, because at least death would be at their own hand, and there was freedom in that choice, and they would be free. Send the dogs with their snarl and wail, bring the pattyrollers with their batons and guns. They knew what awaited them once they were found—their heels clipped to prevent them from running, the devices meant to torture and maim until they were fragments of what they used to be. Do what you feel you must, they dared, because they would. They knew the truth. They would be free. No matter what was done to them, one way or another, they would be free, because they had seen the promise of freedom and would not let it go.

IV.

K IPSEN WAS MOSTLY the same. She'd come across Antebellum
Road, a nickname given to the area of historical mansions
where the privileged few lived. The town was still deeply segregated, but this time driving through the disparity felt more
pronounced. As she drove, she saw more boarded-up houses and
more trash littering the gutters of streets. Mira passed a multitude
of closed-down businesses with the lingering signs of what they
used to be. Not much remained of downtown. She saw a check-
cashing-and-payday-loan store with its name glowing. *Fast Cash
Now* another sign flashed. The existence of poverty was palpable
and unavoidable. The streets were filled with potholes and despite
Mira's efforts, she couldn't keep from feeling the jolts as the car
bumped along.

A new road had been built to bypass all this and take visitors
straight to the Woodsman property. She'd seen the sign for the
exit and as she passed it knew what had been done. Curious, after
she'd driven through downtown she circled back to find the exit
and see where it would go.

The road circled the periphery of Kipsen. On this route a
bed-and-breakfast had also been built, most likely catering to
those who wanted to visit the Woodsman place but couldn't afford the overpriced cottages. Branches hung low enough that she
worried some of their leaves would scratch against the car. She

came to a sign marking the Woodsman Plantation as well as an arrow directing traffic. A gate had been built around the entire property except for a nearby parking lot built for visitors. The parking lot was full of cars with plates from all over the country. Not just from the South but from Texas. From Mexico. She saw a plate from Maine and wondered what kind of stories someone from Maine would come expecting to hear.

As Mira got out of the car, a family trotted along in front of her and she decided to follow behind. They looked like they were on vacation. The wife sipped from a large fountain soda most likely bought from the gas station up the road. The husband and wife wore matching fanny packs around their waists. They had a daughter, a small child who couldn't keep up walking so at one point they stopped and the father picked her up, carrying her the rest of the way on his hip. Mira walked behind them, although she made sure to keep a decent distance, all the while hoping they wouldn't turn around and see her—a black girl in a crowd of white.

People gathered and followed along the path. A busload of children emptied into the parking lot, and they ran past her, hurrying to beat everyone else inside. The chaperones called after them and Mira heard their accents, German, and a profound sadness came over her at the realization that this place would be their only experience of this history, a whitewashed house and grounds cleansed of the lives of the slaves who built them.

Mira slowed her pace to let everyone pass her up to the plantation's entrance. Before her trip, she checked out the website created to draw visitors, hoping to get a good sense of what to be prepared for. She'd read the story about Alden Jones. His ancestors had made their wealth from rice. His great-great-grandfather, Macon Jones, had owned one of the largest plantations in the Carolinas, but after he died his wife learned they were drowning in debt. To make do, she sold off their slaves to owners all along the coast, followed by the selling off their land. The family who bought the property, the Whitetons, maintained the plantation up until the war. Afterward, they returned and lived in the house, passing it down from generation to generation, until the last relative to inherit turned the house into a museum. Those who visited thereafter knew it as the Whiteton House. The Whitetons made no mention of the owners who came before them, erasing Alden's connection to this past.

Alden discovered the Woodsman house after seeing the Woodsman name repeated in several slave bills of sale he'd found when searching through his own family records. Woodsman had been the largest purchaser of Macon's slaves. One bill of sale between them marked the transfer of ninety-two slaves for close to thirty thousand dollars. He decided that with this house he'd rebuild his legacy lost, he'd remake it in his history.

Mira had clicked through photos of the Woodsman house. A mix of surprise and horror at the extent of the renovations kept her from looking away. Gone were the chipped paint and the broken windows, which was to be expected, but several structural changes had been made—a double-sided staircase led up to the front porch entrance, for instance. A new roof with tarry shingles to match its shutters, painted in contrast to the whiteness of the exterior walls and Greek Revival columns. Other structures had been built for effect. A courtyard full of other dependencies necessary for plantation life—a cookhouse, a well, a washhouse, a pantry. Mira had scanned through the images, trying to discern what had been built from what she remembered, but each image was more unfamiliar to her memory than the last. The overseer's house, the slave cabins, she did not recognize, but at the graveyard she stopped and leaned closer to the screen. WOODSMAN FAMILY GRAVEYARD, the caption read. Mira had lingered on the image for a few seconds, wondering what part of her own story lay buried here too.

White visitors hurried past Mira to get their tickets to the Woodsman house. They skipped and trotted and bumbled along. It was a holiday experience for them, a vacation, maybe for some a celebration. They'd come to relax, to enjoy a little revelry, to escape. She was not like them. She did not feel revelry. Nothing about this experience relaxed her. With an unsteady gait, she took short steps, pausing with each one. Her stomach made little lurches signaling to her the unsettled feeling that she might soon vomit on the grass. She did not want this. They wanted to be here and she had to be, but did she? Should she have come? How could Celine have brought her here for this?

Near the entrance an elderly black man sat in a cramped booth. He peered through the glass, glanced at her once to tell her the price before turning to the small computer screen in front of him. His ambivalence toward her, a black visitor at a place like this, was a slight comfort that tempered her embarrassment.

"Are there always this many people here?" Mira asked.

The man focused on her again, this time surveying the area around her to see she was alone before he shifted up in his seat. "It's been pretty crowded since it opened a few months ago. What with all that's happened." He paused, rubbed his chapped lips together, seeming to debate with himself what to say to her.

"I haven't heard," Mira told him, hoping he'd be urged on.

"The man who bought all this, Alden whatever. A couple months ago workers found his body splayed across the grass in front of the house, his face all contorted, twisted up like. Wild dogs had got at his entrails, leaving the remains scattered across that lush lawn he'd paid so much money for. They had to scare away the vultures hovering above, ready and waiting to swoop down for the rest of him. The story is his death was a heart attack, but try telling anyone visiting to believe that. Ever since, people have been flocking to this place, wanting to see if all those rumors are true. It gives them a thrill, I think."

They exchanged a knowing look and the man settled back in his seat. "I'm actually only here for the Hunnicutt wedding," Mira said. "I'm not sure where I need to be. Do I need to go up to the house?"

"Hunnicutt? Oh, yes. You'll need to go to where the cottages are. There's a check-in building. Here's a brochure with a map."

"Okay." Mira took the brochure. The front advertised shows for a cornhusking party happening in a few weeks. She opened it and scanned the inside. The brochure looked like it was for a theme park. *Take a tour of the Woodsman house and afterward have an authentic antebellum dinner, only $89.99,* a caption read. *Want to have some quality time? Take the kids to our playroom and have houseworkers Louisa and Mary watch them for the evening,* another read. The brochure also advertised performance showings. *A disagreement is brewing near the corn crib. Tom's caught Ben stealing a few ears. Will he tell? Shows every half hour. Witness reenactments of field-workers showing the tobacco-picking process! Slave driver Tom will take a break from his work to explain how he keeps his crew in line!*

"There are reenactments in tobacco fields? I don't know who would want to see something like that," Mira said.

"Yeah, they're for effect. Like all the reenactments."

"For effect?"

"That's what this place is. All these stops have reenactments. The whole plantation is meant for people to take part in, to give an experience of what plantations were like."

"So, you mean visitors go out and pick tobacco?"

"Nah, nobody's doing any of that. That's what they got the field-workers for. You just watch. You can dress up too if you like. A few of the visitors do, wanting to feel part of the show. Do you want a ticket for the park? You can see what I mean. Tickets are paid for as part of the wedding."

"No," Mira said, but changed her mind. "Yes, actually." She took the ticket and left the booth to find the cottage.

None of this is real, Mira reminded herself as she went through the park. None of what she saw was real; Alden had it built for show. Mira decided to walk around first. The property was overwhelming in its scope. The majority of the park was structured to be a replication of an actual antebellum-era plantation and all the workers performed their varying roles throughout the day as guests walked around and watched. The exceptions were the spirits bar that had been built along with a restaurant serving upscale renditions of Southern fare. Here was where the experience veered from its attempts at authenticity. A couple of photo booths had been set up where guests could take pictures dressed up in their own antebellum-era outfits. A group of women dressed in their drop-shoulder sleeves and hoop skirts laughed as they skimmed the photo strips they paid for. Along with photos, a music booth with a sign—SING YOUR HOLLER SONG—marked the front. For a dollar, guests could sit in the booth, pick one of the listed field holler songs, and listen. Once they were ready, they pressed a button that would record them mimicking the lyrics. When they were done, they could play it back, hearing a call-and-response between the audio recording and the singer.

Mira recognized the spot on the map for the Big House, but there were spots for other things—the rows of slave cabins, the overseer's house, the gardens, the kitchen, the washhouse, a smokehouse, as well as the tobacco fields. She went to the slave cabins first. A series of eight newly constructed cabins were separated into two rows. The path was constructed such that a person could walk around the circumference of the cabins and stop to peer into each one as they read a corresponding sign that talked about the distinct features of slave life. One sign mentioned that the cabin's construction was made of cedarwood. None of the signs had names of any of the people who'd lived and died on the grounds. It had all been erased.

Mira moved up close to smell the cabin's exterior. The earthiness of cedar overpowered the air and she backed away, choosing to peer in the window. Inside the cabin, wooden furniture had been placed strategically around the interior—a bed frame edged against the wall, and on the opposite were a table and several chairs. Mira walked over to the entranceway, where she noticed the air was cooler inside.

Is that air-conditioning? she wondered, and sure enough, she saw the air vents up above, painted to match the same hue as the wood to appear unnoticeable.

"These don't seem so bad. Hell, I could live in something like this," Mira heard an older man say as she passed him by, leaving the slave cabins to see the rest of the grounds.

Mira stood flustered as the man strolled along, nodding at the constructed lies built as truth. Who could look at this and not see it for what it was? To not see the slave system the cabin represented? Instead of a slave cabin they saw a modest-looking room they could have lived in and ignored the truth. None of them wanted to see anything else because the narrative that had been created affirmed whatever falsehoods people wanted to believe.

Like the clerk said, there were reenactments of certain features of plantation life everywhere. Employees dressed up in antebellum-era outfits performed their tasks for an audience. Slaves dressed in cast-off clothes, ripped and dirty. Tour guides wore clothes like the antebellum elite. They ushered groups around to explain what the visitors were seeing. Visitors followed, pausing to watch reenactments of men and women dressed as cooks, as seamstresses, as blacksmiths performing their particular jobs—cultivating crops, hoeing corn, hauling water, feeding livestock, and performing plantation chores. Visitors could see how candles were made, or they could see child slaves churn butter. Families took pictures, and the workers performed their tasks over and over again.

At the laundry house, a group of black women boiled clothes in a huge iron pot. They all were dressed in the same coarse gray shirts and skirts, but they donned headwraps dyed in a rich array of colors. Indigo and sunflower and ivy and lavender. One of the women wore the deepest maroon, the hue of dried blood. The women varied in age, ranging from teenagers to the elderly as they made a circle, using their bodies to create a separation between themselves and the tourists. They beat the fabric to remove the soap, hung the fabric on a clothesline to dry. They didn't turn to look at those gawking, only focused on each other and their job. Mira watched as spectators tried to break them of their trance. "Are those the master's clothes you washing? Better hurry and finish before you get in trouble." Laughter followed, but the women never broke. The sound of their slapping the clothes against the pot grew louder. A small act of resistance, it had to be, and she smiled in this recognition.

A little boy, maybe five or six years old, ran up to Mira and reached for her shirt. He grabbed it and pulled. "What are you?" he asked as he stared up. She met his inquisitive eyes, not knowing what to tell him.

"What do you mean? I'm not anything. I—I'm just here. Like you."

"Oh gosh, I'm so sorry." His mother rushed up. A chubby woman, with round, reddened cheeks. She wore a red visor with an insignia on the front of it, the outline of the Big House with WOODLAND PLANTATION printed underneath. She yanked her son's arm and pulled him back in a way that felt more insulting than the boy's question. "He thinks everyone is part of it," she said.

The woman rushed her son along and they disappeared among the crowd. "What are you?" the boy had asked and not, "What are you supposed to be?" The ambiguity in the question unnerved her. Had he been referring to what she looked like?

Throughout her life she'd been asked that many times, within the question the expectation that of course she was something else besides black. She glanced at her arm, at her skin, wondering what he'd meant. No, it should have been obvious to him what she was, just like she knew her place in the hierarchy of this revisionist story. This was all a performance dressed up as a history lesson, and everyone who'd bought a ticket was here to play a part. She knew where she was supposed to belong, and it made her want to escape it.

When the sun got too hot or their feet too tired, the tourists migrated to the restaurant or bar for refreshments. They congregated in the distance to sit under the cool shade of the outdoor porch. She decided to follow them in the hope of finding a break.

A lot of money had been sunk into renovating the grounds with the idea that visitors finishing the Big House tour would venture out to have a drink and admire the view, so a bar had been built along the back patio. The bar did not serve much. A few mixed drinks. Bourbon lemonades. Mint juleps. As she made her way over, winding through the wrought-iron tables and chairs, Mira heard a couple, having just gotten their drinks, affirm each other's decision to order the rum punch.

A young black girl tended the bar. While her frame suggested she was barely high school age, the way she manned the bar told otherwise, working with the careful ease of someone who'd been doing the job for years. The girl wore the same uniform as every other service worker Mira saw on the grounds—a short-sleeved black collared shirt tucked into tan slacks. Her hair was pulled tight in a bun at the nape of her neck. She wore no jewelry, no makeup, nothing differentiating or uniquely identifying her from the other employees. Mira watched her as she moved seamlessly between taking orders and making the drinks. She did each in batches to save time, ringing up customers first then shifting over to begin filling glasses with ice before pouring the bourbon.

When it was Mira's turn, she noticed that the girl had no name tag. It didn't occur to her until now that the man she'd talked to at the booth hadn't worn one either. Mira asked her name and she gave a bashful smile in response. "We're not supposed to give our names," she said, but said hers anyway. "That's beautiful," Mira responded, and the girl smiled again before asking for her drink order.

"A mint julep."

"It might be a couple of minutes. I got these other people first. Do you mind if I bring it to you?"

"Sure," Mira said, going to an empty table nearby to wait.

The girl at the bar continued to work. Not long after, she came over and placed a napkin down on the table with her drink. "Here," Mira said, handing her a couple of dollars from her purse. 'I'm sorry I almost forgot."

The girl stared back in surprise. "Oh," she said, flustered as she held the wad of money.

"Is something wrong?"

"People don't usually tip. Thanks."

She tucked the bills deep in her pants pocket and went back to the bar. When there was a lull, she walked around the porch, picking up the glasses patrons had left behind, moving swiftly to gather them before more customers came up to order.

Mira sipped her drink. Looking around, she once again noticed she was the only black person. She wondered if she was the only black person in the hotel. If she would be the only black person at this wedding. Most likely she would be.

No, Jesse. There would be Jesse. He was somewhere, although she wasn't sure if she would recognize him. It had been so long. How much of her was still the same as the girl he had known? What would he think if he were to see her now as she sat on the porch sipping her mint julep; would he judge her for participating in this way, however small? She judged herself, and yet—she was thirsty and it was hot. Even sitting in the shade, the heat melted the ice, watering down the sweetness. She brought the glass to her lips and took a long drink before setting it down.

She should leave but sat for a little while longer, slowly understanding that Celine had ignored what this place was so she could have what she wanted. What must it be like to not see what Mira did? To have the privilege of such a choice? Around her, all the guests had settled into such an easy narrative without even the hesitation of a questioning thought, and Mira wanted to know how they were able to do it—to enjoy a moment like this, drinking in contented peace, while admiring the view. To look out and say—oh, how lovely, and not think any more beyond the perceived beauty before them. To marvel at the twisted limbs of the surrounding trees, their branches climbing toward the sky, toward their heaven, and not see lynching trees. To have their drinks served and not wonder how many of those working for them were the descendants of slave owners. They sipped their drinks and talked among themselves, undeterred by the history of this land.

The bartender girl continued with her work, cleaning up after the messes patrons left behind, and Mira thought of all the workers she'd encountered as she passed through the grounds. Unnamed because they didn't need names to do their jobs, not to the people who'd come. Each one of them smiling and serving everyone they saw, including her. The black man who'd given her the ticket, the black men and women performing their song and dance, the black hostess greeting diners at the restaurant, the black cooks and bussers and servers—they each had treated her the same as any of the other guests, and it made her question what her own role was in this place. She wasn't Celine, no, but she recognized her own privilege in the moment. She watched what unfolded around her and did nothing, and because of that, who was to say she was any better? The dynamic that had been created was not lost on her, this replication of what once was, and because of this, a deep sense of shame came over her. It had been there from the beginning, but the feeling clarified itself as she finished the last of her drink. She felt shame for participating, for coming and being complicit. She felt shame for the circumstances that had led to a place like this existing. Shame for the realization that even after all these years of progress, this was where we'd come, to this corrupted version of the past we all thought we'd left behind.

V.

WHEN THE POLICE found the body on the Woodsmans property, everyone in Kipsen knew who it was. Mr. Loomis, whose breath always smelled like rotten fruit. He was a crotchety man who wore moth-eaten sweaters even in the summer. Dirty, box-framed glasses hung on the tip of his nose. His skin was patchy, dry, with petechiae on his cheeks and neck from the broken capillary blood vessels from drinking too much. He was always hunched over, his body fixed in a way as if it were about to collapse upon itself.

Loomis had lived on the edge of the Woodsman land. The story people in Kipsen told was that one of his ancestors had once been the overseer, who, toward the end of his life, had saved up enough to buy a piece of the land. Land that Loomis inherited.

Other rumors circulated about Mr. Loomis—that he'd been a sergeant during the Vietnam War and had never recovered from the men he'd lost. Or, others said, the men he'd killed. They said that even when he was younger he'd been angry and violent, that he used to beat his wife, a woman who left him long ago. They said he ate wild dogs gone loose. They said he captured children and locked them in his closet. They said he was one of the white knights. They said, they said, they said, with no one knowing how much, if any, of it, was true.

He'd lived most of his life out in the woods in his shack of a house, rarely talking to anyone. He had a Rottweiler chained to a post to scare away intruders. Sometimes, late at night, one could hear the sound of his shotgun as he fired off rounds in the dark.

Mira saw him once in Harold's Grocery. She'd reached for a box of Sugar Smacks and the box toppled to the floor. Mr. Loomis picked up the box and placed it back on the shelf. "Girl like you needs something that won't rot out her teeth," he'd said as he leaned down to meet her face to face. He smiled at her, the silver fillings on his teeth glinting in the light.

"You're the Groves girl," he said.

Mira nodded. He leaned closer, close enough their faces almost touched. She held her breath so as not to breathe in the sourness of his. "You look familiar. I can't place it. Something about your face. I know you. Don't I know you? I could swear I do."

He paused to see if Mira could answer his question, but Mira didn't know what he was talking about. She'd never talked to him before, and could only shrug. Mr. Loomis peered down at her a few seconds more before taking his finger and holding it in front of her face. "Your eyes," he said, staring. The corners of his own eyes held crusty granules of rheum he hadn't bothered to wipe away. "You look like—

"Get away from me!" Mr. Loomis suddenly yelled, recognizing in her face something that scared him. The shift in his tone caused Mira to jump back in surprise, but nothing could compare to his contorted expression of fear. "Get away from me. Get away. I want nothing to do with you."

Every now and then Mr. Loomis ventured into one of the bars in their downtown. He sat hunched in a corner, drinking bourbon shots one after the other. He mostly kept to himself, glancing around periodically before directing his gaze back to the table, too afraid to have anyone realize he was looking. No one bothered him. Loomis told stories of how his father had been a farmer, a sharecropper of tobacco mostly but they grew other crops—oats, corn, wheat. Loomis's father wanted him to leave, to work a better life than one of the field. "When I go, sell this land and get out of here. Don't stay like me. This place will get you if you stay. It'll find a way to own you forever," his father had told him, and so he signed up for the army, thinking that would be his way out.

"Before he died, my father used to tell me they were coming for him. I didn't understand what he meant until I started hearing the whispers," Mr. Loomis used to say, telling anyone who would listen. "It's only a matter of time before they come for us. Sons bear the sins of the fathers, you know, and they're coming to take their due. I should have stayed away like my father told me, but after he died that land became mine. I came back after I served my term to take what was mine. I'm the one who owns those woods. I'm the woodsman now."

For years Mira would wonder why he remained. If he truly believed in what he said, he must have known what would happen to him in the end. That he'd have to answer for what had been done. The land he lived on, land he'd inherited, it belonged to those his family stole it from, and as he said, sons bear the sins of the fathers. It wasn't greed that kept him; he could have sold the land. No, he remained out of his own defiance for what he believed to be true.

While the town may not have cared about Mr. Loomis, they cared about what they were convinced was a murder, and after the police found Mr. Loomis's body everyone began to question. Why had Jesse been out in the woods in the first place? What had he gone looking for in that house? What had he been hoping to find? Their questions were enough to fuel their fear, but in the end the police couldn't charge Jesse with murder, no matter how much they frothed with desire to. They found no weapon. Nothing linked Loomis to the house. All the blood had been Jesse's, and nothing could link Jesse to the river where Loomis died. The coroner listed his death as inconclusive. *Inconclusive.* The word haunted Mira with its lack of finality. Inconclusive. Yet, it was enough. Combined with the rest of it, it was enough for the police to let Jesse go.

Jesse had gotten lucky, but at school he was a pariah. The black kids wanted nothing to do with him, too afraid they too would be targets for the white students' hate, and who could blame them when every day felt like an escalation of the one before? One day Jesse left class to go to the restroom and a group of students ganged up on him, beat him bloody, and left him in a crumpled heap on the bathroom floor. They broke into his locker and stole his drawing book, drew pictures of murdered monkeys on all the pages. Another day he came to class and someone had placed a noose on his chair. After school, they hooped and hollered at him as he walked to his truck they'd tagged with slurs. Jesse, through it all, never complained. He said nothing, and the familiarity of his silence pained her to see, because she knew he'd finally learned the lesson she'd been taught to believe.

Jesse dropping out was the final fracture of their friendship. Mira and Celine had already been drifting apart, but without Jesse the distance between them grew. They were drifting, had drifted, until Mira couldn't figure why they were friends to begin with. Whenever they got together Celine would ask what happened with Jesse that day in the woods and Mira always hesitated. She couldn't help but feel it was between her and Jesse, and Celine had told before, so what was to keep her from letting the truth slip a second time? "Nothing," Mira decided, and each time she said nothing she could feel Celine pulling away.

"Why won't you talk to me?" Celine would ask, not pretending to hide her hurt, but Mira never answered.

Instead she wished she could talk to Jesse. She missed him. She couldn't deny the triviality of her feelings considering what he was going through, but more than missing him she wanted to know if he'd seen what she had when they'd been at the house. If anyone could understand, it would be him.

A few times, she'd gone to his house, lingering at his door in the hope he'd open it and talk to her. She shuffled her feet and kicked her heels and waited. Gnats covered the mesh of the front door screen. If only he would come to the door. That's what she told herself, standing on the porch. She knocked at the door, and the gnats swarmed around her face. She swatted them away before knocking again. Jesse, just answer. Answer and I'll tell you everything you want to know.

One day his uncle did answer. A thin man, with bones and skin hidden under clothes too large for his frame, he gave her a sneer. "You're wasting your time coming around. Jesse's not going back to that school. He's doing homeschooling to take the GED." Grayed stubble covered gaunt cheeks. "He don't want anything to do with you or your little white friend. Both of you are trouble," he said, taking a Swisher Sweet from his mouth and spitting on his porch.

"Will you at least tell him I came by?" she asked, urging. She stepped closer to the door, an attempt to see past in the hope Jesse was hiding in the shadows. "Will you?"

"Like I said, no use coming by anymore," he explained as he blocked her from moving farther. "He doesn't want anything to do with you. Took him long enough. You and your mother always snubbed your noses at black folks like us. Hiding in that house and acting like you was better. All high and mighty. Last I checked y'all black too," he yelled before shutting the door.

Before long, Celine fell in with a pack of other girls, white girls who envied her for her beauty but called her trash when she wasn't with them, and Mira spent the rest of the school year alone.

When spring came Mira found out she'd gotten a full ride to one of the state universities. The day she found out she went to Celine's. They sat together on the bed in her bedroom, a place Mira couldn't remember the last time she'd been inside.

Celine grabbed one of her pillows and wrapped her arms around it, clutching it tight across her chest. "College, huh?"

"I wanted to tell you. You were one of the only people I wanted to tell."

"What about Jesse? Did you tell him too?" she asked.

"No, I didn't. I haven't seen him."

"He works nights at the Pump N' Go. I saw him once when some friends of mine stopped to get gas."

"How is he?"

"We didn't really talk. Wasn't much of a chance to." Celine paused, considering. "He looked good though. Like maybe he was happy. Maybe in some ways it worked out okay."

"You can't think that." Mira's body clenched in response to her reasoning. They'd never talked about what happened, never had a real conversation about any of it, but she wished she had if this was how Celine felt. Celine stared at Mira blankly, with no awareness of what she'd said to Mira. Happiness? What Jesse was doing was surviving and Celine had mistaken that for happiness.

"His life's never going to be the same. Whatever crap options he had are gone. Don't you get it?"

"I get it. I'm not dumb. I'm trying to find a bright side. I wished he'd listened to me about going, but he'd gotten stuck on finding that place and, well, here we are."

"Sounds like you're saying he deserved what happened."

"No, I'm saying—I'm sad, is all."

"I'm sad too," Mira said. Sitting on Celine's bed, she couldn't help but feel like Celine did think Jesse was at fault, but she decided to leave well enough alone and not push. This was probably one of the last times the two of them would spend together and she didn't want to ruin it.

"Wow, college," Celine said, shifting the subject back. "I didn't apply anywhere. I didn't think I'd be able to afford it, not with my grades."

"I'm surprised I got in. I keep thinking they'll send me another letter and tell me it was all a mistake. That they meant someone else."

"No, no. It wasn't a mistake. You were always the smart one. Jesse was the artist, and I—I don't know what I was." Celine stopped, frowning. Mira wondered if it'd been a mistake to tell her. Celine had wanted out of Kipsen as much as she did, if not more, but whatever she felt, she didn't say.

"You should see Jesse before you go. He'll want to know too."

"I will," Mira said, struggling with her response as soon as she said it. He'd made it clear he wanted nothing to do with her, not anymore, and it seemed easier to let it go and leave. If it was what he wanted she'd give him this.

"When do you leave?" Celine asked.

"At the end of the summer. I don't know how I'm going to afford it."

"I thought you said you had a free ride."

"Yeah, but there's all these extra expenses. Like books, and getting there. I told Mom I'd take the bus so she wouldn't have to take off work to drive."

"Hmm," Celine said, then she got up and crouched down on the floor. She reached underneath the bed, feeling in the dark, until she got to what she wanted. She pulled out a tin box, opened it, and took out an envelope, handing it over to Mira. "For you. To pay for what you need."

Mira opened the envelope. A quick glance told her there was close to a thousand dollars inside. A thousand dollars. Enough to buy her everything she needed, for this year and maybe for the next.

"This is too much. I can't accept this, Celine."

"Yes, you can, and you're going to. It'll help at least until you get settled there."

"What about you? This was supposed to help you get out of Kipsen. What are you going to do?"

"You're the one who's actually leaving. You need it more than me, at least for now. Besides, I'll get it back, one way or another. Don't worry about me."

Guilt money for telling, Mira thought as she told Celine thank you and stuffed the envelope in her back pocket. She couldn't give it to Jesse, so she decided Mira would do. She took it, knowing what it was meant to be, but what she didn't know was how much she'd owe to Celine for whatever was to come after.

Mira disappeared for college and there, miles away, hoped to forget about Celine and Jesse and Kipsen. It was the advice her mother gave. "Baby, forget about this town. It's not worth any of the time you're spending on it," she'd told her, and Mira followed her advice. "Surround yourself in something different and new," she'd said, so that's what Mira did. She found people who didn't know anything at all about where she'd come from, about who she'd been, and when they asked, she made up names of cities, names both obscure or general enough that they would simply nod in response before changing the subject to talk more about themselves.

With time, forgetting grew easier. With time, her night-mares faded. And with time, she became what her mother always wanted. She graduated from college, went on to get her master's, and afterward got a job teaching language arts classes at a public high school. When Celine called again to say she was getting married, saying how she wanted the best friend she'd known to be there, Mira believed she had finally made herself anew, but she'd been wrong. What she'd tried to forget had always been there, this piece of her past, this history. Mira had tried, had spent a decade trying, but a person can't run away from who they are. Soon enough, what's been buried will rear itself again.

VI.

AFTER AN HOUR's worth of effort, Mira was ready for the rehearsal dinner. Her hair had curled from the day's heat so she had to press it again with her straightening iron. The sizzle and pop of her hair's submission filled the silence as she finished, and once straight, she brushed it into a side bun, hoping the style would hold for the rest of the evening. She did her makeup and painted her nails a clear polish with flecks of gold. The other women would have professional manicures and she hoped none of them would notice the difference. She wet a razor and ran it over her legs. After she was finished, she put on the dress, a gold-sequined backless cocktail dress she'd paid too much money for and knew she would never wear again. She felt bare and exposed. A shawl would help but it was too hot. Underneath the dress, sweat gathered in the crevices of her body, and the trickling against her skin made her want to undress and forget the whole thing, but she straightened and tried ignoring it.

Mira barely recognized her reflection in the mirror. This was the most dressed up she could remember being. Her mascara already weighed heavy on her lids. Her smooth skin made smoother with the veil of foundation, powder, concealer. A gleam of highlighter on her cheekbones and the tip of her nose. Her lips lacquered with gloss. On her neck a diamond choker, the jewels fake but she hoped no one would notice, and on her wrist a bracelet to match. Who was this woman she saw? One who found herself worried over how she looked for a bunch of people who wouldn't remember her name, if she'd fit in among them, if her dress and hair would make her pass. She didn't owe any of them anything so she shouldn't give a damn what they thought, but that didn't stop her from checking her reflection once more, and though she may not have owed them, she owed Celine.

Celine had been her friend. Awkward and shy, Mira had been bad at making new friends. She sometimes played with some of the neighborhood girls, but she always felt like they were doing it to appease their parents. She never stayed long, was never offered to stay after dinner or sleep over, and Mira would walk home alone as the streetlights blinked on.

Celine was a poor white girl who'd shared her cheese sandwiches with Mira for lunch. They borrowed each other's clothes, Mira wearing Celine's jelly sandals despite them falling off her feet when she walked. Mira didn't care that Celine was white, like Celine didn't seem to care Mira wasn't, and they never thought much about what anyone else said, and Mira had believed none of it mattered until the day at the plantation.

Obligation had brought Mira here because of the friend Celine had been. Still, standing in front of the mirror, it felt like it'd been a mistake to come, to agree to any of what she was about to do. Yet she had made a promise. By tomorrow evening the wedding would be over and she could enjoy what remained of her weekend as best she could. They were not far from the coast, a short drive, and she could go see the beach. She didn't have to go home right away, back to her empty bungalow in the city, nor did she want to. At the very least, by tomorrow she could come back to this cottage and relax. Order room service. Watch their cable. Draw the curtains and sleep until her body got tired of that too. Tomorrow seemed closer than she originally thought, and what lay before her became even more feasible considering, so she took a breath and grabbed her purse, leaving the cottage in haste in the direction of the dinner before she could change her mind.

The dinner was being held outdoors behind the Big House. A tent had been set up. Strings of lights draped from the ceiling. The theme of Phillip and Celine's wedding was "Silver and Gold," partly meant to be a play on Phillip's age and a reference to the Gatsby novel she'd read freshman year of high school, and so the entire space had been color-coordinated. Gold, ivory, and silver décor was everywhere—from the place settings of gold-rimmed crystal to the gold-rimmed charger plates. The tables were decorated with a textured silver tablecloth. All the guests went along with the theme. Mira was not the only one in a sequined dress, but the dress was where Mira had stopped. She saw women with shimmer in their hair, diamond fingers glittering as they waved to greet acquaintances. Even their makeup took it to a level Mira hadn't expected. Heavily pigmented gold eyeshadow lined with charcoal. The men had the same level of extravagance in the details of their suits. Gold and silver tuxedo vests with matching ties. Cartier cuff links. Only the best with every detail. Nothing was subtle.

Mira hesitated. A small crowd mingled around an open bar. The guests, wanting to keep in the spirit of the environment, ordered cocktails they imagined from the Gatsby era—gin rickeys, Sauternes, clarets, or champagne for those who knew of nothing else. Waiters floated through the crowds, parading an endless array of hors d'oeuvres. Oysters Rockefeller, mushrooms stuffed with crab meat, salmon mousse spread on sliced crusted bread. Mira watched as black waiters dressed in white suits lowered themselves while holding out the trays for guests to take, and take they did.

In the center of the room, a gleaming white floor had been built for dancing, but it was empty now. Everyone sat at tables surrounding it, occasionally glancing at the bare tile in the hope someone else had dared to be the first. On the opposite side of the floor were tables for the wedding party. Mira's eyes passed over the men and women occupying the seats, all of them people she didn't recognize except for one—Mr. Tatum, Celine's father, sitting at the end. He'd gotten thinner with age, and wore a silver suit lacking the adornments of some of the other guests. He sat with the rest of the wedding party, drinking and laughing, unaware of the pained expressions of the others for having to tolerate his presence. The display made her wince. As much as any of the guests might not have cared for Celine once, they certainly never did for her father. Hot-tempered and brash, he often gave voice to the worst of themselves, saying out loud what they tried to cloak in hushed gossip. Being white couldn't save him from their disdain, and no amount of money would make them bend toward acceptance.

He shouldn't be here. He'd been a neglectful father at best, and at worst? Mira remembered the nights Celine used to sneak to her window. Her tapping, light but sure, because she knew Mira would always answer, and she did, stumbling out of bed to slide the window pane open so Celine could climb inside. The two of them lying side by side in her darkened room. Some nights, Mira woke to Celine's wild thrashing, nightmares that made her jerk and cry in her sleep. Celine never said, so she couldn't be sure, but she'd seen the mottled marks Celine had tried to cover, and Mira never asked, because what could she do? What could either of them have done? They were poor, she had no one else, and he was her father. She was tethered to him in the way children were to the people meant to care for them. Before morning Celine would slip away, leaving Mira to find the opened window and the trail of footprints left behind. Mira would think about following Celine before stopping, realizing it didn't matter because she knew where they led.

Tatum shouldn't have been here but neither should most of the guests Mira saw. None of them had or did care for Celine.

This was all a show meant to impress, and if Tatum hadn't been invited his absence would have been the subject of every party table's gossip. In view of everyone, he could be ignored as guests concerned themselves with each other.

Mira fiddled with the tag that displayed her name and table number, ready to leave, but she took a breath and she searched for where she needed to go.

"Mira? You must be Mira."

A man stood next to her holding two champagne glasses. He was in his fifties, with gray hair slicked back. He had the beginnings of a beard, the gray hair complementing his tanned skin. He wore a silver suit with a matching tie. That's too much silver, Mira thought, but he wore it all well.

"Yes?"

"I'm Phillip Hunnicutt. Celine's fiancé."

"Oh! It's nice to finally meet you."

She was a little taken aback by Phillip's visible age, but he was attractive in the way older men always are. The kind of man who had the experience to know what he wanted. Self-assured, but with a slight air of haughtiness that wasn't surprising for someone with money. He grasped Mira's hand and held it, not wanting to let go. His eyes remained fixed on hers. "Mira," he repeated, smiling.

"Finally."

"Yes."

The longer he stared the more Mira resisted the desire to pull away from him, too afraid of how he might interpret the gesture.

Finally, he let go of her hand and she reflexively folded both arms across her waist. "I'm so glad we're finally meeting. Celine said you were her oldest friend. That you two knew each other as kids. That's impressive."

"Where is she? I haven't seen her yet."

"Really? Oh, she's around here somewhere." Phillip gave a

cursory glance at the crowd before turning back to Mira, continuing the conversation. "You know, Celine said you didn't want to be in the wedding?" he whispered.

"What? What do you mean?"

"She was going to make you maid of honor but said you told her you'd be uncomfortable doing it, so she asked my sister. Luckily, it worked out. Oh, look, there she is," Phillip said, looking past her at the crowd.

"Mira, I'm so sorry." Celine came over and hugged her immediately. Mira breathed in a mix of bergamot and jasmine as Celine held her close.

"I didn't think I'd ever find you." Mira smiled. Celine let go and they stood before each other. Celine's fake eyelashes accentuated her smoky eye makeup; her deep red lips didn't smudge despite the drink she held. Her hair was shorter, loosely curled into a fake bob. She wore a gold-beaded flapper-style dress with a slit that went up to the thigh, and she carried an ostrich-feather clutch. Celine had kept her jewelry simple, wearing only her engagement ring, which was large enough to be the only thing she needed.

"Do you love your room? It's the nicest of the cottages, and like I told you before it's all taken care of."

"Yes, it's lovely."

"Isn't it?" Phillip interrupted. "When I heard about the changes at the Woodsman, I knew I wanted this to be the venue. Celine wasn't sold at first, but it's beautiful, isn't it? The owner did an amazing job."

Celine didn't mention what Mira expected her to, but it had to be on her mind. She couldn't have forgotten. Mira waited, wondering when Celine would bring up the story with Jesse, but she only smiled and talked more about the itinerary for the wedding.

Phillip stood beside her, an arm clutched around her waist. When her glass of champagne was close to empty, he gave her his own, not wanting her to leave his side to look for another. On the surface, Phillip was attentive of Celine in a way Mira hadn't seen anyone ever be, and she wondered if underneath all this pretense, he did love her and if it was the kind of love they'd dreamed of as kids—honey-drenched, sweet enough to make a body ache. Love full of heartbeat flutter and bewildering desire. Strip away the wedding with its pomp and circumstance and weren't they two people making the same whispered promises to the other? No one saw what went on between them when they were alone, so who could say if it wasn't love? Certainly Mira couldn't. She didn't know about love. Longing, she knew. She'd grown up with its taste in her throat, but love? The kind lasting and true? She hadn't known in any kind of real way.

Before long, it was time for the dinner and everyone gathered to their tables. Celine leaned toward Mira and in hushed words asked her to stop by her room after the rehearsal. Away from the crowds, with them together again, Celine might tell her the truth. The comfort of a future explanation made Mira nod, agreeing, and Celine squeezed her hand before being ushered away to join the rest of the wedding party.

Mira was put at a table with two couples; she'd known both of the women from high school. When Mira explained she'd gone to Jefferson High too, they stared back, dumbfounded.

"I left Kipsen after graduation," she said, relieving them of their discomfort for not knowing who she was.

The evening so far was going how she'd expected it would—poorly—and she had barely made it an hour. She'd been right about the guests. Around her a sea of white faces cavorted with like-minded acquaintances. None of them noticed her, but they wouldn't have. In high school she'd been a poor black girl they'd tried their best to ignore. Just because she sat among them at Celine's wedding didn't make things different.

The women at her own table had returned to the conversations with their partners, leaving her with nothing to do but take slow sips from her near-empty glass. The whole experience already felt like a lasting regret she'd have to bear, and she still had the dinner to suffer through. She sat up in the chair, wishing for another drink, and then saw Jesse. She thought she'd prepared for this moment but seeing him changed all that. Even from far away he looked good, and the sight of him filled her with such yearning she could hardly contain it. And then she couldn't help but smile. He sat at a nearby table farther up, also with strangers. The way the tables were arranged, he couldn't see her unless he knew where to look, but what was important was that she could see him.

He behaved like someone who'd learned to question every decision. Everything deliberate, cautious, back straight, hands clasped together in his lap. He didn't dare drink. A glass of water sat at the table and when there was a lull in the dinner, he brought it to his lips. He looked like he was trying very hard to feel as though he was actually there, that he belonged.

During the speeches at the beginning of the dinner, whenever a woman spoke—Celine, or Phillip's mother, or any of the bridesmaids—Jesse lowered his head, not lifting it again until the conversation had shifted.

Mira couldn't stop watching him through the rest of the meal. She directed her gaze back to the table each time she thought he noticed her, pretending to listen to the conversation. She wanted to catch his attention, wanted him to see her, but she also wanted to see his face when he noticed her. Her stomach was in knots; she could barely eat any of the steak on her plate.

When dinner was close to over, Phillip's parents, the hosts, announced that the floor was open for dancing, and Mira saw her chance to go to Jesse, but Celine's father got to him first.

"You're a murderer," he said, pointing at Jesse. He'd tried to control his tone, as if aware of his place in the hierarchy of guests, but he still managed to be loud enough to cause attention. A quick hush fell over the room as guests processed the scene.

"Dad, it's all right—" Celine started, her face flushed. She got up and moved closer in her own attempt at de-escalating what she saw coming, and it might have worked except Jesse snickered in response. A reflexive action done before he could consider its repercussions, that men like him could be killed for less. A snicker could be a dangerous thing, especially when directed at those who felt the world had already done them wrong.

Clench-jowled, eyes burning, Mr. Tatum wasn't going to stand for Jesse's disrespect, especially among the company he'd spent all evening trying to impress, and he pushed him out of his chair. "I said you're a murderer," he yelled as Jesse stumbled to the floor. "Everyone knows it. Knows what you did. You don't deserve to be here. You've got no right."

Jesse's face shifted from Celine to Phillip, waiting to see if one of them would do something, but neither of them intervened. Jesse raised both hands in the air, palms facing outward, as he stood back up.

"It's okay," he said, "I can leave."

Jesse gave up so easily. It was painful to watch as he resigned himself to leaving. Everyone else's silence made Mira's skin burn. Do something, she wanted to scream. What is wrong with all of you? How can you sit there and let this happen?

None of them cared, that was why. Not about him or anything they'd witnessed happening here. They'd all come for entertainment. This, another show, and Mira had had enough.

She pushed back her chair, stood up to go to Jesse, but Celine reached out for Jesse's arm, touched him before pulling away in the recognition of how it might look to the others in the room. She called his name and struggled over her words. "My father, my dad, he's just—" She stopped before lowering her voice. "Please, Jesse, don't go."

But before them all, Celine made a choice—her father, the real person who needed to go, would stay. His display alone should have been enough to kick him out. Celine must have known how her decision would appear to Mira and to Jesse especially, who stared back with such incredulousness that Celine would be an idiot not to see. Celine's eyes pleaded—Jesse, solve this problem not of your making—and to Mira's astonishment, he did. He got up to go.

"Hey, I'm not done with you yet," Mr. Tatum yelled in a slurry jumble of words. "I didn't say you could go. I'm not finished telling everyone about you and what you did."

"Dad, stop—"

"They need to hear it! They need to hear about how the police found Loomis all bloated and bruised in the river. His hands and feet gone. I knew Loomis and he didn't deserve what you did."

"I didn't do anything."

"You did and you did it at this place. Down by the river. Did you all know that? You should, if you don't. That's why you're back, isn't it? You've come for another one of us?"

"Us?" Jesse repeated. "You think you're one of them? Just because your daughter is getting married to a Hunnicutt doesn't mean they'll ever look at you as anything beyond what you are—a poor drunk. How foolish can you be?"

"That's enough," Phillip interrupted. "Maybe you should go. It seems like you're not wanted."

"Celine?" Jesse said, but she remained quiet. By this point whatever she could have said wouldn't have made a difference.

"Damn right you're not wanted," Mr. Tatum scoffed.

Jesse suppressed a laugh. He scanned his growing audience and Mira could see the contempt he'd tried to hide earlier. Mira thought for a second he'd paused, seeing her, but he moved away before she could be sure. He quickly surveyed everyone before stopping at Celine.

"Well, okay, then," Jesse said. He straightened his posture in an attempt to compose himself.

Silence followed in the few minutes after he left. Everyone awkwardly waited for the tension to end. They passed glances at one another, shifted in their seats. Slowly, a few reached for their glasses, pressing their drinks to their lips to take long sips. Others lifted their knives and forks to cut into their entrées, the metal scraping against porcelain plates as they sliced chunks of beef to put in their mouths. The low murmur soon escalated into a cacophony of voices. Conversations started again. Laughter filled the room. Before long what everyone had witnessed had faded.

"Well," Phillip said to Mr. Tatum. "He's gone. Like you wanted. You want to sit down now? Come on, here's a seat. Sit down and try and enjoy the rest of the night before it's over."

Mr. Tatum went and sat in the chair Phillip had pulled out. He was sullen but he didn't say anything else. Phillip clapped his hands before signaling to the band to play a song.

Celine held Phillip's hand and together they walked to the center of the dance floor. They moved side to side, dancing in rhythm to the music. Phillip pulled her close and she put her head against his chest.

To onlookers, it was a beautiful scene—the glimmer of gold and silver against the dimmed lights, the two of them, clearly in love, holding each other as the music swelled to a fever pitch.

Nearby, employees clocked out of their shifts. They carried the odors of their jobs with them, the sweat and stink of their labors, as they shuffled into their cars or walked the long paths down the dark roads. Their bodies sagged and heaved from the burdens of the day. Their feet shuffled against the dirt. They moved like ghosts in the distant periphery, visible only to those who believed in seeing. They would come again tomorrow, and the day after, but now they made their way home. Mira wondered if they turned to look at what was behind them. She wondered if they thought what they saw was beautiful too.

VII.

Mira ran out from under the tent, hoping to catch up with Jesse. His dark shadow walked on a path ahead of her and she rushed toward it. "Hey, Jesse, wait up," she said, breathing hard when she'd finally reached him. She touched his shoulder, startling him around.

At first Jesse didn't seem to know who she was. His face made a pinched look when he got angry, and she saw what he'd been trying to hide from the others, but then she caught his flash of recognition and his expression softened.

"Mira?" Jesse stared at her, his confusion fading. Up close, she studied the changes in the man Jesse had become. He was tall, almost six feet, but the way he hunched his shoulders made her wonder if at times he felt insecure over his height and the amount of space he took up in the world. He'd grown a beard. His skin was darker, tanned from working in the summer sun. His skin managed to be smooth and wrinkle-free, despite both of them nearing the age to begin to be concerned about such things. If he shaved she imagined people would assume him to be in college.

"The prodigal girl returns," Jesse said.

Mira had missed his teasing. His mouth opened to say something else and she braced herself to hear a joke about her dress or the heels she could barely walk in, but he hesitated, appearing to change his mind. "What are you doing here, Mira?" he asked instead.

"I haven't seen you in ten years and that's the question you want to ask me? How about, 'How are you?'" she responded, trying to keep her tone light in the hope they'd settle into banter. "Besides, Celine invited me, and I—"

"And you—" Jesse interrupted, frowning. "You should go on back inside to the party. It's almost over. Don't want to miss what you came for."

"I've been searching for you all day. Since I got here. You really think I'm going to leave now that I've found you?"

Jesse's dismissive response confused her. After all this time, she'd hoped their meeting would go another way, that he would want to know how she was at least and not be so distant, if not hostile.

Mira caught him glimpse back at what they'd left behind and she realized his anger hadn't been because of her. Without them, the party's evening had continued on its rhythm. Following the future bride and groom, the guests had joined the dance floor. From this distance, the bodies hovered like glittering orbs circling around each other under the lighted tent. A cacophonous harmony of laughter and music swelled into the night. Jesse's eyes held the hint of someone mournful, and Mira imagined in a way he was. Maybe he'd come believing it would have gone differently than it had, that after all this time they wouldn't continue to hold him to his past, but the past was always there. For him, for all of them.

"I'm sorry for what happened back there," Mira continued.

"You shouldn't apologize. It's not your fault. It's theirs."

Jesse tried to play it off, but Mira kept on, pushing further. "Celine should have stuck up for you. She should have done something. I can't believe she sided with her father. Why'd she invite him anyway? After he—"

Mira faltered as she wondered if Jesse knew. He'd have no

way of knowing unless Celine had told him, and why would she have when she'd never even told her? As a child, Celine had been good at covering for her father—Celine rarely invited either of them over, and when she did, it was when he was long gone, making his drive to work at the paper factory two counties over, and they never questioned her actions because they both assumed it was because her father never wanted them there, and they knew enough not to push for more truth, and Celine never offered any beyond what she must have imagined they assumed.

"Celine hates him. Or I thought she did."

"Yeah, well—he's still her family, and you know as well as I do roots mean something to these people, even if the core is rotted."

"I would have thought you'd want nothing to do with any of this. I don't get why you're here."

"I could ask you the same question."

"Celine convinced me. She called and I didn't know how to tell her no."

Jesse laughed. "Sounds right. She was always hard to say no to."

"That's not what I mean. You're right, but I—I think I had to come back. So much felt unresolved. *Feels* unresolved."

"Is that right?"

Instead of answering, Mira listened to the faint call of whippoor-wills. As they stood in the near dark on this once-plantation, with only the dim light of the lanterns in the distance, time felt arbitrary. In this moment looking out onto the grounds, at the path from the Big House leading toward the cottages, she could not tell the difference between this year or one long ago—fifty years or a hundred. The wind's whisper through the trees made her wonder at all they'd once witnessed. What burdens had the trees had to bear?

During their silence a decision seemed to settle in Jesse's mind. He exhaled deeply, and forced a smile. "You want to go for a walk?"

As Jesse and Mira walked along the grounds, she occasionally noticed a few other employees. Kitchen staff, their white uniforms stained from the day's work, passed them on the way to the parking lot. Mira waited for him to start the conversation, but the longer they walked the more Jesse appeared at ease. He'd grown used to the quiet of being alone, was comfortable in the space of himself. If she let him they could walk together and the whole night would be like this.

"If I close my eyes, it sounds like the summers we used to camp outside in my backyard," Mira said, hoping with the memory Jesse would open up. "The three of us with just a couple of blankets to sit on. No tent."

"Of course no tent. Tents were for rich kids," Jesse added.

"And each of us holding flashlights while we tried to use cigarette lighters to make s'mores," Mira continued after hearing Jesse laugh. "With that Marshmallow Fluff because Celine thought it'd be the same as marshmallows but it dripped and stuck to everything."

"Well, you were the one who brought that grab bag of candy. Kit Kats and Snickers aren't for s'mores."

"They were still good though."

"I haven't thought about those days in a long time. I remember how hot I always was, what with those itchy blankets in the middle of summer. I've never been able to sleep in the heat, and I always worried your mother would find me with you and Celine. I always lied there awake in the dark and listened to you and Celine as you slept."

Mira raised her eyebrows. This was not how she remembered it. It always felt like Jesse had been having as much fun as Celine and Mira. He'd always come with snacks and listened to their jokes and gossip. She didn't know what to do with hearing this different story than the one she'd known.

"Why'd you come if you didn't like it?"

"Because it was something we all did, I guess. I don't know,

I did a lot of stuff because of other people. I was too proud then to admit it."

They continued walking, and after enough time had passed Jesse finally opened up about the past decade of his life. He'd lived in Louisiana for the first couple of years. Made an okay living as a derrickhand on one of the oil rigs out on the water. His uncle Ray got sick with cancer and he came back to take care of him. It was around that time when Alden Jones came wanting to buy a bunch of the property in the area.

"I told Ray not to do it, but he had a lot of medical bills. Jones offered more than the house would ever have been worth anyway, so he took it and paid off his debt. What little was left he gave to me after he died. That was over two years ago. I worked a bunch of odd jobs after until I got the one here."

"You work here? At this place?"

"I'm one of the field hands. I also keep the grounds."

Jesse said it so matter-of-factly. Like it meant nothing. After everything, he was working at the place that had altered his life. Did it haunt him to see it every day and know what this place had become? She couldn't bring herself to ask, not yet, and so she asked another. "Jesse, you still haven't told me why you're here for the wedding. I gave you my reason. What's yours?"

"Can't I just have wanted to see what it was all about? Celine—she was always going to do what she wanted, whether or not I said anything, whether or not she thought it was right. You saw that firsthand earlier. Me being here wasn't going to change any of it."

"I would have thought you'd want to avoid it."

"Maybe I got other reasons." Jesse rubbed the back of his neck, a gesture he did when he'd gone too far in saying what he shouldn't. "I don't want to talk about Celine anymore," he continued, cutting Mira off before she could ask. "Tell me how you've been. What you're doing now."

"Well, I teach," Mira said, laughing a little. "High school. Language arts classes."

"How is it?"

"Not what I expected, but then, what ever is?"

"A teacher, huh?" Jesse said. Mira could tell he was trying to picture it—her in the classroom in her blouse and trousers, hair in a loose side bun, her heels clicking against the tile floor as she walked around the classroom. "I don't remember any of my teachers looking like you."

"We usually don't wear cocktail dresses."

"True, true," he said, nodding. "Maybe I would have been a better student."

"From what I remember your grades weren't bad."

"They could have always been better."

Better. Hearing the word caused her face to flush. She hadn't connected it before, but hearing Jesse talk, the similarities between the two of them were apparent. In Jesse, she saw Javion.

"I had this student," she said. "He reminded me of you a little."

"Oh yeah? He give you shit?"

Mira paused and Jesse took her answer for yes, laughing in response. "Well," he said. "He must really be like me then."

Mira found herself telling Jesse the story—how he acted in her class, what she'd said to him the last day she saw him, and what happened with the other teacher. "He dropped out, I think. I have no idea what happened to him or where he is."

"That's not all on you," Jesse said after she was finished.

"But part of it is. Don't we have a responsibility to each other? I had a responsibility to that kid and I failed him."

"You didn't fail him."

"Yes, I did."

Mira had failed Javion because she'd judged him in the same way all the white teachers judged not just him but the other black kids at school, and she'd let her judgments affect how she saw him. She'd never seen him at all, because if she had she would have seen a kid struggling and in pain.

"I thought if he just acted better that the world wouldn't be so hard on him. Who was I kidding? I mean look at all this!" Mira threw her hands up in the air and spun in a circle. "This is what we're up against. A place like this existing to remind us of our place. That we've never been equal. We were never free. Knowing that, don't we have a responsibility to do our best to fight against it, to stand up for each other in any way we can? Maybe all of what happened to Javion wasn't my fault, but you can't tell me I didn't fail him in some way, and—you can't tell me I didn't fail you too."

Jesse was about to respond but stopped, his attention caught by something in the distance. He squinted toward the darkness, but when Mira looked she didn't see anything. "Jesse, what is it?" she asked, and he shook his head and told her it was nothing.

"I thought I heard something, that's all. This plantation is starting to affect me a little," he said, changing the subject. He gave a heavy sigh and kicked the dirt, forming a dust cloud that soon dissolved in the air. "I don't understand how people can't see it for what it is."

"I think they do. That's why they come," Mira said.

"They're going to make millions off this land. It's not even theirs. It's ours. Yours, mine, and every black person. Our ancestors were the ones who built this place. They lived and died to make it, and what did we get in return? I don't even know anything about any of them. I know nothing about who they were."

Mira thought of the story of Marceline. "You know, my mother drove me out here once," she told Jesse. "She took a shortcut on the way home and we went down this road and she pointed and said our ancestors were buried out here, so where are their graves? Where are they now? I didn't remember seeing any graves when I took the tour earlier."

"There is a graveyard. I can show you."

They walked until they got to another smaller trail, leading into a thicket. Mira stopped but Jesse urged her on, saying they were close, and then they came across the graveyard. The area was gated, and seeing this, Mira was about to give up and turn around but Jesse stopped her. "Hold on," he said, leaning down and feeling along a cluster of stones near the door. "They keep a key somewhere. I just got to find—Ah, got it." Jesse unlocked the gate and they went inside. It was dark enough that they had to go to each of the markers and lean down close to see the names, but the graveyard was small so it didn't take long. All Woodsmans, each of the names, and Mira sighed. She came across Roman's plot. BORN 1817, DIED 1884. She passed by the other gravestones, those of his wife and the rest of his family members—brothers and sisters, nieces and nephews—but no one else. After they'd gone through them all, Mira looked back at Jesse, horrified. "This is it?" she said. "There's got to be more. What about the slaves? Where are their graves?"

"Doesn't look like there are any. Not marked, at least."

Jesse circled the graves again. He stared down at one of the plots at the edge of the graveyard. He got down in the dirt to inspect closer.

"What is it?"

"This one isn't like the others. I didn't notice it before. It's a fieldstone marker. The others are marble. You see?" Jesse said.

Mira looked. IN MEMORY OF MARCELINE, it read. BORN 1836, DIED 1885.

"I know this name. This is her. Or—it isn't. I don't know."

"What do you mean?" Jesse asked.

"One of my ancestors had a relationship with one of the Romans. She had children, at least one, maybe others, I don't know."

"You think this is your ancestor?"

"It could be. Or his daughter. Or it could be someone else entirely. I don't know."

Mira stared at the marker, frustrated at the lack of answers she'd been given. There was no mistaking that this grave was not like the others, but she struggled to understand the reason for the distinction. Why was this the only marker of one of the slaves, if that's even what it was? Who had this Marceline been to the rest of them? Had she been Roman's lover? Or was she his daughter? She was important enough to be buried in this graveyard with the rest of the family, but Mira wanted to know why, understanding she probably never would.

"She died after the war, so she made it through that at least," Mira said, noting the date. "A small comfort. She died free, who- ever she was." She ran her fingers along the engraved name before dropping her hand. "If it's her, and she's buried here, that means he must have cared for her, right? That has to mean something. God, I don't want my story to have come from rape. I don't want how I came to exist to have come from tragedy."

"If you look hard enough at any one of our stories you'll find some tragedy lurking." Jesse held out his hand to help Mira up. "I don't think we're going to find the answer you're looking for. Not tonight, anyway."

They left the graveyard. Jesse locked it back up and hid the key. After, they continued walking around the rest of the grounds, killing time because neither wanted to leave the other, to let the evening end. They passed the majority of the other outbuildings and were near the slave cabins. Mira leaned against a railing and peered into a darkened window.

"I've spent my entire life doing what I could to avoid being seen in the way visitors have looked at the black people who work here. I've watched as their faces betray their real desire—for all this to be more than replication. They want us serving and smil- ing and this place delivers. No wonder it's popular. You realize this, right?"

Jesse walked up to the railing and leaned against it with her. "Yeah, I know," he said solemnly.

"Why do you stay?"

Mira asked the question because, the way she saw it, he had no ties left in Kipsen, not anymore, and she wanted to know what kept him living in a town that hated him. "After your uncle," she continued. "You could have left again, gone back to Louisiana. Or anywhere. Why stay? And not just come back, but work here of all places?"

"We do what we have to," he said. It was a pithy platitude meant at dodging any kind of real answer.

"Come on, you can do better than that."

"Does it matter where I am? North Carolina. Louisiana. The scenery could change but I'm still a black man living in America. Being in another state's not going to change that. Besides, if I had left, I might not have ever seen you again."

He leaned into her, giving her body a little push, a familiar sort of tease like he used to do long ago, but they were older now, no need to skirt the boundary between friend and lover. A heart can only take so much yearning. She'd done enough to last. His action, small yet intimate, was enough for her, and feeling bold, she kissed him. She'd meant for it to be quick, not expecting him to kiss her back. His salty sweat lingered on her tongue. He pulled away with an expectant look that mirrored her own.

"I've been waiting for that for a long time," he said afterward. "Since—" He faltered, but she knew what he meant.

The moment would have been perfect if they were anywhere else. One direction led toward the plantation they'd once broken into, and the other led to the river where Mr. Loomis was found dead. As she stood with him on the path, she forced herself not to think of what had happened—of the police arresting him for murder, of the break in their friendship after he'd been released, of the years that had gone by between then and now.

Jesse must have sensed this too. They stood awkward and fumbling underneath the dim park lights. "Are we ever going to talk about it?" he asked when she'd been silent awhile.

"Why do we have to? It doesn't matter anymore."

"Mira—"

"Don't. All that is over."

"But what if it isn't, Mira?" Jesse continued.

"It's getting late," she responded, much to Jesse's disappointment. While they'd have to deal with their past eventually, it didn't have to happen tonight. Better to leave the evening with the feeling they were having a new beginning.

"I should be getting to bed. You should too," she said, trying to smile, and Jesse relented, nodding.

"I can walk you to your cottage. It's the gentlemanly thing for me to do," Jesse said, puffing his chest up in a mock sense of bravado.

"No, I'll be all right," she assured him. "We'll see each other tomorrow, right? I'll see you again?"

"Yes, I'll find you after the wedding. I want to lay low until then but don't worry. I'm not going anywhere."

The prospect of tomorrow buoyed her enough to let go, and Mira said goodbye. She ambled along the path toward the cottages, lingering in the feeling of her restless desire. She replayed the evening. As imperfect as it'd been, the memory was still hers to have. Memories always dimmed after their creation, and she wanted to stay in this one as long as she could. To think, she'd almost decided not to come. She licked her bottom lip, glad for a moment she'd let Celine persuade her otherwise.

VIII.

As she walked back to her cottage, Jesse's condemnation urged itself to the forefront of her mind. *Celine was always going to do what she wanted*, he'd said, dismissing the history of their friendship with one sentence, but it was true. Celine always did what she wanted. There was the time the two of them skipped school to swim at the river, where they'd come across a group of boys skinny-dipping. Celine and Mira giggled as the boys peeled off their sweaty and soiled clothes, naked and free as they plunged into the water.

"Let's join." Celine pulled off her clothes, threw them on the ground, and sauntered toward the group as if she'd always belonged. She talked with them for a few minutes before waving for Mira to join. The boys went to a school in a neighboring county and, like them, were playing hooky, swimming in the river because it was one of the few places they could be alone.

"There's a nicer spot a little farther down," one remarked, a sandy-haired boy with crooked teeth. "We should all go," he offered, and the other boys responded with teeth-filled grins.

Celine and Mira followed until they saw the river cliff, and before Mira could tell Celine they should leave, the boys were daring them to jump. "We've all done it," they teased. "Nothing to be afraid of."

"I'll go," Celine yelled, bolting to the top of the cliff. The boys heckled from below. *She's not going to. What a liar, a tease, she won't jump,* but they didn't know the Celine Mira did, one who could kill a copperhead as if it were a garden snake. They'd play chicken by lying on railroad tracks, and when they heard the rumbling of the train Celine would close her eyes like she was sleeping. She never looked to see who remained, waiting, listening as the train got closer until finally, right when they thought it was too late, she pulled herself up and ran away, her face flushed pink as she asked who won, feigning surprise.

Mira knew Celine would jump, and, breathless, they had all watched her fall, her arms swanlike and delicate, a seamless line of honey hair and milk-white skin. Her body would appear right when they'd lost faith in her, when they decided to move on; that would be when she'd let her body go.

If a person could be defined by a singular instance, Mira would have described the moment she'd seen her jump. This was the girl from Mira's childhood, daring and headstrong, but at the party, Celine had been so willing to conform in the hope of everyone's approval. Mira tried to reconcile the woman she'd seen with the girl she'd known, but memory can shift in its recalling, making the past become not what one remembers but what one believes. Mira had always believed Celine jumped for the simple reason that she wanted to, but when she thought back she wondered how much of Celine's actions had been meant only to prove to everyone she could.

Celine had asked Mira to stop by her room before the night was over, and while it was late, Mira decided to go find her. She walked back up the path to the house and, making her way inside, noticed how much the house had changed. Alden Jones had opted for a mix of antebellum and contemporary furnishings, giving the illusion of the era but with modern comforts. Flat-screen televisions mixed with antiques. Thick, velvet curtains darkened the windows. The main parlor had been converted to a check-in lounge, but because it was late in the evening and all the rooms in the house had been booked, no one manned the desk and the area was roped off. A sign marked the morning hours when the next attendant would be available along with a guest services number to call in the event of emergencies.

Mira passed a large white ballroom. Everything inside gleamed. White floors, white walls, all of it a blinding brilliance that refused to be ignored. Mira couldn't remember this room from when she and Jesse had snuck in. Curious, she went to it, wanting to see what it had been made to be.

Along the walls were a series of portraits of the Woodsman family members. She tried to guess their names before checking the plaques below. Their eyes seemed to follow her as she walked throughout the room, her shoes making light clicking noises amidst the quiet. Mira walked to the center and stared up at the chandelier, its golden fixtures shining from the light. She stood across from the fireplace, above which hung a portrait larger than the rest of them, of Roman Woodsman. The man in the portrait was balding. Thick eyebrows overpowered his deep-set eyes. He had sunken, hollow cheeks, his skin a weathered texture. He sat upright in a chair, his posture rigid and his face straight ahead.

Below the portrait hung two plaques. Roman's name was inscribed on the first. Mira peered at the second to read the description. NICKNAMED THE WHITE CASTLE, THIS ROOM WAS BUILT FOR ROMAN'S FUTURE DAUGHTERS. WHEN HE WAS UNABLE TO HAVE CHILDREN, IT INSTEAD BECAME A PLACE WHERE HE ENTERTAINED GUESTS, AND IT WAS CONSIDERED TO BE HIS FAVORITE ROOM IN THE HOUSE.

The ballroom was meant to be a replication. The Woodsman family portraits reproductions. The furniture and décor inauthentic copies. It was all what was assumed to have existed, or conjured in Alden's imagination to have been here during the Woodsman family era. It wasn't real. Yet, she couldn't shake the feeling it was.

Mira left and tried to get her bearings. She came across one of the staircases and went upstairs, searching for Celine's room.

Each door had a plaque with the name of the room embossed in gold. Mira scanned over each one. THE RANDOLPH. THE CHAUNCY. THE LANDRY. THE SEATON. All plantation owner names. She kept going until she reached the end of the hall and stood in front of the last one. THE CORDELIA.

"Celine," she said, unsure if she'd remembered correctly. She lightly knocked on the door, not wanting to disturb the guests in other rooms. "It's Mira. I just— You said to stop by, and—"

"Oh, I was hoping to see you," Celine said upon opening the door. "Everything was so rushed earlier. There wasn't nearly enough time for us to talk at the dinner."

Celine wore a white negligee underneath a white terry robe. Her hair was freshly washed and the damp waves had made wet spots on the shoulders of the fabric. With her face stripped of the day's makeup, she looked like the Celine Mira used to know, except older. She was still beautiful, but slight imperfections had begun to show. Tiny cracks had settled on the corners of her eyelids and mouth. Her complexion appeared duller, her blue eyes less vibrant.

This could have been one of the rooms Jesse had snuck into when they were younger, but since everything was different now, she couldn't know for sure. Brass wall sconces emitted an amber glow. Bouquets of peach roses filled the vases on the vanity and on both bedside dressers. Celine had ordered champagne for herself, and the crystal tray with the empty glasses and half-drunk bottle sat on the floor near the bed. The bed's frame was a replicated antique, its posts carved with intricate sheaves of rice. After letting Mira in, Celine went to it and settled on the mattress. She ignored the champagne and picked up a brush that'd been hidden under the sheet's folds and ran it through her hair.

Mira walked to the nearby chaise. Like a lot of the furnishings in the bedroom suite, the chaise appeared new, barely touched. She marveled at how much money had been spent, at the gratuitous display of it, both in its attempt to erase and preserve the past. "You're getting married," she said, as she sat down on the chaise's stiff upholstery.

"Do you like Phillip? What do you think of him?"

"He seems nice enough."

"'Nice enough.' Tell me what you really think."

Celine forced a laugh, but Mira knew her enough to recognize her attempts at playing off an underlying insecurity. Celine didn't need her approval but she wanted it anyway. "He dotes on you," Mira offered.

"Yes, that's true. It can get little obsessive though."

"Do you love him?"

Celine appeared taken aback by her directness, as if she'd never considered another possibility, or that anyone would dare to ask her otherwise.

"Why would you ask that?"

"I'm sorry, I didn't mean anything by it." Mira hoped to relieve any possible tension, but Celine was clearly still bothered by the question. She shifted on the bed until her back was against the headboard and placed the brush in her lap. Mira was about to apologize again and leave, but before she mustered the nerve Celine spoke.

"Like you said, Phillip dotes on me," Celine asserted. "We've already started on plans for a house. Three floors. A wraparound porch. Inside, it's going to have hardwood throughout, not that tacky laminate some of the other girls have where you need to be careful about what shoes you wear. Custom cabinetry and marble countertops in the kitchen. It's going to be perfect. Everything I could ever ask for and more than what anyone else here has ever had."

Celine had always desired the life she believed the Kipsen rich lived, whereas Jesse and Mira used to mock them for their money. The year they all turned thirteen, one of their classmates held her birthday party on a luxury charter yacht where she'd invited the entire year. Students had to carpool to Beaufort, and this might have been the reason Jesse hadn't wanted to go. They would have had to find someone to drive all three of them, and none of them knew who would. Jesse was too proud to ask and Mira too shy, so they agreed not to go, convincing Celine to do the same. "It's obscene anyway," Jesse had said, "the way they flaunt their money at us."

Celine had played along at first. "Do you think they know what they have?" she'd asked after they'd quieted down.

"Oh, I bet they do. That's why they try so hard to make sure people like us don't ever get it," Jesse had joked, not recognizing in Celine what Mira had started to see.

Celine didn't need to say it, but she wanted the South she felt was denied to her. She wanted the taste of gumbo thick with meat, crab cakes buttery and rich, slow-roasted barbecue tender enough to fall from the bone. Her childhood had been one of saltines soaked in milk for breakfast, mayonnaise sandwiches for lunch, Vienna sausages wrapped in American cheese for dinner if she was lucky. Food she could make because her father never cooked. Pantry-staple food, salty and never satiating.

Celine wanted cotillion balls. To shimmy a white dress up over her hips. To slide her hands through white lace gloves. To have the dangle of pearls from her neck. She wanted a gentleman's hand holding hers. To breathe the magnolia-scented air as he kissed her under the moonlight-drenched sky. She wanted all the romance and gentility she believed made up their world. Longed for it then, and Mira saw she wanted it still.

"Is that why you invited them?" Mira asked, not hiding her accusing tone. "You wanted to make them jealous? You think they'll accept you now because you have more than they do? This is why the wedding is here too, isn't it? Because of them. They used to treat us like shit and it's like that doesn't matter anymore."

"Can't people change? You're judging them for who they were, but maybe if you gave them a chance, you'd see you're wrong. They're not so bad."

"Yet because of them you're having your wedding here. At a plantation, Celine."

"It hasn't been a plantation for over a hundred years, and it's not like my family owned slaves."

"What about its history? The suffering that built it. That's never forgotten. It's always there. Isn't it always there?"

"If this is how you felt you shouldn't have come."

Mira could see the discussion was going nowhere and it was getting late. She stood up to go. Celine did not move from the bed as Mira walked to the door. Mira hovered as she contemplated what to say before leaving. This would be the last time they'd talk. Tomorrow was the wedding, and after—after, who knew if she'd get another chance to talk to Celine. A gulf stood between the two of them. They were strangers, tied together solely because of obligation for what used to be, out of an allegiance to what was.

If this was it, if they were to never see each other again, she wanted to offer her one last truth, one she knew none of the other girls would give. "You know you don't have to go through with any of this, right? Who cares about any of them? The Celine I know wouldn't. You can still change your mind. Tell them all to go to hell. Don't do this if it's not what you want."

Celine's lips pursed together before forcing a smile. "Who says it's not?" she asked before briefly turning her gaze away. When she looked at Mira again her expression brightened. "Besides," she said. "Isn't that what divorces are for?"

Mira laughed and shook her head. This was the Celine she knew. "You're right," Mira said, softly smiling. "Sleep well, Celine." She closed the door, but their conversation felt unfinished. She thought about opening it again and asking Celine to clarify her answer, but didn't, hearing the sound of laughter from afar. It was the light, airy laughter of a child, and she whipped around to see to whom it belonged. The hallway was empty. No child anywhere. She could have been in one of these rooms, but to Mira's knowledge all the guests Celine had invited were adults. Celine's request on her invitations had read *Adults Only*, printed in a glittery script font. Whose child was it? If no children were here, where was the laughing coming from?

The laugh came again. Unmistakable this time, a playful giggle calling to her, asking for her to take part.

"Okay, where are you?" she answered, and waited. "Is this a game? I don't know the rules. Can you come out and tell me?"

The laugh grew softer, fading, and Mira continued following the sound, curiosity having gotten the best of her over the possibility of a child hiding alone in the house somewhere, especially at this hour. She'd regret not checking if later she learned this turned out to be the case. She snuck up to each door along the hallway and listened, expecting to hear some family commotion to let her know her instincts were wrong, but heard nothing.

"I couldn't have imagined it," she said, confused. She spun around, played the waiting game as she fixed her attention on the empty hallway. Any second the child would give up and appear, either from one of the rooms or from some darkened corner Mira had missed, but as the minutes passed, no one came.

"Last chance!" Mira gave it one last shot in as upbeat of a tone as she could muster, but the laughter she'd heard had stopped. Deciding she'd done enough and not wanting to linger any longer, she left the house.

Outside, the weather had changed; the heat finally died down. The air was unnervingly cold considering how warm it had been earlier. North Carolina weather could be unpredictable, especially this near the coast. A fog was forming, unusual for this time of year. She wished she had brought the wrap. As she walked back to the cottage, she passed the structures she'd seen before, the smokehouse and laundry room and kitchen, now closed up. A quiet cloaked the land. Those staying on the property were already in their cottages. Couples making love in their air-conditioned rooms, settling off to sleep. Mira was the only one out roaming.

Seeing Jesse had sparked a reverie of remembering and she

found herself roaming the grounds. She wanted to find the barn, to see if it was still here. The barn had been the last place she and Jesse had been before their lives fell apart. She let herself think of the feel of his hand as he'd gripped hers tight, leading her through the woods. The slow exhale as they found the barn and crept in. The creak from the springs of the wooden door as Jesse pulled it open. They'd stood inside an abandoned marker of history and it felt like a secret for them to keep.

Any action, however small, carried the weight to alter a life. What if she'd told him about her feelings then, in the barn? Part of her lingered in the fantasy. "Mira," he would have whispered, moving close. His hand touching the small curve of her back, drawing her toward him. He would have kissed her, and nothing after would have happened in the way it did. Who knows how different it could have been?

The closer she got to the tobacco fields, the darker it got. Her heels dug into the soft earth with each step and after a while she gave up and pulled them off, walking barefoot the rest of the way. There were no light posts this far out past the main house. Her eyes had adjusted to the night but it was still hard to see. She re-lied on her memory of the layout from when she'd read the map earlier in the day.

The barn should be near here. Not far this way, only a few minutes more, she thought. She hugged herself against the crisp night air. What if she got lost and ended up wandering around the grounds until morning? She would never get through the wed-ding then.

Up ahead, in the tobacco field, Mira saw a figure, a woman, standing at the edge. Where had she come from? Mira hadn't seen anyone else during her walk. The woman had appeared from no-where. Was she lost like Mira seemed to be?

"Hey, where are you going? Do you need help?" Mira called out, but the woman didn't move. The woman faced the fields and Mira was unable to see her expression. Whatever lay ahead had transfixed the woman. Dressed in all white, in the dark she looked like an apparition, a ghost roaming. Her hair cascaded down her back, and to Mira, she appeared to be an angel, not a ghost, something descended from the sky, something holy, something true, and Mira called out again, asking for her to turn around, but the woman wouldn't listen. The woman took one step and then another, her bare feet gliding through the dirt and mud, dirtying her skin, getting closer to the edge of the fields, and as she got closer, Mira's heart quickened. She called out to the woman in white once more before running toward her, to see who she could be, but when she got to the fields the woman was gone. Mira searched and searched but there was no one, not a single other person anywhere to be found.

IX.

MIRA WAS GRATEFUL for the comfort of her bed. She sighed from the feeling of the cool sheets hitting her skin. It had been a long time since she'd enjoyed a simple luxury like this. Her apartment did not have central air and the box air conditioner was constantly on the fritz. She was always hot. By now she'd hoped to have adapted, but she never got used to the damp feeling of the mattress wet from her sweat. She needed a new one; every morning she woke to a persisting ache in her lower back. In this bed her back didn't ache. The cool air was a welcome reprieve. This, to her, felt decadent, and she relished it. Her muscles relaxed as she settled in and closed her eyes.

It was not instant, not a sudden pulsating rush of remembering, but instead a dull hum, a gnawing that grew as pieces of her evening with Jesse replayed themselves for her in the dark. How he looked. How he'd been. When he'd hugged her, she'd caught a subtle hint of cologne and was surprised he would wear it. She tried to conjure the smell of it again, tried to remember the feel of his body when they'd embraced before separating for the night. His hand had only grazed her waist, but the memory was enough to get her started. She thought of how he'd grabbed the railing surrounding the slave cabins, how his fists had tightened against the rail, and the muscles in his forearms had tensed. All that was left was her ache from longing. She pulled the covers up and over the rest of her body, pressed her head against the pillows.

Mira dreamed. She dreamed of a knife being lightly dragged across her skin. The blade was dull, not sharp enough to do any harm, but the feel of it made her itch. In her sleep, she reached for the places the knife touched, scratching so hard that unbeknownst to her she drew blood, the drops of it getting underneath her fingernails and smearing the sheets. Soon, it was not the knife but something else, insects—blowflies circling her mouth before landing, the feathery hairs of their antennae brushing against her skin, then ants that crawled around her, slowly moving their way onto her body, on her legs, moving up her thighs as they found their way into the depths of her. They were along her stomach, circling her belly button, moving around the slopes of her breasts, crawling on the most vulnerable parts of her. Then the flesh flies came. They were all over her, multiplying along with the others as her body began to bloat, their legs moving rapidly against her skin, going up her neck, tracing the line of her jaw, crawling across her chin and pausing at the curve of her lips, slightly damp from the lick of saliva. They rested atop her eyelids. They stood before the cavern of her nostril, tempting the path inward, the tickling itch of them hovering near her breath. It wasn't enough to swipe them away. She batted one and another took its place. They multiplied, growing to cover every inch of her body. She swatted and shook in her terror, and finally woke to find herself wildly thrashing her arms in the dark.

Mira's heartbeat thrummed in her ears. She was alone in the quiet of the cottage. The only sound was the humming of the air conditioner. The temperature was colder than she'd meant to set it to. The clock on the nightstand showed a few minutes after three. Mira had not been sleeping for long.

It was only a dream that had bothered Mira so. A bad one, but still, a dream. She looked at her arm and saw the marks from her scratching. Her fingertips glided lightly along the broken skin.

She hoped tomorrow no one would notice what she'd done to herself.

Even awake, Mira could not shake the feeling something was after her, whether hiding amidst the folds of her sheets or caught in the tangles of her hair.

A pinprick. A blip of pain in the contour of her neck. Mira reached and felt for the mark. She pressed her fingers together, sat up in the bed to see. The smeared remnants of an insect lay between her thumbprint and forefinger. Mira flicked the fragments onto the floor.

X.

The wedding would be at noon, but it was not yet time. In the other cottages, guests slept. The sun had barely risen; the light had not completely erased the room's fading darkness. There was still time to turn their backs to the sun, to pull sheets further around bodies, sleep a little longer until they too must slip on their dresses and their suits and leave for the ceremony. For now, they dreamed of the reception to come, of the free bar, the hors d'oeuvres and wedding cake they'd cram into their mouths. This was what they'd come for anyway—the party, one they knew would be in gloriously decadent excess, because they knew Celine's desire to impress them with what she believed they wanted to see. Celine was beautiful, after all, had always been, was even more so now, and had managed to snag a man many either wanted or wanted to be. Phillip Hunnicutt of Honey Leaf Tobacco. Phillip Hunnicutt who once said he'd never marry. They'd all tried his cigarettes, for many their first, enjoying the mellow flavor as they inhaled. He was a name to them, a name that meant something. Never mind the rumors, because that's all they managed to ever be.

Upstairs, in one of the rooms of the Woodsman house, a group of women gathered. Dressed already in their matching bridesmaids' outfits, they went over the schedule of the day. Some of them stood barefoot, the straps of their high-heeled shoes dangling from their fingers. Some of them half listened as they snuck out their mirrors to reapply lipstick or make sure their mascara hadn't feathered or their concealer hadn't clumped on their skin. While the wedding wasn't about them they'd be damned if they didn't look perfect for it. Their dresses glittered and rustled as they shifted their bodies, as they finally got up together in search of the lady on whom they were waiting. It was time to get her and begin.

A knock followed by another. "Celine, dear, we're all outside waiting for you. Open up," one of the gathered called. She had practiced her voice, making it airy and light, just like she'd practiced her expressions, wanting to make sure she didn't reveal her true feelings about this day.

"Please, sis," Phillip had begged her. "Celine doesn't have anyone. Can't you do this? Can't you do this for me?" She'd done this for Phillip, and after she'd said yes she'd given herself up to the obligation of it, but as she leaned against Celine's door and waited for it to open she wondered why Celine hadn't asked that black girl who was here to be in her place. The two of them had been friends once, so why wasn't she standing here instead? The more she thought about it, the more unfair it became and the more incensed she was over the whole affair. Her knocking became banging, growing louder and faster with each passing moment Celine refused to open the door.

"She should be up, shouldn't she?"

"Why isn't she answering?"

"Do you think she's there? She can't possibly be sleeping."

"Maybe we should call."

They dialed the number of the room and listened outside the door as it rang. They did this two more times, listening in the hope of hearing the sound of the phone leaving its hook, a voice, groggy, tired, but still heard.

No one answered.

"Someone go to the front desk or find a cleaning woman to open the door."

A bridesmaid scurried away, hurrying out of sight while the others continued to wait for her return. Each round of door taps grew with more force, more urgency. "Celine, honey, you need to answer now," they called to the door. It had been a good half hour of this and they were late, everything veering off schedule because of Celine and her foolishness. None of them wanted to be here. All they wanted was to get through this day, to fulfill the request that had been asked of them, but to do that she needed to answer the door.

The front desk woman came, shuffling as she repeatedly apologized. She looked far too young, a tiny thing, barely eighteen probably, with the smoothest dark skin they'd ever seen. Blemish free without the slightest hint of makeup, and they stood beside her seething at her unaware beauty as she fumbled with the keys to open the door. "Can you hurry up?" they said with a sneer, and the girl stuffed the key in the lock and turned, opening the door for them all.

"Usually I don't do this," the girl cried after the fact, her voice shaky over having to make the decision to break with protocol. "It's not our policy—"

None of them listened. They were already crowding inside, pulling on the sheets to reveal an empty bed. They checked the bathroom, opened the closets, and found nothing, nothing, nothing except the wedding dress on its single hanger, its fabric shimmering underneath the dim light of the room.

XI.

SCATTERSHOT SLEEP FILLED the rest of Mira's night. She spent the remaining hours shifting her body from one edge of the bed to the other. When dawn came and Mira's room filled with the morning light's amber glow, she pulled herself out of bed to get ready. At least by the time she showered and dressed the restaurant would be open and she could get a little food and coffee in her system.

The restaurant was crowded by the time Mira arrived. She assumed most everyone she saw had been at last night's party, and they'd managed to beat her here, filling the dining room and the bar in the hope of brunch cocktails before the ceremony. Mira stood at the entrance, waiting until an empty seat became available, and when it did, she sat down and asked for a menu.

"It's packed," she told the bartender, an older black man who had only enough time to smile back before he had to help other customers. He moved briskly from section to section of the bar, transitioning seamlessly from taking orders and charging credit cards to making Bloody Marys and mimosas. When he came back to her she ordered eggs Benedict, hoping a treat would make her feel optimistic about the rest of the day.

A man sitting on a nearby stool got up to go and he brushed up against her, putting a hand on her bare leg in the process. The touch of his skin against hers made her jump, but when she looked at the man expecting an apology, he looked at her as if he'd done nothing wrong, a smug grin on his face as he turned to go.

"Seriously?" she called after him.

He stopped, pivoted. He leaned into her, his face close enough to kiss her if he wanted. He put his hand on her shoulder, traced small loops on her skin with his finger. He rubbed his lips together before straightening again. "Someone should teach you some manners. You're lucky I've got someplace to be, but maybe I'll see you later," he said, then walked away.

No one saw what he'd done. No one cared enough to catch a glimpse. Around her, customers continued getting drunk, paying no attention to her sitting at the bar alone. Aside from the bartender, Mira was the only black person in this restaurant and while she'd tried to ignore this reality before, the acknowledgment now filled her with fear. Fear told her to get up and go, head back to her cottage, and order room service. Fear made her want to ignore what just happened as well as last night, but she'd already ordered and the food would arrive soon. A scene would make the situation worse, and she feared leaving would cause one. He could still be watching her, waiting somewhere among the crowd for when she'd be alone. She couldn't leave, and so did the only thing she knew to do—she crossed her legs and leaned across the counter, positioning herself in a way to make it seem like she deserved the space she occupied, but no matter how she arranged her body, no matter where she tried to focus her attention, she couldn't let go of what he'd said. She could pretend, but pretending was not believing.

Next to Mira on the other side, two women talked. Each of them wore a pastel dress. Gold jewelry gleamed on their wrists as they brought their champagne flutes to their lips. Mira didn't recognize them from the night before, but she didn't recognize anyone. She assumed they were Phillip's guests.

"What do you mean by 'she's gone'?" Mira heard one of them

ask. She tried not to eavesdrop but she was close enough that despite her best intentions she heard anyway.

"Disappeared," the other responded. "You know. Left. Got cold feet. With that heel I would have left too."

"Heel? What did he do?"

"That man will go to town on anything in a skirt, if you catch my drift. He wanted to settle down but no one would have him."

"I didn't know about that. I only knew from Darcy that he could be a bit hot-tempered, but you know Darcy—she thinks a man who curses has gone too far."

"It wouldn't surprise me if he was too much to handle and that's why he'd been single for so long."

"I feel like a little fury is sexy, you know? Like when Rhett takes Scarlett in his arms and kisses her. I love that scene. He knows she wants him and is willing to take her. Every woman wants a man who'll be forceful like that, but in the right kinds of ways."

"Yes, that, I think, is the difference," the first woman said. She poured the rest of her drink in her mouth and pushed the glass to the edge for the bartender to collect. She ran her tongue across the front of her teeth before making a sucking sound and continuing. "That girl Celine was the only one around here left to give him the time of day. Trash meets trash if you ask me, but she must have smarted up. You know, people think he's got all this money, but tobacco's not doing well. No one smokes that much anymore. Even consolidating, most tobacco farms can't match the scale of production of any of the big companies. That's why he started that practice, for goodness' sake. I heard he put most of what he had in this wedding because he knew how important it was to her. He did all that and she's gone and he's gotten himself broke over it."

"How much do you think they spent?"

"I don't know, but it's got to be a fortune. What a waste."

Mira heard Celine's name and had to interrupt. "I'm sorry, I didn't mean to overhear, but are you talking about Celine? The fiancée?"

"Oh, you haven't heard?"

"No, I—I haven't heard. I'm sorry, but what happened?"

"That girl's gone. No one can find her anywhere. She's gone and disappeared."

Mira couldn't cancel her order, so she paid for her meal and left, making her way to the main house. A small crowd had gathered around the entrance, but with nothing to see and nothing to do they just circled around the lawn. Others had gone and sat on the porch chairs. Guests sat with their hands clasped in their laps, their eyes scanning in search of further gossip.

Mira passed them all and went upstairs, heading straight for Celine's room. She wanted to knock on the door and see for herself, but when she got up there the door was already open. Phillip sat on the unmade bed. He ran a hand through his disheveled hair. He was dressed in his nightclothes. Dark blue silk pants and an unbuttoned silk shirt. On his feet a pair of black slippers.

"No one can find her," Phillip said, shaking his head. "No one knows where she is."

"What happened?"

"When she didn't make her hair appointment, Kristina"—he gestured to a woman sitting on the sofa behind him—"came over to see if maybe she'd just overslept. She knocked on the door but no one answered and so she got one of the staff with a key to let her in, but this was what she found. Everything left like this, with her gone. The bed was unmade so she slept here, so she must have gone somewhere this morning, but no one has seen her."

"Not exactly," Mira interjected. "I came by last night and she'd already messed up the bed."

"You came by? What time was this?"

Mira paused, trying to think. "It was late. At least an hour after the party ended. I'd gone for a walk and then came up to check on Celine. I wanted to talk with her one last time before the wedding."

Mira left out the part about Jesse. She wasn't sure why, but the decision was a reflex. Phillip shook his head again. Seeing him now in the light, he looked much older than he'd appeared last night. His worry made the wrinkles in his face more prominent. The confidence he'd exuded the evening before was replaced with a wearying sense of dread.

"How long has it been?"

"A few hours," Kristina interrupted. "We were supposed to meet her at eight and it's past ten now."

"I don't know what to do. Should I call the police?" Phillip directed the question at Mira, his voice betraying a pleading for her to tell him yes.

"It's too early for that, I think," Mira told him. "She's probably out on the grounds somewhere and lost track of time."

"The wedding party has split up and are tackling different areas. The other bridesmaids are asking guests in the cottages if they've seen her. The groomsmen are going through the rest of the buildings. Most of the staff know too and they're keeping an eye out for her. We've got everyone looking," Kristina said.

"Then I'll go look too," Mira offered. "Okay, Phillip? I'll see if I can find her. There are all kinds of places she could be."

"Has anyone told her father?" Kristina piped up.

Mira tensed up thinking about Mr. Tatum. "Has anyone seen him?" she asked, and both Kristina and Phillip shook their heads.

"Someone should try and find him. To let him know."

"I'll go look," Phillip said, his voice sounding calmer now that he was faced with a task.

"No, Phillip. I think you should stay and wait here in case she comes back. After last night, Mr. Tatum is probably passed out drunk in his room, or he probably went home. We should focus on finding Celine first."

"You're right," Kristina agreed. "Somebody needs to be here, and, Phillip, if you go outside everyone will see you and it'll make things worse. Right now, all they have is rumors, but if they see you they'll know something's up. This way we can keep everything contained until we can figure out what's going on."

Mira appreciated Kristina's help, although she disagreed with her reasoning. Still, Phillip decided to stay, keeping watch inside the hotel suite in case Celine came back.

With a plan in place, she left the room and went outside to figure out where she should try to look for Celine. The truth was she had no idea where Celine could have gone. She couldn't say she knew Celine anymore, however close they used to be when they were younger. She wondered if the two women at the bar were right, if Celine had really bailed on her wedding. Mira thought back to the expression on Celine's face last night. Her flippant joke. Had Celine been trying to say something else, something darker? Despite the distance between them, if Celine truly had been unhappy, Mira hoped Celine would have said something. If Celine couldn't, then what did it say about who they'd been to each other after all? Celine had to be fine, Mira reasoned, and so she walked out into the sun in the hope of finding her.

XII.

KRISTINA HADN'T MENTIONED searching the fields, so Mira decided she'd look there first, partly because she felt a beckoning to return. She trudged along the path away from the Big House, pausing every few minutes to get her bearings. In the light of the day, the layout of the grounds confused her, and she had a difficult time gauging which direction she needed to go.

"Excuse me. I'm looking for the tobacco fields?" Mira asked a man she came across on the path.

"What do you want to go out there for? There's no showing today because of the wedding, although that doesn't look like it's happening either."

"Please, I don't have my map and I don't have time to go back to my room and try to find it. Do you know which way?"

"The fields are that way, I think," he said, pointing south, and Mira started in that direction.

While she tried to think about Celine and where she might be, she couldn't escape the image of the woman in white. Mira had been too far away to recognize her face, but whoever she was, she'd been alone, and no one came out to these woods unless they were looking for something or someone was looking for them. What other reason could a person have, especially with the night's darkness surrounding them? The woman's attention had been fixed on what lay hidden deep among the tobacco stalks, something Mira had been unable to see, and she wanted to find what last night she might have missed.

It was a long walk, longer than Mira remembered it being, and the farther she went the more she regretted not changing out of her clothes for the wedding. The dress was too constricting, and the material made her itch in the heat. At least she had comfortable shoes, flats she'd slipped on instead of the heels she'd felt pressure to wear. She continued on the uneven path, trying her best to recollect the way she'd gone.

With the plantation closed for the wedding and most everyone still at the restaurant, the grounds were whisper-quiet, a stark contrast to what she'd witnessed yesterday. Without the conversations of strangers or the sounds of the machinations of plantation life, she heard the sounds of the woods. Its hums and calls. With each step she heard the low whistle of wind or the trill and buzz of insects hiding in the dark.

The foliage grew dense and lush as she continued into the heart of the woods. The trees' branches above clouded the summer light, and she worried she'd cross a point of no return where she'd be lost forever. It didn't seem she was getting any closer to the fields but closer to a world unfamiliar.

"This isn't right." Mira stopped, finally admitting to herself she was lost. Everywhere she looked the path appeared the same, and she had no idea anymore which way to go. Her worry became a fear as she started again, quickening her pace, her chest tightening as she ran faster in the hope she'd stumble upon something she would recognize. Soon, she had to stop. The sound of whispers rippled through the trees. Whispers swelled to murmurs. She couldn't resist following the sounds. Murmurs shifted until she heard talking. Then, singing. A haunting call trailed by the chorus's response.

Now see that possum he works hard. Hoe, Emma, hoe. You

turn around, dig a hole in the ground. Hoe, Emma, hoe. But he can't work as hard as me.

Mira followed. The trees fell away and she came upon a clearing where a few feet ahead of her a group of black men rotated, digging a large hole in the ground. They struck their shovels deep in the ground and threw the dirt in the air. Mira watched it fly. As they worked, they sang, their deep voices bellowing as they dug again and threw. She sank behind some brush to watch, hidden from their sight.

Hoe, Emma, hoe. You turn around, dig a hole in the ground. Hoe, Emma, hoe. He sits a horse just as pretty as can be.

Mira could not see into the hole, only the end of the shovels as the dirt they carried was released into the air, but she did see the men who'd climbed out to rest. They were dressed in plain clothes, mostly torn rags that were darkened with sweat and covered in dirt. Many didn't have shoes, walking through the grass and mud barefoot. When they climbed from the hole, they glanced up at the sky, their eyes searching for something to deliver them. Nothing ever came and soon they were told to get back to work, and they fell once more into the hole, continuing on with their pace.

Hoe, Emma, hoe. You turn around, dig a hole in the ground. Hoe, Emma, hoe. He can ride on and leave me be.

This was not like the reenactments she'd witnessed before. These men were gaunt, nearly starved, mud-slicked skin shining as they kept on. She waited for them to falter or stop, to say they'd had enough. They'd been digging all morning by the looks of the hole; it must be past break time now and any minute she'd hear the call letting them know to quit. Mira listened, but as the time passed she was forced to face the possibility that it wouldn't come at all.

One man climbed out of the hole and pulled off his shirt to clean his face. Mira saw a mark on his chest, the skin dark and raised, a wound long-since healed but the mark distinct, the lines embedded in the shape of the letter, a branding to warn others to whom he belonged.

They'd see her if she stood up. It seemed almost impossible none had already caught her crouching in the grass. Although, didn't they want to be seen? That was what these reenactments were for. To be witnessed. She should stand and watch, at least get a better view, but she remained still, barely breathing as she let the brush be her cover. Standing meant acknowledging what was in front of her in a way she wasn't prepared for, not out here, not alone, with her their only audience. When she was surrounded by the crowds watching the reenactments, it was easier to wipe her hands, to shrug in the admission that *this is how it is and how it'll always be*, but alone she couldn't ignore it. Alone she had to face the reality of what she saw and her own participation in it, because watching was participating, wasn't it? Allowing it to continue? Any movement might disrupt the veil, the one that kept her invisible, watching. Her whole life, she'd existed on this side of it—keeping quiet, following rules, doing whatever possible to continue in the safety of being unseen, fearing the slightest transgression would put her on the other side. How many times had she watched as people like her got their spirits ruined from the unfairness of this world? She'd lived in the false promise that because she was invisible, she'd be spared, and while she knew now this was a lie, she stayed crouched to the ground, hidden from view, too afraid of any other choice beyond watching as they worked.

A white man supervised in the background. Young, clean-shaven, with dark hair. He carried the look of a man who'd never been told no, who acted as if the world had been built for him, and for most of his life it probably had been. In this heat he still dressed in his finest clothes because a man like him could afford to. He wore dark trousers with a matching frock coat. Underneath he wore a single-breasted blue-and-green-checkered vest.

On his feet were ink-colored leather shoes, which he tapped impatiently against the grass.

He yelled at the others as they dug, impatient, yet his gaze betrayed a sense of gratification in watching the men as they struggled. "How much longer?" he barked.

"Almost done, sir," a voice down in the hole yelled back. "Almost done, sir. Almost done," he repeated. His tone was of someone who'd lived a life of acquiescence, someone who'd become intimate with the strain of a bowed head and bent back. Like the other men, they did what they were told because they knew of no other choice. They dug their hole. A hole for graves or a hole just because. They dug.

The white man nodded and walked off out of sight. When he returned, he had a band of other slaves following behind him in teams of two, with each twosome carrying a large burlap sack. They grunted as they walked, straining from the weight of what they carried. He signaled for the slaves to drop their sacks and they pounded against the ground. Then, he called to those in the hole. "Enough," he said. "I'm done with this. I've got other plans for today than to watch you all work."

The slaves were pulled out, and the hole was empty.

"Which one of these is him?" he said. "Do any of you know? The one who organized it?"

"He's here, sir," a slave said, eager to achieve some small favor as he pointed to the final sack.

"Pull the cover away. Let me see."

The others crowded around, blocking Mira's view, as they pulled off the sack. Mira couldn't see his face but she could see the expression of a few of the others as they recoiled in horror. One could not contain himself and turned away, retching in the grass.

"You're going to look!" the white man told them all. "Look, and see what your future will be if you try to escape again. Look hard now. All of you. Look."

Mira watched as they stared down at what was once covered.

Their faces sullen, pained, angry, but whatever they felt, they never expressed a word. When the white man was satisfied, he called again to one of the slaves. Mira thought it was over but the slave brought an ax and handed it to him.

"This will be a lesson to all of you," he said, holding the ax high in the air, the blade's metal blinding her from seeing more.

Fear told her to do what she'd always done—run, and she did, running as fast as her legs could take her through the uncertainty of the woods. She ran, putting as much distance as she could between her and what she'd left behind.

Behind her, the singing continued, a chorus rising.

Master he be a hard, hard man. Hoe, Emma, hoe. Lord strike down Pharaoh and set them free. Hoe, Emma, hoe.

Those who stayed behind found their own ways to resist. A burned field at night meant no crops to harvest come morning, and a burned barn meant no crops for their master to sell. To slow down work they ruined themselves, since a broken leg couldn't hoe a field. Broken fingers couldn't pick tobacco leaves. Over and over they suffered the pain of fractured bones, of mutilated flesh. They'd always known their weapons were their bodies. They stuffed cotton roots down their throats. Forced down turpentine and indigo to make the life within stop. The path to resistance was through what their bodies could do, and so they found ways to refuse at every turn.

They made do with what was given. They dyed rags to their liking and wrapped them around their hair. Colors vibrant and daring, colors that gave them a sense of pride despite the shame of their circumstance. They adorned their clothes with cowrie shells and glass beads, smiled at their gleam refracted in the sunlight. They made beauty out of nothing and wore it like the finest jewels.

They took what homeland practices they could remember and used them on their rations. Golden hoe cakes cooked out in the fields, their edges crisp and glistening. Okra stews thickened with sassafras leaves and rice. Hog maw bits cooked with peas. The food was meant to sustain the long days, but soon came new traditions loved and passed down.

When they were told to pray, they prayed. They prayed

to a god now told was theirs, but they understood that even this god knew the morality behind keeping someone in chains. This god, their god, would one day save them, and so they snuck out into the woods to pray—for freedom, for salvation, for retribution, but when even this was soon denied, when they could no longer speak aloud their Sunday prayers, they turned to their hearts, silently praying their secret desires in the hope they'd finally be heard.

They blessed their children. The river water washed over their skin and they were born anew. They were saved so that if ever lost on earth, in heaven they'd be found.

Despite these efforts, each day they resigned themselves a little bit more to this life of servitude, of serving, and every day they wished for their god to finally strike down and end it for them all.

Yet, there was a story they heard, one spoken during their weakest moments when they could do no more—a fish's heart could beat after it had died. You could sever one, dig your fingers past the skin to find the flesh and organs, and find the small clump of red. Reach in and tear it out, hold it in your hands and feel its viscous softness. Toward death and even afterward it continues to fight. Watch as it throbs, this heart, pulsating and still full of life.

XIII.

WHOA, HEY, MIRA, stop!"

Mira collapsed into Jesse, her body falling, knees buckling, until both of them were tangled on the grass. She remembered the glint of the ax. She remembered the ropy scars as she laid her head on his chest.

"What are you doing here?" she asked, bewildered by his sudden appearance. His arms gripped hers and she realized it was because she couldn't stop shaking.

"I went for a walk. I couldn't stand being around everyone at that plantation. It's a shitshow back there. Gossiping about what could have happened with Celine. None of them cared about the wedding to begin with and now they're using it as an excuse to get day-drunk and party. Never mind that something could be seriously wrong."

Jesse's contempt was palpable. Now that they were far enough away from the others he seemed to feel free enough to express it, or perhaps he had reached his breaking point, unable to hide it any longer. He was the one who worked with people like this day in and day out, every day dealing with the same frustrations. It had to get to him, and if it did, he couldn't express it, never in the way Mira imagined he wanted to.

Blades of grass were scattered all over his suit. Mud streaked his jacket sleeve. "The wedding," she said softly. "You were still planning to go?"

Jesse watched as her fingers rubbed over the worsted wool. "Celine invited me," he answered. "It doesn't matter now since there isn't going to be a wedding. Everyone is saying she bailed. Phillip called it off."

"When was this?"

"Over an hour ago."

"An hour? What time is it? Do you know?"

"It's past two."

"Two? Jesus. That can't be right. That means I've been out for a couple of hours. I had no idea I'd been gone that long."

She'd wasted a lot of time searching for Celine, worried Celine had gotten lost or hurt, but it seemed she might have actually taken Mira's advice and run off. While relieved, she wished Celine had told her she was unhappy. Last night, Mira had given her an out. All she had to say was the truth—that she'd changed her mind, that she wanted to end it, and needed the help of her friend. Celine could have told her but chose not to, and Mira had to admit she felt a little betrayed by this revelation. Celine had gone through so much effort that Mira wondered what the point of it had been if this was supposed to be the outcome. *You have to be here for my wedding, you just have to come,* Celine had pleaded on the phone, guilting her with their past so she would say yes. *I want my best friend,* she'd said, but when it came to it, she couldn't tell her the one thing that might have given credence to her words.

Celine's intentions had been a sham, Mira reasoned, but hadn't Mira's own been as well? She stared at Jesse and had to face the fact that she was here for him, had come for the possibility of him.

"What were you running from?" he asked. "Was someone following you?"

"No," Mira told him, and the image of the men returned.

Downtrodden frames fixed on the burden of their task. They'd had no choice; the expressions on their faces made that clear. She'd seen the same look many times. The students at her school were filled with the same resigned anguish for a system designed to break them before they'd barely begun their lives.

"I went to look for Celine and I got lost. I found this group of men digging this large hole, like some sort of mass grave. It was so big. They had to have been digging for hours. Another man stood watching and yelling orders at them all. After a while he told them to stop and the men carried over these large sacks. I think bodies were in the sacks. It looked so real, but it couldn't have been. Could it? No, that's ridiculous. It must have been another reenactment."

"There wasn't supposed to be any reenactments today, or least not any before the wedding, but now that's not happening, I don't know."

"A rehearsal for one maybe?"

"Maybe," Jesse said. He was calm, relieved almost, as if he'd been expecting to hear what Mira had told him. His face scrunched up as he turned back to the woods. "Do you think you could show me where this was?" he asked.

"I'm not sure. I don't even know. I thought I was lost. Jesse, there were so many bodies. Why were they dragged out to a place no one could see? And the man watching them, he had an ax and I saw him—"

The gleam of the blade as it flashed from the sun. His frame leaning over the grass, his gaze steadfast as he brought the ax to the dead flesh. Mira had run before she could witness anything else.

"We have to find where you were," Jesse resolved when Mira didn't finish. "You have to show me. Try to remember the path you took. I need to see what you saw."

Mira agreed, not out of any kind of desire to go back, but because of Jesse's doggedness. She led Jesse on through the woods.

Neither of them talked as they made their way. As Jesse followed her, she could not stop thinking about how familiar this all felt, except this time she was the one leading him, but what exactly, was she leading him toward? What lay ahead this time, ready and waiting to change their lives?

Mira followed the path as best she could remember. They walked until Jesse began to lag behind. "Okay, Mira," he said, stopping. "Maybe we should get back."

"Tired?"

"No, it's just we've been going for a while, and if I'm right we're getting near the river."

The river. Mr. Loomis. Of course he wouldn't want to be reminded, but now that they were here she could see they were close.

"It's not that much farther. Up this way."

"You sure?"

"Yes," Mira said with a newly found determination. "I remember this. It's up this hill. Come on."

They walked up the hill until they got to the clearing where Mira believed she'd been, but when they reached it she saw no men, no digging, and no hole. Mira kneeled. "This was where I was," she said. Her fingers traced over the markings in the dirt, trying to prove to Jesse they were her prints from earlier. "I crouched here, and over there the men were digging the hole," she said, pointing to a grassy clearing that existed in the place of the hole. Woodlands encircled the area. What earlier had felt like reprieve from the day's heat now felt closed in, and she stood up in response.

"This was where you were?" Jesse asked.

"Yes. It was right here. All of it. The ground—a hole was right here. Right where my feet are standing. Right here."

Mira stamped her foot against the grass. She did it over and over and then got down on the ground and clawed at the dirt. Her fingers dug into the rich earth, pulling up chunks of sod and throwing it behind her. "I don't understand. It was right here.

This wasn't grass. It was a hole. They couldn't have finished it. It couldn't have—it just, it couldn't."

"Mira, stop."

"I don't get it, Jesse," she said, stopping. She hit the ground a final time. She felt ridiculous. They were so far away from the main grounds, and for what? Maybe she'd seen nothing after all. She'd been out in the heat for a long time, walking around in these woods. Sweat soaked her clothes, and now that they were standing there together she thought maybe she'd been imagining what she saw.

"Maybe I was wrong."

"No, I believe you. You hear me? I believe you."

Jesse asked her if she wanted to get lunch.

"Come on," he said. "There's some stuff we should talk about. Some other things, I think, it's time you knew."

XIV.

J ESSE HAD OFFERED to take Mira off the plantation but she
didn't want to leave in case Celine came back. As a compro-
mise, they ordered a late-afternoon lunch at Mira's cottage. The
room service menu was all distorted versions of the food Mira
remembered from her childhood. The glimpse of familiarity excited her, and Mira let herself order what she really wanted. Hush
puppies, fried golden and crunchy. Pan-seared shrimp and ched-
dar grits with andouille sausage. Buttermilk biscuits, flaky and
crumbling. Jesse ordered chicken fried steak with potato puree
and a side of collard greens. It wasn't until the food had been delivered and the room had filled with its smell that Mira realized
how hungry she was. She relished the meal, not talking much as
she dug in. Jesse too was quiet, and as they ate they listened to
the sounds of traffic outside—guests opening and closing their
cottage doors, the sounds of conversations fading in and out.

Mira relaxed a little from the heaviness of the meal and the
time that had passed. Earlier, while waiting for their orders to
come, she'd changed her clothes, putting on a T-shirt and jeans,
and had taken off her shoes. Jesse had stripped off his tie and left
it draped over the edge of the couch where they both sat. On the
coffee table in front of them, the unfinished remains of their food
were getting cold. Mira's stomach ached. She watched as Jesse cut

into another bite of his steak and brought it to his mouth before sitting back on the couch, pushing the plate away to keep himself from eating any more.

"I hadn't eaten here yet," Jesse said after a while. "Until today, I mean. It's not bad."

"It's expensive," Mira said. "That's to be expected though."

"It's also not the same as anything you'll get outside of this place, but that's to be expected too."

Mira returned Jesse's smile with her own. A pang of nostalgia hit her. "We should have gone to Catfish Joe's. Remember how we used to go on the weekends? Celine and I would share a fish plate and you'd always steal my hush puppies even though you said you never liked them."

Catfish Joe's. She couldn't count the number of times they used to go. Run by a retired black couple, it was a small shack of a building several blocks from the downtown. Not much to look at, but who could care when the fish was freshly caught every morning? Only the people who knew its worth went. During the day it was mostly regulars on their lunch breaks. You ordered from the window and later one of the owners would bring out the food, glistening from the grease. It was all outdoor seating of patio chairs and foldable tables. Jesse, Celine, and Mira would go when they'd gathered enough money to spare and sit and eat. They always went near closing, once the air had cooled and most everyone who was going to eat had done it already. By that time the lot was empty and it could be just them, sitting under the setting sun sharing a meal with no one else to bother them.

As Mira talked about Catfish Joe's, a lingering fondness sprung up in her voice. Back then it had just been a place they'd gone to, but it held a significance to her now.

"Catfish Joe's is gone," Jesse said bluntly.

"What? When?"

"A few years ago. Joe's wife, Helen, died and he couldn't keep up the place himself. I guess didn't want to maybe. The building is still there but like a lot of things in this town, there's only the ghost of what was."

"What a shame."

"Yeah, but I don't know though—people in town seem to think this Woodsman place is going to change things, bring money into the town, revive it again, and maybe they're right. Lord knows jobs are sorely needed here. I just wish there was some other way."

Mira agreed. She hated the idea that the main source of Kipsen's economy would now come from the Woodsman Plantation. Despite whatever the original intentions, the echoes of slavery were difficult to ignore. A new system had been created, one where the poor people in the town, faced with no other option, took jobs at the Woodsman because any job was better than nothing. It had not been lost on her that most of these jobs were service ones, and most of the people who'd taken them were black. And the visitors were mostly white; it was all haunting in its history.

The mood shifted. Mira tried to think of a way to lighten things, but failing, kept quiet. Jesse, taking the initiative, saw Mira's plate of food and reached over, grabbing the last hush puppy and popping it in his mouth.

"Still the same. Always stealing my food."

"Yeah," Jesse said, laughing. He swallowed, then reached for one of the mints that had come with the meal. Mira heard the hard crunch of him chewing it down. "Remember how I used to tell you they got their name because an owner got tired of hearing his barking dogs so he hushed them up, ground their meat with meal, and fried them up?"

"Oh god, I remember! I believed it too. For the longest time I believed it. That's why I never ordered them. I thought you two were eating dog."

"But you ate them!"

"Yeah, well, they were still good."

"I've missed you," Jesse confessed.

"Me too."

Mira sipped her water and sat back on the couch. Jesse's gaze stayed fixed on her, the heat of it making her feel blissfully, radiantly alive. When was the last time a man looked at her in this way? She could not remember but felt like she should. One should know the last time they were desired by another. It had been too long, and the recognition of this absence enabled a sudden and intense longing; already she was imagining the way his hands would trace down the spine of her back, touching the curls of her hair, touching every part of her, feeling every curve and muscle and bone of her body.

Mira moved closer to him on the couch, close enough that she could smell the musky scent of his cologne, and before either of them could say anything to ruin the moment, she moved so her body was on top of his. She kissed him, a deep-throated kiss that held an unexpected urgency. She pressed her lips to his and her tongue tasted the lingering mint of his mouth. He kissed her back, and she felt the flutter in his chest, the wild, furious beating that mirrored her own. This response made her braver, and soon her hands were touching every part of him—the tender parts of his face, his cheeks, moving down to his chest and down farther to his pants, searching for the cool metal of his belt buckle.

"Mira—stop. I need you to stop." Jesse coughed, his body becoming stiff, and Mira, embarrassed, quickly got up and moved to the other end of the couch. After she was off him Jesse reached for the nearest pillow and placed it in his lap, covering what was obvious to them both.

"I don't understand," Mira said, her voice low, almost a whisper.

"I wish you hadn't come," Jesse said. "Not like this. Not for all this."

Mira, frustrated, stiffened in her seat, bracing herself in case Jesse said he would leave. He didn't. He reached over to the coffee table for his glass of water and gulped it down, placed the glass back on the table, then took a napkin to his mouth. After he wiped his lips he balled the napkin up and threw it on the table with the plates of uneaten food. Mira watched him and waited. He couldn't say what he had without some sort of explanation. She would wait until he gave it to her. Jesse sat on the edge of the couch, one foot tapping against the wood floor, a nervous tic she recognized. "Mira," he said, so low that she almost hadn't heard it at first. He gave a forced cough before meeting her face again, and then finally he asked what he'd been working himself up to say. "What do you remember about the Woodsmans?"

"The Woodsmans? I remember the stories people told. Gosh, there were so many."

"There were," Jesse said, nodding. "Like how Roman Woodsman used to have rape parties with slave women. I heard that one a lot."

"Yes, I remember that one too. Or the one about his wife drinking slaves' blood to make herself live longer. Or that they had a torture room somewhere in the house."

"Everyone loved that story. I remember Michael Petrewski saying once how they tortured slaves and then when they died sold their bodies to pay off debts."

Back and forth they went, retelling the stories from their youth. They laughed at some of them, remembering how much they believed or wanted to believe. What neither of them mentioned though, what they refused to remember, was how it was those stories that brought them into the woods that day.

"Mira," Jesse said as he edged closer to the reason behind his question. "Those stories everyone used to tell—I think they were true. You asked me why I came back. This is why. To find out the truth. That day when we snuck onto the property, there was someone else on the grounds. I felt it. I knew someone, or something, had been inside that house, despite what the police said. I just couldn't prove it. At first, I thought it'd been an actual person, someone hiding I couldn't see, but then I remembered those stories. The ones about the ghosts. Hauntings. When I heard about Alden Jones buying the Woodsman property and wanting to build his tourist attraction, I thought it could be my chance to have access to this place and see if they were right."

"But they couldn't have been," Mira said abruptly. "Jesse, come on. What you're saying. They're not real—"

"I've seen them, Mira."

"What have you seen?" she asked. She crossed her arms to keep her body still so Jesse wouldn't see she was shaking.

"Well, you know I've been working here long enough that you get to know what everyone does. Every person has their role and they rarely change up. One night I was the last to leave my shift and I saw a group of men. They wore the uniforms but I didn't recognize any of their faces. They were walking to the cabins, but I couldn't figure why. They should have been following me toward the exit to go home, since the day was over. What could they be doing? I should have followed but I thought it wasn't my business and left. I never saw them again."

Jesse paused to take a breath, but his story reminded Mira of the woman she'd seen on the grounds, and she needed to ask. "I've seen a woman," she began. "Dressed all in white. Young. With long dark hair. Have you seen her? I wish I could describe her better but I couldn't really see her face. She wouldn't look at me. She kept staring out into the fields. I don't know what she was looking at."

"No, I haven't seen anyone like that. Not a woman."

"Oh," Mira said, frowning in disappointment. She questioned if Jesse had really seen anything. It could have been new employees he'd seen that evening, and maybe they'd quit soon after, which would explain why he never saw them again. How much of what he said to her now was because he wanted to believe her, and not because it was true? She couldn't be sure, but felt it made a difference.

"Just because I haven't seen her doesn't mean—doesn't mean

it's not—" Jesse hesitated. "I think you're seeing them too, like that day when we were kids. You wouldn't tell anyone then, I guess because you didn't think they'd believe you, but you can tell me now."

This broke her. "Jesse, I tried. I went to the police station but they wouldn't listen. I should have done more. I should have told you. I'm so sorry," she stumbled out. It was an apology she'd waited years to say, and hearing it released something deep within her and she began to cry. She'd held it in all these years and now she couldn't control it anymore. Her whole body shook as she cried into his shirt. She was sorry she hadn't tried harder, she told him, sorry that she'd left Kipsen and attempted to wash her hands of everything that had happened. Sorry for trying to forget. She was sorry for so many things, too many to even begin to explain, so she kept repeating the words in the hope that it would be enough.

He reached for her hand. "I would have believed you if you told me. I hope you know that. None of this is your fault," Jesse said after she finished. "It never was. It's their fault for not seeing the truth, for not believing you. They should have. I wish they had. They should have believed you then."

They remembered the feeling of their beloveds sold, the shouts of hallelujah! for the money bartered, *and their children's cries as they were shuffled into the arms of another, onto the wagon they went, and they remembered the moment when the coil grip of their fingers loosened, and the* don't you let go don't you do it hold on hold on *screams until the skin slip, last touch, and their hollering wail quieting as the wagon jostled along the road, and days months years of the sound continuing to echo in their hearts, subsuming all other noise. No sorrow song could quench a loss such as this, no, but it could dim it enough so they could survive, and that dulled ache they carried with them.*

You can make another—the words panted out in between clutching a handful of their dress, reaching underneath and up, handling them as if they could never hurt, and it was like that moment right when they were thrown on their backs, legs spread wide, right when they could feel the push as they muffled the urge to scream. They clenched their teeth and bore it, but right before, they told themselves to remember this injustice done—the way they were ruined until they bled, their insides bruised and swollen, and the half-cocked smile asking if it was good.

They remembered the rising lurch in their throats when it was long past dark and one of them didn't come home, the night hours moving slow as their eyes stayed steadfast to the door, and when they could wait no longer they joined the search, their hearts full of hope and hurt as they trudged on, until at last they came upon their sons and daughters and saw their necks broken, eyes bulged, bloodstained from their beating and hanged from the branches above.

Or those times of weakness when they smarted back because they could no longer contain their resolve, the seconds between the words escaping their mouths and what came after—the crackerjack strike of the whip against their backs, or if they were lucky a hard slap across the face, but before all this there was the single space of a moment stretched before them between an action and its punishment, between their rising defiance and their forced submission; before the snuff of recognition there stood a brief glimmering moment in which they understood that a person's hold could not last forever.

Every day for them was the feeling that it could swing another way, followed by the pain of what lay true. For them it was like this, always, and yet always the early morning after, the sight of dawn breaking and knowing there would always be more, more to suffer through, more to resist, more to pull them down, knowing that today is tomorrow is yesterday, it was the fear of believing this was the way it would be, forever and ever amen, and what remained were only the beleaguered days ahead.

But what if when faced again with that space in time they decided to choose another path? This was what they asked *themselves—what if we resisted further, refusing to stop? What if we clamored and yelled, fought in every way we could? And what if we weren't alone? What if it was all of us together rising? Can you imagine it? Can you imagine what we could do?*

XV.

A FTER THEY'D CLEANED up from lunch, had gathered the plates together and called room service to get them, Jesse said he might have an idea of where they might find Celine if she'd bailed on the wedding. A Hail Mary plan he'd called it before asking if she wanted to go. She agreed, thinking it might at least be a good idea to leave the plantation for a bit. Jesse said he needed to change his clothes first, so he left to find the spare jeans and T-shirt he kept in his locker and they decided to meet up in the front parking lot.

After Jesse left, Mira picked up the phone to call Phillip. The afternoon had come and gone without any calls from Phillip and she wanted to know what news, if any, there was. She dialed for his room number first and listened as it rang and rang. When the phone eventually clicked off from no one answering, she tried Celine's room. "He can't possibly have been waiting there all this time," Mira said as she glanced at the clock, but Phillip picked up at the first ring.

"Celine? Celine?"

"Phillip, no—it's Mira," she said, feeling the need to instantly apologize. She refrained and instead told him she was calling to check in.

"Oh, Mira. Yes. You still haven't seen Celine?"

"No, that's why I was calling. So she's still gone?"

"Yes. I've been calling her cell phone but it always goes straight to voicemail."

Phillip's voice sounded strained, as if he was trying hard to keep it from cracking. He told her that the other bridesmaids had gotten a group together to search the property for Celine but that was hours ago. He'd called her father, thinking maybe she'd left with him somewhere, but her father also wasn't answering the phone.

"I heard you called off the wedding."

"I didn't know what else to do. It's been hours. I thought I could hold out a little longer but there's been no sign of her. I've just been waiting in this room expecting her to open the door any minute now. Or even to call. I don't understand why she couldn't even call. If she didn't want to get married after all—I could understand her leaving, not wanting to tell me, but to not even call? No note or anything? It doesn't feel like her."

"I don't know, Phillip."

"And she didn't say anything to you? About the wedding or me? About having doubts or—"

"We weren't as close as we used to be," Mira explained. "I think Jesse would know better."

"Jesse?" Phillip asked. "You mean that boy from last night? The one who got kicked out?"

Mira flinched. Boy. She fumbled over an answer to Phillip's questions. "We were all best friends once," Mira said in spurts of anguish, "and since he lives here and I moved away—I just thought, you know, between the two of us, she would have had more of a chance to talk to him over me, but I don't know how close they are, if they even are friends. She may not talk to him at all anymore."

"Well, she invited him to the wedding."

"Right," Mira said. She regretted mentioning Jesse, as Phillip began to ask her more questions.

"Where is Jesse now? Have you seen him?"

"No, I haven't."

"He works here, doesn't he?"

Mira didn't like where Phillip was taking the conversation or the assumptions he was beginning to make, but she didn't know how to steer things in a different direction.

"Listen, Phillip, I think Celine will call eventually, or we'll figure out where she is. Everyone's out searching for her, so she's going to turn up sooner or later. You're right, it's not like her. I'll try and keep looking too. I'm sure we just need to wait a little bit longer. We have each other's numbers, so that's good. I'll call you if I learn anything else."

Mira hung up the phone before Phillip could say more. Even if they managed to find Celine, it was long past time the wedding would have started and ended. She gathered her things and left to find Jesse.

As Mira walked along the plantation grounds, she expected the environment to feel somber and quiet, but it wasn't. With no ceremony to attend, the guests relished in their vacations. Many had already changed out of their wedding attire. Some of the guests wore outfits bought from the gift shop, having fun dressed up in their costumes while they got drunk and played pretend. Or were they visitors to the plantation? Mira couldn't discern, but they mingled with each other. The bar was so crowded that patrons had spilled out onto the walkway in front of it, sitting in groups on the grass and drinking. Others strolled the grounds. Mira passed a cluster of couples near the slave cabins.

One of them climbed the railing to get inside a cabin. The others held back, watching and laughing, their glasses sloshing. Guests were becoming reckless and emboldened in the freedom of the day.

Mira had meant to keep her gaze down, out of shame for what she saw but also from fear of being recognized, but as she looked around in the hope someone on staff would see, she realized no one was around. Mira guessed they were overwhelmed with everything going on, or maybe they'd decided it'd be easier not to interfere, to let the damage be done, knowing Celine and Phillip would take care of it in the end.

Mira looked again in the direction of the group by the cabins and this time she recognized one of the women. "Kristina?" Mira called, remembering that she was in Celine's wedding party, a bridesmaid.

"Oh," Kristina said, swallowing another gulp of her drink. "I know you. Yes. Celine's black friend. That's you."

"Obviously," one of the men snickered, and the rest of them laughed.

"Mira," she corrected, but they all paid her no mind. "Kristina, what are you doing? I thought you were looking for Celine?"

Kristina waved her hand at the mention of Celine's name. "Look, I tried. I've asked everyone who might have had an idea but they either don't know or don't care. Who knows where she is? If she doesn't want to be found, who am I to bother? Let her come back when she's ready. In the meantime—" Kristina raised her drink in the air and took another gulp. The others followed suit.

"Hey, you all got to see inside here. It's kind of cozy. All we need are some pillows or something."

Mira looked at the guy who'd gone inside the cabin. He popped his head out of the window frame, smiling at his sense of accomplishment. "Thomas, you want to go back to the cottage and get some?"

"Yeah, cool."

"Also, see if you can get one of those servers to come down here. I'm kind of hungry."

"They're kind of swamped though," Kristina interrupted. "We've got some snacks."

"Get them! And maybe some beers at the bar. Yeah, this place is great. Cool in here too. You need to come inside and see."

All of them except for Thomas crawled across the railing to get into the cabin. Mira heard their clamors of excitement as they stole inside. She walked briskly away, passing the tent from last night's post-rehearsal ceremony, only now it was set up for the wedding reception. A few girls sat at the tables guzzling champagne from the abandoned bar. "I should have known Celine would stand him up," one of the women complained. "I don't know what we're all sitting waiting around for. Celine is gone. No way she's coming back now and risking everyone laughing in her face. We should just go home."

"I wouldn't come back now if I were her. Not with that fiancé of hers running around like he's lost his favorite toy. The man needs to buck up and realize she didn't want him. It's not happening. The wedding ship has long since sailed. But at least there's free booze for us," the other said, taking another long sip from her glass.

"True. We'll stay until it runs out and then I say it's time to get out of here. Besides, it's starting to get hot."

Mira left the women and passed the gardens. The guests around her had become more brazen. Fueled by alcohol and dizzy from the heat, their recklessness began to feel destructive. A group of men were laughing. They were dressed in matching black suits with silver ties. Mira meant to ignore them but she recognized them: the groomsmen. They stumbled over themselves, slurring their words as they whooped at another man who ambled over to a flower bed a few feet away. His pants bunched at his feet, he held his penis, moving it around in small circles as he peed on the flowers. His face was flushed pink from laugher. "I'm just doing my chores, is all. Watering the flowers. Yessir," he said, grinning. The others slapped their hands against their knees in their own howling fits of laughter. "Make it rain!" they yelled back.

Mira hurried past the men. She wanted to get off the grounds as soon as possible, to leave for a little while and return once things had settled down, if at this point, they even could.

Eventually, Mira got to the gate where Jesse waited. Jesse wore a white cotton shirt and pants and large brown boots caked with dried mud. The image of him brought up the memory of the Woodsman workers, their bodies hunched over as they picked tobacco during their reenactments, but also of the men she saw earlier digging while they sang, keeping up their pace. She also couldn't forget the men she'd first seen out by the highway while driving here. All those anonymous men. And now Jesse. She stopped walking, feeling sick. Jesse caught her stare and asked if something was wrong.

"I thought you said you had another set of clothes," she told him, her voice shaky.

"I should have clarified," Jesse said, shrugging. "It's fine for where we're going. Hey, you all right?"

"Yes, I'm fine," Mira lied. In the distance, she could have sworn she heard the hum of singing. *Master, he be a hard, hard man. Sell my people away from me.* "You hear that?" she asked, listening to the whispered chorus.

Both of them stood still as the chorus grew louder. Jesse gripped her hand, and their fingers interlocked as the rhythm and hum filled her ears.

"You hear it too, don't you, Jesse?"

Lord, send my people into Egypt land. Lord, strike down Pharaoh and set them free.

"Let's get out of here," Jesse said, and Mira agreed, following him to his car.

XVI.

MIRA DIDN'T ASK where Jesse was driving her. He said it wouldn't take long. She sat in the passenger's seat as his car bumped along over the potholes in the road. She closed her eyes and let the breeze from the open window cool her face. Jesse didn't talk as he drove, nor did he turn on the radio, and Mira didn't ask him to, preferring quiet. After the commotion at the Woodsman Plantation, it was nice to listen to the silence; she hoped it would calm her for whatever was to come.

In the silence, the memories she'd collected of him flooded back to her, like a strong current she couldn't keep at bay. School bus drives as he told jokes to distract her from the other boys' teasing. Birthday ice-cream sandwiches using money they'd saved and pooled together to celebrate on one single day for them all. Jesse's idea since Celine's father never cared about her birthday and Celine refused to tell them the date. Jesse with his hair pick in his constant attempt to grow out his Afro. His barely there freckles. His always skinned, sometimes ashy knees. The way he dreamed of his life, as if what he wanted could be possible if he loved it enough. She looked at this boy, now a man, and wondered how much of her memory of him had remained.

Jesse drummed his fingers along the steering wheel, a nervous tic to pass the time as he drove, and Mira glanced at his hands. Thick calluses had formed on his knuckles. A jagged scar was etched in the skin of one of them and she wondered if it was from when he'd broken the window, but she was too afraid to ask. His nails were stubs, bitten down to the quick. Rough and tanned, his hands gave away the signs of years of his work outside in the sun, aging him far beyond his years.

The marks of the world are on us, Mira thought. It's often as simple as looking at a person's hands to know who and all of what we've been.

Jesse's car slowed. The woods outside the window seemed like the same expanse of woods she'd seen when they'd left. It looked like they'd gone nowhere. "Where are we?" she asked.

"I have spare boots in the back. Grab those and put them on," he said after he'd parked the car and got out. "We got a little bit of walking to do."

Mira did what was asked, slipping off her shoes and reaching in the back for the boots. They were several sizes too large but she tied them up anyway, and when she was finished she got out and walked with Jesse down the path. It didn't take long before the path merged with a large graveled trail that paralleled a water canal. Still, it didn't register to Mira what it was and where they were until a couple appeared with matching kayaks floating along the canal, heading in the direction of the swamps.

"I can't believe I grew up in Kipsen and never knew about this place." They were on the edge of the Great Dismal Swamp, close to two hundred square miles of swampland. Jesse's boots made sense now. She had to be careful where she walked. She moved slowly, each step deliberate, and listened. There were bears to watch out for, as well as snakes hiding in the thicket. Mosquitoes and thorns ready to pierce the skin. Terrors lurked in what she couldn't see.

"I didn't either. I learned about its history a few months after I first moved back. I mentioned it to Celine and we used to come whenever we both could get time off. It became our place for a bit. Someplace we could go. The canal isn't that far and it'll take you to Lake Drummond, the heart of the Great Dismal Swamp. We rented a kayak to see it once. The water was like black tea—clear and dark. We paddled out to the lake and when we got there the sun had begun to set and an orange glow shined over the water. It was so quiet and still. That's what I remember about it. It felt like we were entering another world."

"I wouldn't think she'd even care, not the Celine I talked to last night," Mira said. "She seems too wrapped up in the security of her new life to want to risk any threat to it."

"Huh, yeah," Jesse said, and Mira worried he thought she meant him being the threat and not the act of the two of them sneaking off into the woods. Mira was about to clarify but Jesse continued. "It might have been the stories of how they all sort of disappeared. I'd told her about how slaves escaped and created maroon colonies in the swampland. Remember, Celine was always wanting to leave Kipsen? She liked the idea of disappearing like them. They built communities by living on these small plots of high ground. Not much land at all. Twenty acres at most. They built cabins using wooden posts. Grew rice and grain that they sometimes traded. They just made do, but they lived. Managed to start a new life for themselves. That appealed to her. The idea of having some sort of control over your life. They didn't actually have control though. They were still slaves outside of what they'd created, but they came to this swampland and found their own autonomy. They created their own rules, their own lives, found their own freedom. I think she liked the idea of escaping. Disappearing and starting over as somebody else."

"Maybe that's what Celine wanted to do. Escape, but from what? She has more now than either of us ever will."

It was a whisper of contempt Mira had let slip in her moment of honesty, but Jesse noticed. He raised his eyebrows in the expectation she'd say more, but she felt it unnecessary to spell it out for him. They'd both seen the expense taken for the wedding, money that could have changed either of their lives, now wasted. Celine wanted to start over, but didn't everyone want to start over in some way? People with less than Celine still suffered through, and what exactly did she want to leave? Celine had gotten everything she'd ever wanted, that's what she'd told Mira, so what made her want to go?

Jesse said they needed to go farther on the trail. Mira went on ahead, picking up her pace as she ventured deeper, but she didn't know where to go or where they should be looking. Soon the thicket grew dense enough that she was forced to stop, afraid she'd get lost and end up alone. She turned around and saw Jesse was right behind her. "Okay, what are we doing? We can't search the entire swamp for her."

"No, we can't."

Mira expected him to tell her his plan, but he kept on the trail. It eventually curved to the left, separating from the canal. This was where Jesse stopped, leaving the trail and going toward the water.

"What are you doing?"

"Celine?" he called, low at first, and then louder. He did this for a few minutes with Mira watching.

"Celine's not here," Mira said when he'd stopped for a minute. "We're alone."

"This was where we used to come. This spot. Here."

Jesse circled. He peered in the brush, searching, as if any moment he half expected Celine to appear out of her hiding place, but no matter how hard he looked there was no one to find. Mira wondered what other secrets they'd both kept from her.

"I still don't get why now, out of anywhere else, you'd think she'd be here," she said.

"I just know."

"Okay, but, Jesse—how? How do you know?"

"When I moved back, we became friends again." He paused.

"This canal goes all the way to the swamp, but in the other direction, down that way, it connects to the river. The one by the Woodsman property."

"Okay, and?"

"Celine liked this spot. We took a wrong turn kayaking once and ended up going in the other direction, connecting to the river that led us to the property. We didn't realize it at the time, thought we were still on the nature reserve land, and left our kayaks on the riverbank to stretch our legs. Celine started walking off ahead of me and I picked up the pace, to catch up to her, but deep in the woods we got separated. I called and called for her, and when I found her again she was in shock. She wouldn't stop shaking. She told me she saw a group of black men, each of them carrying hatchets in one arm and in the other—they carried decapitated heads."

Jesse looked out into the trees, appearing unsettled. He lowered his voice to tell Mira the rest of it.

"She said the men didn't notice her at first. They ran right by, moving in another direction. She froze, watching, and they'd almost passed by without her being noticed, but then one of them turned and looked right at her. She bolted, running until she found me. After she told me the story we both ran out of the woods, found our kayaks, and got out of there."

The familiarity of Jesse's story was not lost on her. Did Jesse realize it? Had he noticed the echo from what had happened to the two of them?

"Once Celine found out we'd been on the Woodsman property she wanted to come out here all the time. I think part of her was always a little jealous over that day you and I had gone without her. I took her because I was happy to have someone else interested in the Woodsmans, even if she didn't know the whole story. It's been lonely not being able to share with anyone about what happened for all these years, and I could tell she was lonely too. We never saw anything like Celine had that first day again.

Then Celine met Phillip and we stopped coming as much. When Alden Jones began building his park the only way to get on and off the property besides the main entrance was the river. If she wanted to get off the plantation without being seen, if she wanted to disappear, this would have been the only way to do it."

"Well, she's not here. There's no sign of her having been anywhere near this place."

Jesse climbed back onto the path. Mira sensed there was so much more Jesse wasn't telling her. She hoped if she waited long enough he'd finally tell her, but he continued to stare in the direction of the swamp water, as if somewhere lurking underneath its stillness was an answer he needed to know.

"Maybe we've gotten this whole thing wrong. We've spent most of the day looking for Celine but maybe she doesn't want to be found." Mira was tired, dirty, and wanted to go back to the cottage so she could take a shower and crawl into bed. Following Jesse had taken her nowhere. They weren't any closer to finding Celine.

A few yards away a couple appeared from the trail. Mira and Jesse were quiet as the couple passed them by, nodding as they hiked along the path in the direction of the entrance. Mira watched them as they disappeared. "Jesse, it's what makes the most sense. Maybe she didn't want to marry Phillip after all. Not sure I can blame her, to be honest, and she left because she was too afraid of facing everyone about it. Maybe that's all this is. All those people back at the plantation, they're not concerned at all about Celine and where she could be. Maybe they have the right idea. Maybe she's just gone."

"I'd really hoped we'd find her, Mira. Like she'd be waiting to tell us this whole thing was a huge prank on everyone. Or at least we'd see some signs she'd left, deciding not to go through with it after all. I wanted to believe she was different. That she wasn't the type of person who'd truly want to have a wedding at a place like the Woodsman Plantation. Otherwise it means she hates us."

Mira balked at Jesse's conviction. Celine couldn't have hated her. Mira thought about all the times as children when Celine had stood up for her, had been her friend when others wouldn't. *We could be sisters*, Celine used to say, giggling as they sat on Mira's bed, Celine reaching over to give her a hug, to pull Mira close. Hate? She would have never done that for someone she hated. No, *hate* was too strong a word.

"I don't know if I'd go so far as to say hate."

"Why not?" Jesse responded, raising his eyebrows. "How isn't it? Think about all the people who died. They were exploited. Punished. We went to the graveyard and you thought one of the graves was of your ancestor. Imagine what was done to her. We don't even know the full story, but think about what we do know and what was done to them. To ignore that—"

"I asked her about it. Last night. She said she hadn't owned slaves. She'd had nothing to do with the place's past and so it wasn't the same."

"She may not have had anything to do with the past but what about now? She didn't care about the hurt her actions could cause. For me it's the same. It's like the difference between drowning someone and not caring if someone drowns nearby. In both scenarios the person ends up dead. Celine may not have known all about the Woodsman history but she knew what happened to me, to us, and yet none of it mattered. She didn't care about what it might mean to us. Look, Mira, I get it. It's easier with the others, you expect their hate, their disregard for your existence, but Celine? We all were friends. We grew up together. For her to be this way, to have this wedding like this—it's worse, I think, because it means she never saw who we were to begin with. How could she ever have seen us? You're trying to tell yourself it's not the same because it's hard to reconcile with the truth. I don't know how to live with it either."

XVII.

J ESSE SAID HE needed to show her something else before he brought her back to the plantation and that he would have to drive her to his house. "One last thing," he'd convinced her when they'd gotten to the car. Mira wanted to know why he couldn't just tell her what it was and he said she needed to see to understand.

Jesse lived on the top floor of a house, which had been converted into an apartment. The owner, a retired woman who mostly kept to herself, lived below. His hand grazed her back as he guided her to the entrance.

"It's not much, I know," he said, apologizing after he'd led her up the narrow staircase.

"It's all right." Mira observed the surroundings. The apartment was small and mostly empty of furniture. Wood-paneled walls were reminiscent of a seventies-era aesthetic. The shag carpet came out in some of the corners and she could see bits of floorboard underneath. A well-worn sofa sagged in the living room. Bookcases lined the walls, all filled with black authors, a lot of whom she recognized but some she didn't. An oak table sat in the breakfast nook. In the kitchen an efficiency burner stove was next to a utility sink, which, he said, was the reason he rented the place. Down a narrow hall Mira saw his bed, unmade, with a sheet balled up near the headboard.

"You're taking photos again." Mira noticed the collection of images plastered on one of the living room walls. Photographs covered over the white paint, lining almost every inch of the wall. Mira had to go slow to view them all, wanting to see all of what he'd done.

Jesse had progressed to mixed media. His work involved juxtaposing slave narratives taken from the Works Progress Administration, or the WPA, with contemporary portraiture, specifically photos of Kipsen's black residents, contrasting his images with the written quotes from the once-lost stories. The WPA slave narratives were oral histories from ex-slaves conducted by the Federal Writers' Project, a unit of the Works Progress Administration, both of which were New Deal initiatives to help provide jobs for the unemployed during the Great Depression. Few of these accounts were tape-recorded; instead they were written reconstructions from the WPA interviewers who'd relied on their own memories and field notes. Because of this, the narratives reflected the bias of the interviewers, often depicting the slaves as content and docile, as well as the plantations they had lived on as idyllic. In the 1970s, thousands of other slave narratives were discovered, which depicted the harsh and cruel treatment by the slave owners. It turned out that the state FWP officials chose to bury these narratives rather than forward them on to the Library of Congress.

Jesse's face lit up when he told her this, and in hearing him talk about his work she saw the boy from her childhood, with his camera and photo books, now grown up. "I have some of the audio recordings of the narratives too," he said. "The ones that have been digitized and are available online, but I don't like listening to them. I wish I could hear the actual tapes because the voices sound like ghosts of the original audio. I'm reminded that I'm listening to a hollow reproduction, a shell of the original."

Jesse said he wanted to publish a book of his collected pieces and he was working toward that. Mira listened as he talked about another project idea. He wanted to work with the Lost Friends ads. The ads were written by former slaves who were looking for their relatives after the Civil War.

"They're fascinating to read. Relatives were forced to contain a whole life into the span of a few sentences, all in the hope another person reading would be able to recognize that life as once their own."

Mira looked intently at each of the photographs, at the town she once knew. She saw her old neighborhood but in a different light. Elders sat on the porch fanning themselves in the shade. A pair of children played a clapping game on a front lawn, the photo capturing them with their hands midair. A cluster of kids played hopscotch. Another, double Dutch. He'd found people leaving church service. Wide-brimmed hats blocked the Sunday sun. Women were boldly dressed as they smiled toward the camera. He'd gone to the community pool during their slowest hours, which were also the times black families would frequent, and seeing those photos—the mothers sunning, baring their soft bodies for the world to see, and their sons and daughters splashing in the water, jumping off the diving board, eating slushies that stained their teeth red, all their happiness on full display—it made her insides twist up into something fierce. Jesse was able to look at their town and see it in a way Mira hadn't.

"If I ever get out of Kipsen, this is what I want to do. Photograph more towns like ours. Document people living day to day and show the beauty of their lives. We got poverty, but there's joy too."

As she passed over the photographs, the focus shifted to images of the Woodsman property. A few were taken from the road, the sort of distant shot popularized on keepsake postcards that made the place look sweeping and grand. In one, Mira recognized the same house exterior but the photo depicted what looked like a large-scale game of pick-up sticks, except with piles of fractured wood and metal bars.

"There was an accident," Jesse said, answering the question for her. "The scaffolding collapsed and a couple of workers died. I saw it happen."

"When was this?"

"A year ago, maybe."

"How were you able to get so close?"

Jesse laughed. "I have a good camera. Besides," he said. "I don't think anyone cared enough to notice me even if they had seen."

Jesse had a few of his earlier photos up too, the ones he'd taken when they were young. These were, in some ways, what had started it all, and she'd never gotten to see what he'd wanted so badly to capture through his lens. She saw a photograph of a vulture, its wings spread wide. He'd taken a picture of the broken chandelier, the glass glittering like a hundred fractured diamonds sprinkled across the ground. He'd taken photos of the architecture of the Woodsman house, both inside and out. She saw the white ballroom but with its faded paint a dull, dusty white and not the brilliant gleam it was now. She saw each of the rooms, empty and derelict, and she thought of how much had changed.

She got to one photograph and lingered. The light from the window made some dust particles glow, but there was something else, something by the wall near the window. "What is this?"

"You tell me what you see."

Mira couldn't be sure. The way of the light, the camera, she couldn't be sure. She looked closer, reached out to touch it, but hesitated. It looked like a little black girl standing there, wearing a plain slip dress. She was barefoot. She looked young, a child, considering her stature and size in the photograph. Her face was blurry.

"You do see it, don't you?" Jesse pushed.

"Is that a girl? Who is that? When was this taken?"

Jesse leaned against the edge of his couch, taking in the rush of Mira's questions. "I took that photo the day we snuck onto the Woodsman property. You were outside and I was roaming through the house taking photos of each room. I got to one room and I—I don't know. The air changed. It got colder, but I shrugged it off. I was walking around, not paying attention, and I tripped, stepping on something on the floor. I looked up and I saw the dust moving through the air and I wanted to take a photo of it. I held my camera up in the air, trying to focus, and that's when I heard you scream. I must have clicked without noticing, taking the photo. I never knew I did, what with everything that happened—I stopped taking photos after. I never developed the roll. I put it all away and tried to forget. I left my camera and everything when I moved to Louisiana. It was years later when I found this stuff again. I was going through the house, trying to clean up everything after my uncle died, and I found all my old things. I found the camera and the film, decided what the hell, and tried to develop it, and that's when I saw this photo, all the ones I took that day, but what could I do?"

There was more Jesse wasn't telling her. He went over to the wall and lightly traced his fingers over the image. "Here's the thing, Mira. No one was in the room with me. I was alone. This is a picture of someone who wasn't there."

This was what Jesse had been leading up to. It was why he'd shown her the swamp, why he'd brought her to his house, all for this story he was trying to tell her now. "Who is she then?" Mira asked, but she already knew the answer. Last night when she left Celine's room she'd heard a child laughing. A beckoning meant for her, but she'd waited and no one ever came. She never saw a girl, but maybe she should have waited a little longer.

"Her name's Lucy," Jesse said. "She was sort of a pet of the Woodsmans, mainly for the wife."

Jesse told Mira to sit down while he went into another bedroom. When he came back he carried a scrapbook full of photocopied pages, notes, and scribblings on Post-its stuck on photographs. He placed it on the table while explaining it was a collection of all the material he'd been able to gather about the Woodsmans. As Mira looked through it, he told her the story of what he'd learned about Lucy. She was a slave Roman Woodsman bought his wife, Annabelle, and served as a sort of de facto daughter. "Lucy was kept in the house and at night slept on the floor beside her."

"How did you find all this out?"

"In a journal Annabelle wrote. She was very detailed, keeping records of everything—names and birth dates, deaths. Here, see?" Jesse skimmed through the book, pulled out what he wanted to show Mira, and placed it on the coffee table. "The script is kind of hard to read at first. It took me a long time to get a sense of reading the handwriting from that era, but you get used to it after a while."

"This is so much research. It must have taken a lot of time."

"I wanted to know more about the Woodsmans. There's a whole Woodsman collection in the archives of the library. I never thought to look through it when we were kids. I found the journal there, and some other things. Look."

Jesse handed her some pages. He'd highlighted sections he found important. It was hard to tell if any of it even was, but Mira looked through it anyway. The first page was a family register. Mira read over the names. She pictured the steady hand focused on writing each of the birth dates in the cursive script, the move of the pen across the paper in sure, fluid strokes. The action was filled with the promise of a life, but on the right-hand side of the page another date was listed, the death date, many the same as the birth.

"All these deaths. She'd been trying to have children for years. Almost a decade. And they all died."

"It was probably why Roman bought Lucy. To get her to finally let go of the possibility."

On another page were the lists of slave names. In neatly written script, Annabelle had written the births and deaths of hundreds of slaves, all under the heading of "Negroes." *Lizzie, born August 1854,* Mira read. *Pleasant, Till's babe born February 1855. Bell's boy Bull S., born April 1855.*

She ran her fingers along the page, tracing over the names of the unfamiliar and the lost. "There's no Lucy here," Mira noticed after she'd reached the end.

"I know," Jesse said. He handed her another page. It was an 1858 bill of sale for an eight-year-old girl named Lucy with "yellow complexion and black eyes."

"So this is her," Mira said. She took the copy and went back to the photograph on the wall. She looked at the image once more, trying to picture her face, but as hard as she looked she couldn't see anything. The image looked like the outline of a girl, a ghost image haunting the frame.

"This is why you came back. Why you got the job at the Woodsman Plantation. You've just been—researching and gathering all this stuff, because of some trick in the light that looks like a slave girl."

"You and I both know that this is more than just some trick in the light," Jesse said. He seemed a little taken aback at her reaction, but still—all of this, all this gathered material, photos and news articles and records. Piles of research. This was more than trying to understand history.

"Okay, but even if— So what we're saying, what you're really saying—" Mira stopped herself. The words choked inside of her. It was too much to wrap her mind around. She needed time, but there wasn't any. She could see Jesse's eagerness for her to believe, but he'd been thinking about this for years.

"All I'm asking is for you to consider it."

"Let's say I do. They've come, or are coming back. None of that explains why. Why are they here? What do they want?"

Jesse's face lit up, and he talked faster, spilling out the story in pieces. There was a revolt, Jesse said, on the Woodsman land. A group of his slaves had started an insurrection, but one of them told Roman of the plan. The slaves were all caught in the middle of the night, and to make an example of some of them, Roman made the slaves dig the graves of those who'd been caught. Afterward, he decapitated the leaders and put their heads on pikes along a five-mile stretch of road. Negro Head Road, people called it after, as a warning to other slaves. Now known as Antebellum Road.

"Those graves are out there. The clearing we went to, it's why there even *was* a clearing. I'd been to those graves this morning. I saw the men who'd created them. A group of slaves digging. It had to be those graves. I thought it was a reenactment, and I guess it was. They were ghosts trying to show me their story," Mira said.

"Who else did you see?"

"Just the slaves. Oh, but also another man. Young. He was the one giving orders."

Jesse stopped listening and shuffled through his stack of copies once more. The papers were getting everywhere, falling off the coffee table and onto the floor. Mira held a stack of them in her hands and she flipped through them, skimming the pages and pages of listed names in census records and slave records.

"Is this who you saw?" Jesse held up a page, a copy of a tintype image. Mira squinted at the picture of the man in the photograph. "This is Mr. Loomis's ancestor, Henry," Jesse said.

"No," Mira said. "I don't understand though. Why do you have a picture of his ancestor? How does Mr. Loomis fit in with all of this?"

"He died on the property too."

"I know that."

"Right, but it's how he died. The police said he drowned by the river. The river. I had to research it, but Mr. Loomis's family, his great-grandfather to be exact, was the overseer. It was his job to supervise the slaves, and he failed. They planned their revolt and some of them made it to the river and disappeared. Mr.

Woodsman let him keep his job and he remained on the land, was able to buy his own plot. But, Mira, he had to be committed. The family moved away after that, disappeared, until two generations later when the property got passed to Mr. Loomis's father, and then eventually to Loomis. He tried, I'll give him that. For a little while he tried to make something of that land. There's an article here somewhere of when he first moved back, a human-interest piece about his farm. He gave it a good shot, at least. Didn't know what he was up against."

"He was haunted by his failures."

"Or haunted by something else," Jesse said, and Mira flashed to when she was a child and the way Mr. Loomis had leaned toward her face. His look as he stared into her eyes, one of confused familiarity as he tried to reckon with how he knew her followed by the torment of the answer. It was her blood that scared him, blood from the bodies of her ancestors his had helped to spill. He saw in her what his family had done, and, forced with the truth of his history, he had to look away.

Jesse leaned across the table and ran his hands over the photographs, spreading them around as he searched for another. He found the one he needed and grabbed it, picking it up to hold in front of her. "Here, what about him?"

This man was slightly older than the one she'd seen, with a thick mustache, but his eyes—when she looked closer she saw his eyes were the same.

"That one. Who is that?"

"This is Roman Woodsman," Jesse said, confirming her thought, and she was quiet, seeing the resemblance to the white man she'd watched earlier in the day. It was Roman Woodsman who'd ordered those men. Roman who'd forced them to dig the hole and fill it with the bodies of the dead. Faced with this evidence, Mira had to believe the story Jesse was telling her. She couldn't deny this photo.

"Here's one you'll be more familiar with," Jesse said, handing her a copy of the portrait hanging in the Woodsman ballroom. "This is one from when he was older, right before he died."

"How did he die? Do you know?"

"See, that's the thing—in one of his wife's letters she writes that he went mad. He told her he started to see 'movement in the shadows,' as he put it, and had nightmares so upsetting he was afraid to even sleep. He would do anything he could to keep himself up at night by"—he made air quotes—"'taking whatever herbal remedy he could find.' When those didn't work he got so desperate he went and found one of the torture devices he used on his slaves. It was a type of collar that had these spikes that pointed inward so he couldn't lie down or they'd pierce his skin. He put it on but when he wanted it off he couldn't find the key. He panicked, searching the house trying to find it, but it had disappeared."

"God," Mira said, horrified. She was afraid to ask for the rest of the story, but Jesse continued.

"It took another couple of days to get to a locksmith and have him make a separate key, but by then he'd been up several days and was suffering the effects of prolonged sleep deprivation. His wife found him in the bedroom, having run headfirst into a wall. He was on the floor surrounded by a pool of blood."

"He deserved what he got, but Jesus."

"That's two people, Mira. Henry and Roman. Two that went crazy. I think both of them saw the ghosts. It could explain what happened with Mr. Loomis too. Maybe he saw them and wasn't convinced they were real. Maybe he died because he denied them their history."

"I don't know, Jesse," Mira said, but she did know. Right in front of her was the answer to it all. *Crazy old Mr. Loomis*, people used to say as they mocked him, but what if he'd been right? The ghosts had been after him for what his family had done, and he stayed out of defiance, refusing to believe in their existence until they finally killed him.

"If it was only those two deaths I'd let it go, but it's not just them. Look, I've mapped it all out. There's a pattern of people dying on this land. You know about the construction workers, and Mr. Loomis, but there's Alden. So many others. A whole history of families with unexplainable deaths. Freak accidents. Family members being committed and turning to suicide. I've made lists and marked each one, but the thing is—and I didn't realize this until recently—they all tie up to the plantation. Every single one."

"You're telling me the ghosts are retaliating."

"Yes, that's exactly it. Slowly, but surely, they've been waiting for their revenge. Any descendants of those who harmed them or their kindred, they're seeking them out, killing them if they venture on the property. And now with the wedding, they're all here. Almost everyone at the wedding is a descendant of slave owners. All of them the great-grandsons and -daughters of planter aristocracy, and there's something else. Here, I'll show you. Look."

Jesse handed her another copied page, a newspaper clipping about the plantation's renovation. It was a fluff piece, done to drum up interest in the park the place would become. At the bottom a line briefly mentioned the revolt. "Figures," Mira said, commenting on it before folding the paper back up and placing it on the table with the rest of Jesse's research.

"You don't get it. Don't you see, Mira? Look at the date. The anniversary of the slave revolt is tonight."

Hours upon hours of work sat upon the table. Crumpled pages showed failed attempts at tracing other family trees, names written and crossed out before being written again. At the library, he'd searched through the microfilm for any listing of the Woodsman name, saving whatever he could find. Photocopied daguerreotypes of the extended family members lay scattered about. Some had names marked at the bottom, but many were nameless figures, ghost images, their blank expressions staring back.

Mira saw a few pages of Jesse's own family tree, an attempt

at trying to connect his own story with the Woodsmans. If Jesse hadn't meant for these pages to be there, he didn't let on. There were a lot of empty spaces for where the names of his family members should go, and it made her wonder how much of this was him trying to give his past some sort of meaning, making it bearable, as if hidden in all this was an answer for everything that had happened to him. Like her, his life was haunted by the past, had been marked by it, and maybe this was his attempt at finding a sense of agency over his story.

Mira placed the clipping back on the table with the rest of the information he'd gathered, and in doing so, caught a glimpse of another portrait. She'd almost passed over the photograph, but tucked underneath the others was the one he'd taken of her when they were kids. He'd shot two that day—one of her with Celine, but also another, surprising her with the flash as she heard him call her name—but this was the one he kept. When she looked at herself in this photograph, she felt like the girl looking back at her was a stranger. She saw a girl young and vulnerable, with a curious, open stare. She saw the threadbare T-shirt with the holes on the hem she wore when her mother wasn't around to see. She saw the frenzied, wild mess of her hair from their run through the woods. The recognition of how she'd once allowed herself to be overtook her. Mira's fingers traced over the photograph, as if somehow by touching she could reach out to the girl she'd been.

XVIII.

CELINE MUST HAVE known about this. No way could this be a coincidence," Mira told Jesse after she was finished going through all of his research.

Jesse swallowed a couple of times and leaned back on the couch. He wouldn't look at her face.

"You told her, didn't you?" she accused. Mira went through the events of the day: how Jesse instinctively knew to take her to the swamps, his assuredness hiking through the trails, knowing exactly where to go, and then his flash of disappointment when they'd gotten to the spot he'd wanted to take her. Jesse's shoulders turned inward and as he nodded she quickly put the rest of it together. The revolt, the ghosts; he'd told Celine too.

"I did when I found out about the wedding. I thought it would convince her to change the venue, but then she told me she knew about the anniversary and had told Phillip she *wanted* it on that day." He shook his head. "She'd laughed when she said it, and that's when I saw it'd all been a joke to her. Remember that day when we decided to sneak onto the property? She was too scared to go. I don't know what made her change. Maybe it's because she felt like we'd kept something from her about what happened to us that day, and she was acting out because of that. Trying to prove I was wrong. I don't know. I just thought in the end she'd be better than that."

"She told me you were okay with it. On the phone, when she invited me."

"In her mind she might have convinced herself I was—because I could have told her no, probably should have, but I had to know the truth behind this photo. I wanted to know if there were others. I wanted to know so bad I didn't think about anything else, so in the end, Celine and I both used each other to get what we wanted."

"Jesse, I wish you'd told me all this before."

"That sounds familiar." Jesse said it in a teasing way, but when he glanced at Mira and saw her face he sighed. "I was mad at you for a long time, for not telling me what you saw. I didn't understand why you wouldn't tell me. I get it now. You were too scared to face it. I also get why you left and never came back."

"I wanted to forget. I thought it'd make things easier again to push it away and move on."

"We all do that, to some extent. It's hard to live with certain truths of this world, so we ignore what we can. Choose not to look. We have to do it because otherwise we have to deal with the burden of knowing. I struggle with it. Living here, working at the Woodsman place, being reminded every day. I used to keep my head down and try to push away what I saw, but that's the wrong way to be. We can't ignore it. Otherwise, we'll never be able to fight."

"Fight who?"

"Mira," Jesse said, pausing over what he would say next. "What if—what if we didn't go back to the plantation?"

"What? What do you mean?"

"You know what I mean. What if we let the night play out?"

"We can't do that. We can't—"

"Why not? It's not our problem, is it? I mean, what responsibility do we have to tell any of those guests anything? We don't owe anyone there anything."

When Mira looked at his face, she saw he was serious. He

didn't want to go back. He didn't want to warn them about what they'd learned because that's what this whole wedding had been for, why he'd bothered to come. His interest in the wedding had been a pretense meant to test his theory, and he hoped now that his theory was true.

"But to let all the guests—to let them all be murdered? That's what you're saying, what you're telling me, that in reality they should all be murdered? Come on, you couldn't—you couldn't possibly want to be complicit in that. Wait," Mira said, stopping herself as she realized something else. She thought back over the course of the day and how Jesse had found her near the tobacco fields. It was his idea to leave the plantation and go to the Dismal Swamp, his idea to come to his house afterward. "Have you been stalling this entire time?"

"If I'm right, you wouldn't want to be there. Mira, I wouldn't want you to be there."

"God, Jesse. This is—we have to go back."

"I forgot. You're a *good* girl. You're so good you've let the desire to be it overtake you. It's defined who you are. That day we came to the Woodsman house, I loved you for finally admitting something true to yourself, that you wanted to go, despite it being wrong. Despite it being bad. It was the first time you let what you wanted get in the way of how you felt you needed to be. You've always believed being this way was going to somehow save your life, but it has stolen it instead. Let me ask—what did being good ever do for you? For any of us? You can be good and it doesn't matter. It never mattered."

Jesse got up from the couch and gathered all the papers spread out on the table. He was furious but was trying very hard to contain it. He piled the papers on top of one another and stuffed them in a folder. A few slipped out and fell on the floor but he didn't bother to pick them up. Instead he took the folder and threw it down. He rubbed his hand across his wrinkled forehead. "You don't know what it was like," he muttered. "I was the one they blamed. Not you, me. I was the one they tried to lock up, and after— Once, I came off a shift at work and saw that my tires had been slashed. All four of them, the rubber gashed with a knife. I tried to let it go because what could I do? Go to the police? The police who'd just as soon lock me up again? So I ignored it, hoping it'd all die down, but then strangers started showing up at the house. I heard some hollering one night and then a loud bang, saw after they left that they'd bashed the mailbox. Once they threw rocks and broke the front windows. Glass shattered all inside. In the morning I went outside and they'd hung a noose from one of the trees. I took it down and a few days later another appeared. I asked the neighbors if they saw who'd done it and none of them would tell me. None of them wanted to. They were too scared to say anything. Even my uncle—eventually he said to just leave it, so we left it there for weeks and weeks until one day it was finally gone. I couldn't take it anymore. My uncle said he had a friend that could get me some work in Louisiana if I went there. Said he'd help me out with a place to stay too. So I left. I never meant to come back, but when my uncle got sick, I had to, and then— Well, you know the rest of it already."

Mira sat listening, finally, to the rest of what he'd kept from her. Here was the final piece of his story, and she could not blame him for what he wanted to do. None of it should have happened. But she couldn't just let them die.

Outside, the sun's orange glow dimmed, signaling the twilight hour. Night was coming. Whatever was bound to happen would begin soon. They needed to leave and she had to warn them before it was too late.

"Why can't you consider for a moment that maybe—I mean, think about all the harm they've done. What they continue to let happen right in front of them. You've seen the photos. I've told you some of the stories, and there's so much more."

"None of the people there are part of this."

"You're wrong, they are. That's what I've learned." Jesse pointed at the mess. "We're all tangled up in this history. They think they're absolved from the past, but it's their past too. All our lives have been shaped by it, but they're the ones who've ignored how, even though the past has made them who they are. They need to face what's been done and we need to let them. And you know if the situation was reversed they'd leave us to die. You know it. You just don't want to see it."

"We're no better if we do nothing. We can't sit and do nothing. I won't."

"You've always done nothing when it needed to matter. Why can't you do it now?"

"That's not true," she started in protest, but stopped because he was right. Flustered from the shame of remembering, she thought of all the times she could have defended Jesse to her mother but didn't when they were kids. She'd never spoken up as her mother judged, not just Jesse but all the other black kids who didn't fit into her way of being. How much over the years had she let her mother's judgments affect how she too saw the world? How she saw herself?

Earlier today, at lunch, Jesse had said he wished she'd never come, but she understood now why he'd said it. In many ways she was just as complicit as all those who remained at the Woodsman house. Jesse was finally calling her out on this truth.

Okay, she thought, let's let it all burn. We can go, leave Kipsen for good. We can start over and never look back. She'd done that before and could do it again. *Come with me*, she could say to Jesse, and they could go far, far away, but Mira knew there was nowhere they could go where this past wouldn't haunt them. Jesse, for all his talk, would regret it if they didn't return to the Woodsman house. If he was right about the ghosts and chose to do nothing, he'd have to carry the weight of any deaths on his conscience, and she wouldn't let him do that.

"Jesse, we can't be like them. We have to go back."

Mira stood up and headed for the door, assuming Jesse would follow, but when she turned around he was still on the couch. Reluctantly, Jesse got up.

"Are you sure this is what you want to do?" he asked. Mira didn't answer and he sighed, picking up his keys. "This is a mistake, but all right. Come on. I'll take you back."

XIX.

JESSE TOOK HIS time driving to the Woodsman Plantation. He must have thought she wouldn't notice he took the long way, making a loop around downtown instead of through it, or that he went five miles below the speed limit the entire time. Mira kept her mouth shut anyway, because at least he was getting her there, and she hoped that despite his stalling they'd still make it before dark.

By the time Jesse pulled into the parking lot the streetlights had flashed on. The glow illuminated the gravel of the parking lot. Jesse parked at one of the available spaces near the entrance.

"Well, we're here," he told Mira as he shut off the engine. They sat in the uncomfortable silence until Jesse began to jingle his keys, making them go around and round his finger.

"I've been thinking about what you said about joy," Mira said. The whole car ride Mira kept bringing herself back to the photographs Jesse had taken, the joy unseen, and she wondered about her own life, their childhood, and how it had been.

"Oh yeah?" Jesse asked, not hiding his surprise.

"It made me remember how we used to spend weekend mornings at the dollar movie theater showings."

"I forgot about those! They had that quarter soda machine too with the knock-off brands. We'd sneak in a bunch of Squirts and Dr. Perky's and stay in there all day."

"Until the manager noticed and kicked us out."

"Yeah, true," Jesse said, nodding. "Man, we used to do some dumb stuff when we were bored. Remember when we borrowed your mother's garden hose one summer to spray ourselves cool and we came up with the genius idea to do a slip-and-slide with trash bags and dish soap?"

"That was a terrible idea all around, both because Mom was mad we took her hose but also because we ruined the lawn."

"And our behinds." Jesse laughed, unable to control himself, and Mira joined him. They both filled the car with their laughter and Mira wished it had been like this between them from the beginning. Mira laughed until her stomach felt sore and the silence returned.

"We had joy too, didn't we? Before the rest of it," Mira asked.

Jesse coughed as he contemplated her question. He turned to face her, his expression now serious. "I think it's easy to forget sometimes, but sure. We did."

Mira smiled and looked out the window, unable to meet his gaze as she asked her next question. "I've also been thinking about that other thing you said. The part about loving the girl I was."

She was asking once again if he could love her, if he did, and the rush of her vulnerability on full display made her want to disappear. The seconds passed, and she tried to find a way to brush off what she had said, but she couldn't, wouldn't. As much as she hated the way she felt as she waited for him to answer, she also wanted him to answer, because she wanted him, and wanted him to want her too.

"I don't know you," Jesse said. "You don't know me. Neither of us knows the other. We know who we used to be, but that's not enough. We can't love ourselves in the past, or whoever we thought we were. We got to love ourselves in the now."

"I get it," Mira said, feeling the crushing blow of his response. "I shouldn't have said anything."

Jesse seemed to sense her disappointment. After a moment

of hesitation, he opened his mouth to speak. "But maybe after all this is over we could take some time to figure it out," he said. "You're not leaving right away, are you? You could stay a little while longer and we could learn who each of us is again. Would you do that? Would you do that with me?"

Mira told him yes, she would stay, and felt the surprising power one word could hold. Yes, she'd said, holding on to its promise of what her life could be.

The clock on the dash showed it was almost nine o'clock. She needed to go and do what she'd come for. She glanced toward the entrance, at the gate surrounding the grounds. Her hand reached for the door's handle but as soon as she touched the metal she let go.

"What's wrong?" Jesse looked at the entrance and then back at her before coming to his realization. "You can't do it, can you?"

"No, I can," Mira asserted. "I just—"

"You're afraid because they won't believe you," Jesse continued. "Who would? It's crazy."

Mira needed to get out of the car and find someone to tell, but who? Where could she go? Phillip, she reasoned, since these were mostly his guests. Phillip was the one most likely to believe her, and maybe she could convince him to make everyone leave.

Mira took a deep breath and briefly closed her eyes. She knew Jesse was watching her but she ignored him. She inhaled again in the hope of slowing her pulse, of calming herself so she could continue.

Jesse blew a raspberry and leaned forward in the seat. "Maybe I'm wrong, Mira. About all this. I could be."

"You want to live with yourself if you aren't?" Before Jesse could answer, Mira saw people running out of the entrance. Wedding guests hurried away from the grounds as they searched for their cars, dragging their suitcases behind them. Mira watched as what became two or three couples became four, five, six. Soon it was a small crowd of them, all with the same panicked look. They tripped over themselves as they ran across the graveled lot.

"Something's wrong," Mira said. "Everyone's leaving."

This was enough to make Mira get out of the car. She ran to the entrance and along the path toward the house. The path went past the gardens, eventually coming to the side of the house where it split in two directions, one around the front and the other heading toward the slave cabins, the restaurant and bar, and the cottages. Mira stopped at the fork in the path, catching her breath.

"I don't know where to go," Mira told Jesse, but he wasn't there. "Jesse?" she called, although it was pointless. She knew Jesse was back in his car, had probably roared the engine the moment she'd left, driving back home, escaping whatever fate awaited this place.

Farther up along the path a crowd of guests gathered and Mr. Tatum stood in their center. His eyes were wild, bloodshot. With a face reddened with fury, he clenched the stock of his rifle, sputtered, and shook his head as he listened to the clamor of the rest of the group. He'd gathered men from the town—laborers, it looked like from their clothes, men like him who existed on the fringes of the town. Dried mud caked the bottoms of their overalls and boots. A few wore straw hats to block out the sun. They held bottles of liquor, the froth dripping down their chins as they gulped down the drink and threw the bottles in the dirt. They huddled around each other, their stammering growing to interloping yells.

Mira did not want to go near these men. Their anger was palpable. She didn't want to get closer, afraid of what they might do. Soon they all shifted their gaze on her. She froze in response. Her heart raced, fearing they would come for her. Backing away, someone grabbed her arm and she turned and saw Phillip.

"Oh god, Mira," he said, and the smell of his hot, yeasty breath made her want to choke. He gripped her shoulders hard enough that she gave a yelp, but he couldn't hear her; it was too loud. "Celine is out there. Oh god."

Mira stared down at Phillip's hands, speckled rust all along the palms. It didn't register at first, it took her a few seconds, that the stains on his hands and on the front of his shirt were blood. "Celine is where?" she asked Phillip.

"In the tobacco fields. She was in the fields. I've just come from there. God, it's terrible. I hadn't meant to go out there, but I heard singing. Some sort of chant. It felt like it was leading me to her, and then I saw—"

"My daughter's dead!" Mr. Tatum yelled, interrupting. "We need to get him. He killed her."

Phillip quickly told her the story. It had started as a walk to clear his head and he'd made a wrong turn, ending up near the edge of the tobacco fields. That's when he heard the song. It didn't take him long before he got lost. The longer he was out there, the more frantic he became about not getting out, and soon instead of walking he was running. He ran and ran, going in circles, with the tobacco leaves cutting his face as he whipped through them, hoping that all he had to do was go a few more feet and he'd be out. He ran and, not noticing the ground below, tripped and fell into the dirt, hitting his head. It knocked him out. When he opened his eyes again, he sat up, wiped the sweat stinging his eyes, and stumbled up. He started to get up but noticed a shoe in front of him. A bedroom slipper the color of cream. He picked it up and rubbed his fingers over the fabric, and then walked a few steps in the direction he thought he'd come from. He took a couple more steps and then saw her—her body facedown in the dirt, negligee torn up to the hips, eyes closed. "Celine?" he called, crawling over to her. He got closer but the smell caught him off guard, forcing him to turn away.

"I shouldn't have," Phillip said, shaking his head. "I shouldn't have seen her exposed like that." With this, Phillip's body collapsed. His knees buckled and he fell to the ground. He stared at the patch of grass in front of him as his eyes watered.

Celine was dead. Mira could barely stand. She wanted to sit but the men crowded around her forced her to stand. These men surrounded her, screaming for justice, working themselves into a frenzy over the desire for it, and Mira stared at their froth and spittle, at their flustered faces burning in anger, and feared what their vengeance might do.

The ghosts must have lured her into the woods, wanting to show her the horrors of their lives. Come and see, they'd whispered, wanting to show her the knitted scars, their bruises and cuts. They held up their hands and showed the empty spaces where fingers used to be. They told her to come, following deeper, showing her where they were captured and slaughtered. Come and see. Their heads on pikes, the skin of the chin sagging, the hollow caverns where the eyes were gouged out, mouths open but nothing inside, tongue cut, teeth stolen, every part taken except the shell of a face. Come and see, come and see, come and see.

Had she seen? She must not have, refused to see what they'd tried to show her, and they killed her for it. If they had come for Celine, then they were coming for them all.

"Don't you worry," Mr. Tatum said, putting a hand on Phillip's shoulder. "We're going to get him."

Him. This got Mira's attention. "Get who?"

"Your boy. Jesse. Where is he? You got to know where he is. Y'all like to stick together."

"Who are you talking about?" Mira was confused. Whatever they thought was wrong. It was the ghosts. They needed to go out to where Celine was, see whatever it was the ghosts had been trying to show her. "No, you're all wrong. We need to get Celine. Phillip, is Celine still out there?" Mira asked, but he wouldn't answer, continuing to look blankly ahead. "Phillip, do you think you could find her?"

"I don't know," Phillip said, but his tone changed. He stepped away from Mira, as if he was afraid of her, of what she was asking of him.

In the background, Mira saw the golden-green leaves of the tobacco fields and she knew Celine had gone in the same direction

Mira had, because just beyond their reach were the graves. That had to have been it. The ghosts had lured her there to show her the graves. To unearth the bodies of those unknown men and women. To make known what had been done. This had to be what all this was about and Mira needed to finish it—find the graves, their bodies, and maybe they would be saved.

"They're coming," Mira almost screamed. She'd tried to control herself, to keep her voice calm, but calmness was not going to work with these men and they were running out of time. She had to convince them to follow her. They had to see.

"Don't you understand? They did this to Celine and we need to find them or it won't stop."

"Who?" Phillip asked her.

"What we need to do is find that black boy," Mr. Tatum boomed. "Where is he? Anyone seen him? He's done this before. He killed that man years ago."

"That's not true," Mira yelled. "You know that. The police let him go. Mr. Loomis drowned."

"The police couldn't charge him but I know the truth. That boy had something to do with it and now he's hurt Celine. Where is he? Jesse's his name. Where is he?"

Mira saw the way these men looked at her. They were looks to remind her of her unimportance. Looks to make her feel small. It was the same look the policeman had given her when she'd tried to help Jesse, his face full of amusement at first, because why would a girl like her have a point worthy of being heard? Then annoyance, which turned to anger. The way he'd raised his arm at her, close to hitting her, when all she'd wanted was to tell the truth. He didn't want to listen to her. He never would have. These men, they weren't going to listen either.

Still, she tried. "I'm trying to warn you," she said again, this time her voice weaker, because they had long stopped hearing.

"He's not getting away this time," Mr. Tatum muttered, quickly joining the throng of other men.

"You don't understand," Mira stammered, but they'd heard enough. It was chaos, a chorus of voices growing louder as each of them yelled places to go. The men shouted names of streets, all unrecognizable to her, and decided to split up to cover it all.

"No, stop!" Mira yelled, hoping with her last plea they'd listen, but they had already started running away from her, with Phillip and Mr. Tatum following behind. There was no way she'd find Jesse in time, but she had to warn him. She ran back to her cottage and stumbled inside. In the safety of the room she searched through her purse for her phone.

"Jesse," Mira shouted after hearing the beep of his voicemail. "Celine is dead. They found her body. Mr. Tatum thinks you had something to do with it. He's looking for you. Him and a group of other men. A mob. If you're home get out of there. God, I hope you get this."

The voicemail beeped, ending her message, but unsatisfied, she dialed his number again, hoping this time he would pick up.

"Mira?"

"Jesse! Thank goodness." A wash of relief fell over her as she heard his voice. "Where are you? Are you home? If you are then you need to get out of there."

"Why? What happened? Are you all right?"

"I'm fine. Listen, they found Celine's body in the fields. There's a mob that thinks you hurt her. They're coming for you."

"I can't hear you. Who's coming? Were we right?"

Jesse sounded like he was in a tunnel. She could only hear part of what he was trying to say and that was muffled.

"You need to get out of there!" Mira yelled. She shouted in the phone for him to leave his house but he couldn't hear her clearly either. She moved toward the window in the hope the service would be better, but Jesse continued to fade in and out. She had to get outside, to get a better signal, and she told him to hold on as she went to the door.

"I'm coming, Mira. Do you hear me? I'm on my way," Jesse

said, and before Mira knew it, her phone's screen had gone black and Jesse was gone. At least he wouldn't be home, she thought as she threw the phone on the couch.

Mira glanced at the sky through the cottage window. There was still time to fix this; not enough, but she would head out to the clearing anyway. She needed a shovel first and left to find one. It didn't take long. At the gardens she found one lying against the shed. She picked it up and started running.

By now, all the guests had heard about Celine. "What do you think she looks like?" she heard a group of them ask as she passed by. "How bad do you think it is?" They gripped their phones, ready to take their photos, as they disappeared toward the trees in their search to find Celine.

Others hurried to their cottages and threw what they could into their suitcases. They flooded the pathway leading to the parking lots. As Mira left the gardens carrying her shovel, more couples rushed past her to the parking lot. None of them paid her any mind, their eyes fixed on the exit, on their cars, and on the looming safety of the highway.

The shovel dragged along the grass as Mira ran. Everyone would see the truth, she just had to get to the clearing and dig. They had to know what laid buried in the dirt. If she did this, the ghosts would stop.

She ran until trees surrounded her and she could no longer discern the path. "Where is it?" she asked, stopping. Which way was right? In the dark, who could tell? She started in one direction, hesitated, doubting herself. The sting of sweat made her rub her eyes. She was wasting time. "Where, where, where?" she called.

Just as quickly, as if an answer to her question, she heard movement in the brush. A breeze, subtle, but Mira felt the air on her skin, making her senses alert, alive, and it was enough. She began to run again. Someone was following her, or something, and as she picked up the pace she felt it telling her where to go, telling her to hurry, almost there, hurry, and she ran, going farther and farther still, until she saw the clearing and stopped.

This was it, where the slaves who'd rebelled were buried. She would find them and they'd be free.

Mira dug. Around her, the whispering call grew louder with each pierce of the shovel in the ground. A clamor of voices rising, pushing her forward, beckoning for her to find them.

She forced the blade into the earth. She lifted one foot and with her heel pushed down on the blade. It took a few tries to get it deep enough. Her arms lifted the broken dirt and threw it behind her. She repeated the process, again and again. Dig, push, lift, throw. She did this job with a desperate sense of urgency, because soon the day would be over, and she had to be prepared for whatever was coming.

Her muscles ached from the struggle but she kept on. Her breath was sparse and she choked on the summer air but she didn't stop. Hair matted, sweat beads dripping, sliding down her neck and into her crevices—give up, her body told her. Give up and go, but she wouldn't.

With each lift she got better, and soon she fell into a rhythm. Each lift of the dirt brought her closer.

She dug through the topsoil, disrupting the grass and weeds. This was the hardest part and she struggled to get through.

She dug, hoping to finish before it was time. Dig, push, lift, throw. She repeated the movement, each time saying the words. They became her own mantra, a prayer, a song, as she dug. Dig, push, lift, throw.

As she dug, Mira thought of the inmates she'd driven past along the highway. Their image came to her as she lifted another scoop of dirt from the ground. Their bodies hunched over, eyes focused on the ground. She thought of the boy who had turned to look. So young. A child. What had he done to warrant such a fate? What had he done? Or any of the others? She wished she could save them, but they were long gone, lost.

Mira dug. An hour passed. She stood in the shallow pit she'd created, exasperated and tired. Her clothes were coated with the muddy earth. Dirt smeared across her arms and her face.

"I must be getting close."

Just dig a little farther and maybe you'll get there, she told herself. It had to be here. Had to be. She had to see this through.

Around her, the voices rose higher still, and as they gained momentum she heard a hymn. The work song sung before, and she dug along with their cadence. Soon, she joined in, her mumbled singing turning to hollering as she threw the shovel into the ground, lifted the dirt, and threw it over her shoulder again and again.

She forced her shovel down in the dirt once more, but this time the shovel got stuck. This must be it, Mira thought, relief spreading through her at the realization she'd hit across the bones. She dropped the shovel. Her body fell into the dirt, on her knees, and she began to claw with her hands. She clutched fistfuls of the muddied earth and threw them behind her, picking up her pace, getting closer, and her heart raced. She found what her shovel had hit and she leaned closer to look. It was just another piece of rock.

Mira grabbed a chunk of dirt and threw it across the grass in one final, exasperated burst of energy. Her chest heaved as she struggled with the scene before her. "I don't understand," she yelled in between breaths. "I thought this was what you wanted!" Mira had gone searching for the graves but the hole she'd dug was empty. No bones lay buried, no graves to be found. None of them were here. Nothing at all.

XX.

It was long dark by the time Mira left the fields. She could barely see in front of her and what she did see she didn't recognize. Something had happened and all the lights were out. She walked slowly, tentatively, afraid of what lurked in the shadows. Fallen branches crackled with her weight. Gnats kept finding their way to her face. She felt the crawl of them on her skin and quickly wiped them away.

Fear kept Mira going. When she thought of the mob of men reaching Jesse's house—their cries of "Open up!" as they pounded on his door—who knew what they would do when they found him. Maybe he'd left in time. A foolish hope, but one she clung to as she made her way through the dark.

After escaping the fields, Mira decided to go back to the cottage and wait for Jesse. It was the first place he'd go looking for her. She reached the main grounds and stopped at the smokehouse. With the realization that she had made it out okay, her legs weakened and she collapsed on the grass. She was so tired. She didn't know if she could go any farther, if she could make it to the cottages. Her body wanted to lie on the ground. She wanted to rest, to just lie here and rest.

Nothing she'd done had worked. The slaves hadn't been found. They remained lost out in the fields. She knew she'd never find them, even if she were to go back again, if she were to try again. Darkness eclipsed the sky. She lifted her head, searching for the light of the moon or the glimmer of stars, but when she looked she saw only blackness. Because of this, Mira didn't see the woman at first. She was so far in the distance. Dressed in all white, she looked like a faint apparition hovering in the night. Her arms flailed above her, waving, waving for Mira to come toward her.

Mira knew her. It was the woman from the night before. The woman was heading in the direction of the cottages. She was leading her away from the fields and through the grounds. Mira got up, brushed her hands across her jeans, and began to follow.

After a few steps she stopped, doubting herself and what she saw. She'd been wrong before, misjudged what she'd been so sure of. What proof was there that this too wasn't just her mind playing tricks on her?

"Hello!" Mira called. She raised her hand and waved in response. The woman waved back, this time with a stronger sense of urgency, and began moving again. "Wait, no. Who are you? Where are you going?" Mira yelled.

The woman kept walking. Mira picked up her pace to catch up to her but she couldn't seem to get close. "Wait," Mira said, hurrying, but her feet were sore, her arches ached, and as hard as she tried, the woman kept moving farther and farther toward the darkness.

Mira was determined to reach the cottages and find Jesse. He had to have gotten here by now. She'd gather her things and together with Jesse would leave this place, neither of them ever returning.

Mira stopped to catch her breath. She choked in the stagnant air, suffered it down, and then tugged on the hem of her shirt, pulling it up to wipe the sweat from her face.

The grounds were silent and still. Champagne flutes and beer cans littered the ground. Everything was empty. Everyone was gone.

Mira saw the Woodsman house up along the path. A single bedroom light was on, a beacon amidst the surrounding darkness. The only sign she wasn't alone was this light from the window urging her.

Mira wasn't sure how she ended up over on this side of the grounds, how she had managed to bypass all the other structures on the property. She must have gone all along the circumference until she ended up at the front entrance of the house instead of making a direct route through the grounds. In any event, she had made it, and that was all that mattered.

The light soon went out. She stepped forward, then stopped, suddenly worried about what lay ahead. She wanted to be off this property. Let whatever secrets existed stay hidden, but what if the answer was there? She hesitated, her attention focused on the window. The question of *what if* lingered. What if Jesse had been right after all? She shouldn't risk it but she needed to know. Her desire to know overpowered everything else. She would not leave without finding out the truth, without knowing once and for all what was in the house.

The scream that came next was unmistakable. A wailing echo. She picked up her pace, running up the path to the Woodsmans house.

Then she heard the scream again.

It took the babies drowning for the rest to say, Enough. *They hadn't been the first to go; many others had killed themselves, hoping for deliverance. Often it was the young girls newly come. Warned of the fate awaiting them, they took to the river rather than face the shame of what their futures held. Each time, those who'd stayed behind hoped that they had escaped, until their bloated bodies rose to the surface and they knew what had happened instead. Over the years, both men and women alike had disappeared into the river, but never had it been children, and never by those who'd borne them.*

These mothers gave their children a baptism of death before deciding they would follow too. They let the water wash their spirits to their promised land, that's what they'd forced themselves to believe, yet the others knew they lived in a world where the only promise was this life meant to break. They broke bread together in the morning and their spirits were broken by evening, hunkering down on the floor, cloistered together, their sweat-stunk bodies from the heat, hoping by night the air would cool but it never did, off to sleep for another day and another. Can see to can't, morning to evening, every day until they could do no more.

It was the murder of the children that finally made them join together in their struggle. Not when they all were taken, bound in chains and forced in ships across the water. Not when they were made to stoop and bend, naked, while checked for wounds, their skin pinched for the muscle underneath, their mouths pulled on to show their teeth. Not when their mothers and daughters and sisters and wives were groped as they danced and curtsied on the block before being separated forever. Nor was it when they were brought to the fields, many collapsing to their deaths from the work as the high-noon sun basted their rotting backs. The bullwhip crack hadn't been enough. All the blood that soaked these fields hadn't been enough. Even after death, when their desecrated remains were stolen from the graveyards meant to be their final place of rest, it had not been enough to make the others see. What it took was the murdering of a mother's most loved—of finding them facedown in the murky river, bodies limp and floating, with their outstretched arms forever reaching for the other—before they finally understood.

XXI.

S TANDING OUTSIDE IN the hallway, Mira watched as a group of
women crowded together in the ballroom. Their skin stood
in stark contrast to the blinding white of the room. Rococo white
marbled mantels. Frieze molding, painted a brilliant ivory, lined
the ceilings. Corinthian columns supported triple arches. White
tiles on the floor. In the corner, a cream-colored piano.

The lace curtains that framed the windows were drawn. The
women stood, shoulders slumped, faces downcast, their arms
hanging limp by their sides. They ranged in age, but the oldest
seemed to be in their forties. There were young girls, teenagers,
maybe even younger, their thin frames lost in the fabric that covered them. All the women were dressed the same, wearing white
cotton shirts with hems that fell to their hips. Their legs and feet
were bare.

They made sure to keep their faces turned at the floor, refusing to look at anything in the room or at each other. Like statues
they stood, silent and still, waiting for instruction from the men
in charge. Occasionally, one of them, usually the youngest, would
raise a hand to wipe the crust of sleep from their eyes, but soon
after, another would remind them not to move and the hand was
quickly lowered.

"What are you doing there? You're supposed to be with the
others," a man behind Mira barked, and, terrified, she joined the

other women in the ballroom. No one appeared to notice that she was dressed differently than them, or they didn't care. Unlike the others, Mira focused on the white men in the room. They all wore black masks that covered their faces. They stood at the doorway, their heads turned out toward the hall, and waited in a cluster as one by one they were searched. Their weapons, if they had any, were taken, exchanged for a paper stub that the men stuffed in their pockets. After they were searched, they entered the ballroom to view the women on display.

The women ignored Mira completely. She heard sniffling, and behind her was a young girl, barely a teenager. Tears fell down her face and she reached a hand to wipe them away, to hide best her emotion, but the act only caused her to cry harder, until she was choking down sobs.

"Hush up," a black woman standing near her called. The woman was close to Mira's age. She was tall; the fabric barely covered her muscular legs. The woman's brown eyes were wide, a look of warning to the girl but also to Mira, and she quieted.

Men gathered, soon filling the room with their pants of want. She stared at the black masks that covered their faces, but these weren't made of fabric. When the men got close, Mira noticed they were made of some other material she couldn't discern, fashioned into a mask. They'd been painted black and a ribbon had been pulled through a hole on each side so the wearer could tie the mask on. The men filed into the room, walking the circumference as they observed each of the women. Mira could not see their faces but she recognized the look in their eyes as their gazes passed over woman to woman. It was a look of entitled desire, of a man who would take without fear of retribution or reprisal. These were men who wanted, and what they wanted was these women, and they knew they would get what they wanted.

Some of them got close enough that Mira could smell the odor of the fields they'd worked. Their breath hovered in her face as they asked questions about her body. They wanted to touch and a few of the men did. Mira watched as their hands felt up a woman's thighs, moving to touch what was underneath the sheets they wore. Unsatisfied, wanting to see more, one of the men ripped off a woman's shirt, revealing her bare skin for all the men to see. She quickly reacted to cover her chest, but the man who'd forced Mira into the room went and struck her, and she let go of her arms, relenting, and the men all stared at what she had to offer.

"How much?" they asked, and for each of them a price was yelled. Men thrust their money and paid. Afterward, they each took their woman and left the room, going off to another part of the house Mira couldn't see.

"Her, I want her," a man said, pointing to Mira. He had blond hair wetted so he could make a side part. Behind his mask blue eyes fixed themselves on her. His skin was tanned, most likely from working all day doing whatever fieldwork necessary for his living. He was dressed plainly, but many of the men in the room wore similar clothes.

"Marceline's not on the table," another man called. This man entered the room wearing a mask like all the others, but he carried himself with a different air. His clothes were more formal, as if he were attending a ball, and his dark shoes made a loud clack as the heels hit the floor.

"I'm not Marceline," Mira said to them both, but the men continued on with their conversation, ignoring her.

"If she's not on the table then why is she here?"

"She's been waiting here for me. That's why. Look, Tatum, I'm not going to argue with you. Either pick another girl or leave. Your choice."

Tatum. Had she heard right? The man pouted, giving a once-over at Mira, and she wished she could see his face. Without thinking, she raised her arm to take his mask, to pull it off him, to see him for who he was. He backed away from her, deciding on another woman nearby.

After he left, the other man, the one with the clacking shoes, walked straight to Mira and gestured for her to follow him. He led her out of the room, down one hall and then another. As they walked, Mira noticed that more of the scenery had changed. This was not the house she'd seen before.

He led her into one of the rooms and cornered her toward the bed. "Shhhhhh," he said, spittle dripping onto her chest. "Unless you want to play our game? We could play that game too, if you want."

He wanted her to succumb. To lie back as he stripped her of her clothes, as his calloused fingers rubbed against her skin. "Stay still," he yelled as his hands reached for her body, his order to obey coming out like a hiss. In other rooms were other women, women who knew what would happen if they fought, and so they lay on their stomachs and backs while these men got on top of them, stinking of booze and the crops they tended. In other rooms were other women, each one rented out by masked men who wanted to relinquish their desires in the safety of secrecy.

"Marceline, stop it now. Stop!"

Mira would not yield. She would not quiet or succumb. She'd spent an entire life doing nothing—of sheltering herself, of not speaking up, of hiding, of letting others go before her, of denying what she wanted—and looking at this masked man filled her with rage from all of it. Her hands reached for his face, wanting to claw at the skin, wanting blood.

The man's mask loosened and it fell off onto the floor. This made him jump back, shocked at this sudden revelation of his face. It was Roman Woodsman. Mira recognized the same eyes, the same squint-eyed expression that had been in his portrait. "What are you doing? This isn't how we do this. This isn't how we play."

Roman's face quickly shifted from confusion to anger when he realized that her resisting wasn't part of whatever game they played.

"You should know better," Roman said.

Mira reached to grab for Roman's mask but he blocked her

with his body. He laughed, seeing her distress. His laughter grew louder, maniacal, and when he lunged toward her she darted away, grabbing for the mask and heading for the door. He tried to stop her but Mira was quick, opening the door to escape before he could hold her down. She took one last look behind her and almost gasped. Another woman was on the bed—the same woman in white. Her eyes held a vacant stare. She was gone, somewhere other than here, and Roman towered over her, his pants lowered to his ankles, his bare buttocks thrusting with fury.

Mira ran down the hall of the house, hoping to get as far away from the ballroom and the other men as she could. The clacking of Roman's shoes resounded in her head, chasing her, until Mira had to stop. Her body shook as she tried to shut out the noise, but the *rapraprap* would not stop. She closed her eyes and waited, silently counting the seconds, and eventually all was silent. Mira opened her eyes. When she looked down at her hands the mask she thought she'd taken was gone.

XXII.

A CHILD'S LAUGHTER CAUGHT Mira's attention next. A little girl appeared before Mira, or maybe she had been there all along. She wore a plain dress, the fabric faded and worn. Someone had attempted to fix her matted hair but had done so poorly. A loose ribbon held a puff of her hair at the end. She had an amused expression on her face. The corners of her mouth were slightly upturned and her round eyes stared intently at Mira.

"Did you lose your parents?" Mira asked, looking down at the girl. She crouched so as to meet her face at eye level. "Do you need help finding them?"

The girl nodded and Mira held out her hand but the girl shook her head in response.

"I don't understand. Don't you want to go?" Mira held out her hand again but this time the girl made a screeching sort of sound and pulled the dress she wore over her head. The sound continued, growing louder, and Mira looked around for someone to help her, but she was alone. "It's okay. It's all right," she said, in as calm a voice as she could muster. "Shhh, shhh, it's all right."

The girl quieted, much to Mira's relief, and pulled her dress back down. "See?" Mira said. "Everything is fine. You're okay."

They were in a part of the house that was unfamiliar to her. She worried that walking in the wrong direction would lead them back to the men from the ballroom, and what if they saw her with this child? What would they do to her?

"I need to get you out of this place," Mira whispered. She glanced down one end of the hall and then back toward the other, not sure which direction was the right one. The girl, however, decided for her, retreating down the hall away from Mira. Nervous that the girl would get away and fearing what could happen to her, Mira followed. "We have to go. Please, take my hand, and we'll go," she said, moving toward her, but the girl picked up on Mira's urgency. She sprang away, and Mira, not wanting to lose her, ran after her. The house was a maze, far larger than she remembered it being, and the girl was fast.

"Wait," Mira called, hoping for her to stop while praying others in the house wouldn't hear. "Don't go. I can get you out. Come back!"

The girl didn't look back. Mira followed her as she ran up a staircase. Mira began to go up, but the stairs creaked with her weight and she stopped. Carefully, but as swiftly as she was able, she went up the steps. When she reached the top, she was faced with another long corridor with a series of rooms. The girl must have slipped inside one of them.

The sconces on the wall flickered as Mira tiptoed along. With each step the light dimmed further. Mira held her breath as she stopped at each of the bedroom doors, pausing to listen and see if she could hear her inside. She moved toward the end and with relief heard the sound of laughter again.

Mira leaned against the wall and then lowered her body toward the floor. The door hadn't been closed completely and she peeked through the crack, careful to make sure the door didn't fully open by accident. The girl stood in the center of the bedroom, her arms folded behind her back, waiting for something or someone Mira couldn't see.

"My nig, where did you go?" Mira heard a woman's voice call

in the bedroom. "Oh, there you are!" the woman exclaimed. "You know you shouldn't run off like that. I get so worried."

The girl nodded. She let out a light giggle.

"Are you hungry? Do you want a treat?"

The girl made a high-pitched squeal and jumped up and down at the word *treat*. The woman smiled, appeared overjoyed at her response, and then walked over to the dresser and picked up something off the table.

Through the mirror's reflection Mira saw the woman's face. The resemblance fit the images in the photographs Jesse had shown her and Mira knew it was Mrs. Woodsman. That meant the girl was Lucy, her Lucy.

Mrs. Woodsman put the treat in her palm and balled her hand into a fist. "Spin," she commanded, and Lucy lifted a leg and turned herself around, spinning her body in a loop. She finished with a little kneel and Mrs. Woodsman exclaimed, dropping the treat for Lucy to pick up off the floor. "Oh, good job," she said. "Do it once more. Spin."

Lucy did as she was told, spinning in another loop, but this time Mrs. Woodsman didn't let her stop.

"Spin, spin, spin!" she yelled, and Lucy spun round and round, laughing at first, but the longer she had to do it the quieter she got, and Mrs. Woodsman kept yelling. Lucy twirled around, becoming more unstable with each turn until she lost her balance and fell to the floor. Her face was scrunched up in pain and confusion.

"No treat for you," Mrs. Woodsman said. "I didn't tell you to stop. What have I told you about not listening? You need to do better. You don't want to end up like those—"

Lucy's eyes welled up, and seeing her face, Mrs. Woodsman stopped. "Well, next time. Maybe you'll follow directions," she huffed.

Lucy nodded again. All of Lucy's answers were either nods or simple gestures with her hands. She wouldn't speak, barely made any sort of sound at all.

"It's time for bed," Mrs. Woodsman said. She moved toward the other side of the room and Mira was able to see her. She was dressed in her nightclothes and her long thin hair fell down her back. She walked around the bed and went to Lucy, patting her hair lightly before going to something else Mira couldn't see. She heard the clicking sound of a latch opening, and the squeak of rusted hinges. Mira lightly pushed on the door so she could get a further glimpse.

"In you go," Mrs. Woodsman said, waving her hand, and Lucy followed on command. Mira pushed the door again, craning her head to see.

Lucy got on her hands and knees and began to crawl across the floor. She crawled toward what looked like a wire cage. It was barely big enough for her to fit. The metal brushed against her back as she squeezed herself inside. She was unable to stand so she curled into a ball on the floor with her arms wrapped around her knees as Mrs. Woodsman closed the door and locked it shut.

"Sleep," Mrs. Woodsman ordered, and Lucy closed her eyes. Mrs. Woodsman stood next to the cage, watching Lucy and waiting. She gave a light tap to the cage. "There, there. Such a good little nig. Unlike all the others, but they are getting what they deserve. Go to sleep now. Sleep."

After a few minutes more, Mrs. Woodsman disappeared to the other side of the room again. She heard the sound of metal clang against a surface—the key, Mira reasoned—and a few seconds later the lights blew out and the room went dark. The sheets rustled as Mrs. Woodsman crawled onto the mattress and sighed. Soon, her body was still except for subtle breathing. Mira took this opportunity to enter the room. She crawled along the floor, afraid of standing lest Mrs. Woodsman wake in the night and see her. Her clothes made shushing noises as she moved along past the cage where Lucy was kept. She needed to get to the other side to the key. Her eyes focused in the dark, looking among the shadows, and she soon settled on the outline of a dresser. The woman must have placed the key on top of it. Mira crawled around the front of the bed, moving over to the dresser, and then she stood up and carefully felt around for the key.

Got it, Mira thought once she grasped the cool metal handle. She held the key in her hands. All she had to do now was let Lucy out and get them both out of here.

A vanity mirror was attached on top of the dresser. Mira caught a glimpse of her reflection in the mirror's glass. She was about to move away but something caught her attention. She squinted, trying to focus on the shadow, and as her eyes adjusted she realized that the shadow was a man's.

Mira opened her mouth but no sound came. She couldn't scream, couldn't risk waking up Mrs. Woodsman and being caught. She couldn't move. Could only watch as the shadow crept in the dark. He went first to the cage, saw the lock. His hand slipped into his pocket and he pulled out his own key, a copy, made for this moment, and he pushed it into the lock and opened the cage's door. Lucy's eyes opened and she crawled out almost immediately. She must have known this whole time, must have been waiting for him to come and release her. The man pointed toward the door and Lucy disappeared through it.

He went to the bed next. As he moved closer, Mira got a better look. He was young, thin, with a thick beard that obscured most of his face. He didn't appear to notice Mira as she stared at him, too concerned with Mrs. Woodsman sleeping in her bed. He stopped when he got to the side of the bed, pausing to watch her shift.

Mira stood, frozen. Even if she somehow managed to sneak out unnoticed, she couldn't bring herself to do it. Part of her knew what he was about to do, but still she stood, waiting to see if she would be right.

The man raised a hand in the air, a signal to God. He lifted his head and whispered a few words. When he was finished with his prayer his hand went to his hip. The knife he pulled out managed to gleam despite the room's darkness.

His hand gripped the knife as he leaned over the bed. He brought the knife inches from Mrs. Woodsman's throat and stopped. Mira held her breath. She expected any moment he would drag the blade across her throat, and she prepared herself for the gurgling sound it would make, Mrs. Woodsman choking as blood poured out, staining her clothes and the sheets.

It would be quick, if he were to do it. He needed to make one single, smooth stroke and then it would be done. He was so close, and yet—he stood silent, unmoving, unable, or unwilling.

What is he waiting for? Mira thought. His hand wavered. Mira worried he would drop the knife, but he managed to hold on. Why won't he do it?

He stepped back, tried to regain his courage. He straightened his posture and breathed in. Then, when he appeared ready, he brought the knife to her throat again. This time he would do it, Mira believed. He steadied himself and closed his eyes.

Outside, a shot fired, the single pop followed by the howl of dogs. The wild calls of men filled the night. Mira tried to slip away, but it was too late. Mrs. Woodsman had woken, saw a black man standing over her holding the knife, and she opened her mouth wide, letting out a shriek loud enough that Mira was sure those outside could hear.

She had minutes before the men found their way inside the house, to her. She needed to find a way to get out. She ran down the first staircase she saw, moving faster, going down another staircase, paying no attention to where she went just as long as she was moving and no one had caught up to her. Down the staircase, down, down, down, and the light around her dimmed, growing darker, chasing her as she ran farther down. At the sight of a door she pulled it open with such force she stumbled back, taking a few seconds to stabilize herself before running outside into the night. She ran, hoping to follow in the direction of the plantation's entrance, but she tripped and fell. Her head banged against something hard.

XXIII.

WHEN MIRA WOKE, she felt a searing pain in her forehead. She reached up to touch the wound and her hand was wet with blood. She wiped herself clean using the front of her shirt.

Wherever Mira was, it wasn't outside. Inside a barn maybe. She must have run far enough away to get to one of the barns on the southern side of the house.

The air was stuffy and damp. A putrid mix of feces and urine, of decaying flesh. Of rot. Light streamed in from slits in the wooden walls, and Mira could see two tables, one with an array of paddles, whips, and a cat-o'-nine-tails, the other just a table-top. All the instruments were stained a brownish-red color, dirty from blood.

Mira got up from the ground and walked over to the door. It was locked. She jerked on the handle, pulling a couple of times in disbelief. She couldn't figure how she'd gotten locked inside. How long had she been unconscious? It couldn't have been that long, but then the light must mean it was morning. She began to bang on the door, crying for help, hoping someone would come.

Soon enough, Mira heard men's voices from outside. She started to bang again but the sound of a loud wailing scared her enough to stop. The men's voices grew louder. They were heading toward her. Mira crawled quickly across the floor to a corner to hide, burying herself as much as she could in a pile of damp straw.

The door opened and two white men entered. They dragged another man and threw him on the ground. The man on the ground was black. His clothes were ripped, and his shirt was stained a deep red on the side. His wrists were tied with rope. He tried to get up but one of the white men immediately grabbed the whip from the table and struck him down. He fell instantly and gave out a muffled cry.

"What's that?" one yelled, and the man on the ground winced quietly, appearing to want to deny them the satisfaction of hearing his pain. The white men loomed over him and Mira held her breath, afraid that they'd hear and be emboldened to do more damage.

The two white men were almost identical in their dress. Both wore dark vests over white collared shirts. Belt buckle badges flashed. Wide-brimmed hats covered their heads. Their boots were caked in mud and the bottoms of their pants were darker than the rest, damp from the river where they'd hunted. These men were pattyrollers, self-appointed with the task of maintaining order. They carried themselves with a sense of righteousness as they enforced their judgments.

"He's one of them that orchestrated this mess. That's what they're saying. He's the one."

"What about the others?" a third voice called, and Mira saw Roman enter the room. He walked in leisurely, as if on a stroll, as if the entire day had been saved for this. He appeared unbothered by the stench in the room. The expression on his face was one of ambivalence, perhaps an air of slight annoyance that was directed more at the two white men.

Roman Woodsman. He was the common horror in all of this. He had orchestrated those women, gathered them together to profit off their bodies. He was the one who'd forced those men to dig what she'd thought were graves, but maybe the task was a futile one, the act itself meant as punishment. They were slaves after all, their life of labor worth more than death, and it was their labor that had made him. The bending of backs until they broke. Their blood had made his money.

"Soon enough we'll get them all. Don't worry," one of them assured Roman.

"What happened to this one?" Roman asked.

"Got hit by one of the bullets. Won't last much longer. He'll be gone before he's rightfully punished."

"A shame," Roman said calmly, his demeanor in complete opposition to the other two men's.

"Where'd you find him?"

"Bill here found 'im out on Keener's property, in the cornfields. Heading toward the swamps."

"They're all out there. We'll wait 'em out."

"We need to send a message," urged the pattyroller who'd whipped the slave. "Make a public display for all the others so this never happens again."

"This wouldn't have happened if you were doing your job, Henry," Roman said, briefly betraying his own contempt. Henry lowered his head in shame. Roman ignored him, focused his attention on the kneeling man. "I already know what I'm going to do."

Henry waited for an answer but Roman refused to elaborate. He asked to be left alone and then Henry left. He wouldn't be able to see what would happen next. Bill stood, awkwardly.

"You can leave too now."

"What about the money? You said if I caught you this one you'd give me the money for the land."

"You'll get your money. Leave me be."

After they were gone, Roman walked over to the table, paused at each of the devices. The slave continued sitting on his knees, shoulders hunched, his body in clear pain.

"Jeffrey, I know you can't help running away. I've heard of Cartwright's theory. That it's an illness. A type of madness. Annabelle seems to believe this too, which is why she treats you all the way she does. 'They're like children' she tells me, 'they can't help themselves.' She's always carrying on, and I was inclined to believe her, but a child wouldn't do this. A child wouldn't do what you've done."

Mira looked at Jeffrey's face. She recognized his panicked look. She wished she could do something, but she remained frozen in the straw, watching in horror as Roman mused over each of the tools on the table.

"On a trip to Philadelphia, I saw a man with the finest shoes. They were a lustrous black and didn't creak when he walked, and I was so curious about them that I stopped the man in the street and asked him what shop they came from so as to make a purchase for myself. Would you believe"—he paused for effect—"would you believe me when I say that he told me they came from the skin of Negroes? He told me that and I laughed because it sounded preposterous."

Jeffrey squirmed on the ground. He wrestled with the rope, trying desperately to loosen the bind. He didn't try to plead with Roman, nor did he apologize for the revolt in the hope Roman would show some sort of leniency. He laid all his hope on the dim possibility of escape.

"They tied it tight, didn't they?" Roman asked. He appeared unconcerned with Jeffrey's efforts, instead picked a thin blade from the table. "Turns out he was correct. There's a whole market for human leather, and not just for shoes."

"That's what you did to the others, isn't it?" Jeffrey muttered. "I heard the stories, but I didn't think they were true, but they are, aren't they?"

"I'm told that the best leather is right here," Roman said, ignoring Jeffrey's question. He took the blade and pierced it on Jeffrey's thigh, forcing a small pool of blood to form. Jeffrey winced again and Roman smiled.

"A buyer by the name of Aldridge has already paid me because he wants a pair of loafers fashioned from your flesh. Many will pay good money for a piece of you. Your tongue. Organs.

Teeth. Skin. I've gotten so many offers. A man's got to know what his property's worth. So you see, I am going to sell every part of you and all the others. Every piece I can, and whatever's left I'll feed to the dogs. Even after your death you'll still be of use to me. I want you to know that. Even dead I'll have a use for you yet. Don't worry, this will go quickly since I won't have to cauterize the wound. I imagine it'll go quickly for you as well. You'll pass out from the pain soon enough, and your body will fail from the blood loss."

Roman's thumb ran along the smooth exterior of the metal blade. He kneeled before Jeffrey, stared directly into his eyes. He then whispered something to Jeffrey she couldn't hear and Jeffrey closed his eyes, mumbled a few words before quieting. He was still after that, resigned to his fate. Roman pulled a rag out of his pocket and stuffed it into Jeffrey's mouth.

Roman pushed Jeffrey so he was lying on the ground. He stood over him before sitting on his chest to keep him still. He took the knife and pressed it against Jeffrey's face, beginning at the top of his jaw. He was careful not to press too hard. Jeffrey bellowed. Mira wanted to close her eyes, but she knew she had to learn the final piece of the story she'd pushed away. This is what Jesse had meant. *Every day I see I struggle.* She told herself not to look away. This was what was needed from her. To look. To see. She watched in horror as Roman guided the knife around Jeffrey's face, beginning with the fleshier parts along the bottom. She hoped that by the time he'd moved from ear to ear Jeffrey would lose consciousness. Jeffrey writhed, but between his tied arms and the weight of Roman on his chest there wasn't much he could do. However much he squirmed, Roman was stronger, and Roman worked with the skill of someone who'd done this before. He was focused and patient as he slid the blade around Jeffrey's face.

Roman was right. It did not take long before Jeffrey stopped moving, either from passing out from the pain or having finally succumbed to death. Roman briefly stopped at this point, saying a prayer for the spirit who'd passed. When he finished his task, he stood up. All of his clothes were covered in blood. Blood on his pants. Blood on his shirt. Hands dripping with blood. He dropped the knife, unconcerned now if it wasn't within his reach. He stretched his back and the crack of his joints echoed. Then he leaned down and picked on a piece of Jeffrey's face, pulling on the skin as it peeled off. He held it in the air in front of him, this skinned face. Jeffrey's face. It looked thin, like wet paper. Blood fell from the hanging flap into the dirt. Roman let it fall, waiting for the last of it. When the blood had slowed, he brought the flesh near to his own, slowly breathed in the scent. He closed his eyes and inhaled. He took another breath before bringing this mask of skin to his face, layering it on top of his own.

There was more to be done.

When Mira was a girl she had once stood outside while the boy she loved roamed this plantation taking photographs. After, he'd asked her what she'd seen and she couldn't bear to speak it. Some horrors were unspeakable, unimaginable even, but weren't they all until they happened?

While she had waited for him to come back to her, she'd seen a man wearing the stolen face of another. Hidden deep under the straw, Mira saw the man again.

Tools meant for work became seen as weapons. Fingers ran across the sickle's serrated edge to test its sharpness. Clipping shears were cleaned free of their animal hair. They collected what they could to use—the scythes and trowels, rakes and hoes. Any object that glinted in the sun they stole because even a shovel could wound with enough force.

Their days were filled with a different dream. Of sparing none as they crept up the stairs in the hope of finding their masters. To stand in the shadow of the moonlight before they thrusted the metal into the soft flesh. Blood pooling, soaking the fabric of their clothes and sheets. Death would come quick because they'd be quick, for there would be more to meet before their night was through.

Just because you want to doesn't mean you can, their brethren warned when they heard of the plan. You don't know what's in your heart until the moment comes.

In response, their hands gripped the fashioned weapons. Coarse and weathered-looking, with embedded cracks in the skin and thick calluses along the sides, these hands were unremarkable, ordinary, and as they glanced at them they wondered if the fears were true. Yet these were hands that had picked the burrs from cotton as dew stuck to their bloodied fingers. They had stripped tobacco leaves, milked cows, slaughtered hogs, gripped battling blocks, and beat their clothes clean. They had shucked and planted and sowed. They had chopped down trees for firewood and carried the heavy logs through the winter snow so the others wouldn't freeze. They were hands that had helped those who'd suffered the tail of the whip. They had comforted and healed, these hands, and later, for those who'd died, they were the hands to bury the bodies of the lost.

Take one of these hands and bend the fingers into a palm, curling the fingers inward. Bend the thumb until it is against the others, and a hand, once unremarkable, once ordinary, now becomes a fist.

Better to blunt these thoughts instead and be grateful for what you've been given, their brethren tried to convince them, but this was a lie told to justify the refusal of what must be done. No shuck and jive would ever break their chains. They'd never yessir and mistah their way to freedom. Even prayer may have once given hope, but they understood hope was a thing to take. No one would give it. Not someday, not ever, so they would make their someday now. It was time to make it and be free. No one else was going to save them. They were the ones. Always had been and always would be. They were the ones who must save themselves.

XXIV.

Mira screamed, unable to keep it in any longer. Over the years she'd tried so hard to forget his face—the way his hands kept touching the skin to keep it from falling off, the way the skin glistened from blood as it dripped down his neck, how he'd smiled as he licked his lips over the carved flesh. The muscles in Mira's chest tightened. Her throat constricted. She let out as much sound as she could before her body's response from the trauma took over, and then, defensively, she clenched herself into a ball and sobbed.

"Mira? Mira, I'm here. Are you all right? Can you hear me? I'm here. It's Jesse, Mira. Come on, open your eyes and see. It's me."

"Jesse?" Reluctantly, Mira opened her eyes and saw Jesse on the ground beside her. She was no longer in the barn. Roman and his torture devices were gone, gone was Jeffrey's bleeding body. Mira was outside on the grass. The air smelled like the height of summer, the sweet mix of alcohol and pollen. She breathed in the grass below her, the odor of her own sweat, almost choking on the smell of it. It's over, she thought, relaxing for just a moment.

Mira's shovel was only a few feet away. Somehow, she had ended up where she'd started. Maybe she had run back to this spot without realizing. It was not far and she could barely see anything in the dark. The Woodsman Plantation was behind her, the back door closed shut. The window, the one that earlier had beckoned her inside, was dark now. The entire house was dark. Empty and abandoned. Remembering the terror inside, what she'd seen, she backed away on the grass.

"What's wrong?" Jesse kept asking her.

"The light was on," Mira answered, keeping her gaze at the house. "I heard screaming and I—I ran inside, and I saw—"

"You saw what?"

"Did you hear it?" Mira asked instead. "What about Roman? Did you see him?"

"Roman? Mira, what are you talking about?" It took Jesse a couple of seconds to understand, but when he did, he turned solemn. "Tell me what you saw."

"I saw what Roman did," Mira said in a rush. "Oh, it's horrible. All of it is so horrible. I also saw Lucy. They kept her in a cage. I saw one of the parties Roman had where he rented out the women to men of the area. Anyone who could pay. They wore these masks. Oh god, the masks. I know why the slaves tried to fight back, and I saw what happened to the ones Roman caught."

Mira abruptly put the rest together. The graves were empty. Nothing had been there. The slaves had dug those holes for the white men's fun, and those in the sacks were the ones who'd started the revolt. Roman hadn't buried them, instead skinned their bodies and used the flesh as leather. The soft inner thighs and arms used for shoes. The knotted marks of the lash on their backs a decoration for wallets. The masks the men had worn—they'd been made from the slaves he'd wanted punish.

"Did you not see any of it?" Mira asked with a pleading.

"No, I didn't."

They sat there on the grass, both of them exhausted, their bodies hunched over, defeated. "You believe me though. Right? Someone has to believe me."

"I believe you," Jesse said, and relief washed over her.

"Let's get out of here."

Jesse helped her to stand. She wiped what dirt she could from her clothes, a futile effort but she did it anyway.

Far off in the periphery, a cluster of lights glowed bright. Mira's gaze narrowed on them as she feared they were the mob, coming back for them both.

"The mob is coming for you," Mira said. "For us. We need to get out of here but I don't know where to go. If we go back to the entrance we'll be running straight into them."

They stood frozen as the crowd of men grew larger. Their faces were a blur, but she knew who they were. She looked out at the looming crowd and saw the years of men like these inflicting their violence. They would not rest until black bodies lay crumpled below their feet as they stampeded over their broken bones and bruised faces. They carried their pistols close to their chests, ready to fire, and they made their way through the woods searching for Mira and Jesse. Together, the mob was young and old—husky men who huffed with each leap as they tried to keep up, the fitter ones shouting as they ran, sweat running down their flustered faces.

Why had Mira tried to convince such men? Why had she believed there would be any outcome other than this? She should have known, should have seen it, but she saw that they were the devils, the murderers, the true thieves in the night. How many communities had men like these destroyed to rubble, leaving only ash from the burning wreckage as it billowed toward the sky? They escaped to their untouched homes while black people were rounded up on the streets and locked away. The elders left to remember had to be urged to tell of the damage done, too afraid if they spoke it would come to pass again. Bodies beaten, men and women with nooses tied around their necks as they were dragged through the streets. Mira saw the history of her people, of this country, of all the violence forgotten and ignored. It was here again. No, it was always here. What she saw before her could have been this year or last, ten years ago or a hundred. The scene was the same, the story the same, and she knew its ending.

"We could try and wait them out," Jesse offered. "Morning's not too far off, a couple hours, and then—"

And then? Mira had no answer because there was none, not for them. There was nowhere they could escape where the mob wouldn't eventually find them. They were never going to make it to his car. They could hide out in the fields, get down low under the tobacco stalks, and pray they could disappear. Maybe make the mob believe they were gone.

"We're not going to make it until morning, and by then they might have decided to get the police on us too," Mira said, pulling on Jesse's arm. "The river. That's where we need to go."

"What do you think is going to happen when we get there? It's not like we can escape. We don't have a boat. You want to hide in the water?"

The river was where this had all started. Mr. Loomis's body was found by the river and Mira suspected if they could get there, whatever had come for him would come for these men. If Jesse was right, Woodsman's slaves had once escaped to the river, following it to the swamps. If they were going to come back, if they had returned to collect their revenge, then they'd be waiting at the river to start their insurrection. She finally understood that she needed to join in their struggle. Her whole life she'd looked away, but she saw everything clearly now and what she saw was these men, full of unhinged fury, the descendants of a long-soiled line. More pain would come unless she fought. She had to stop them. She would lead them to the river to meet their necessary fate.

"I just have a feeling," Mira told Jesse. "Can you trust me?"

"Yes, I trust you," Jesse said, relenting, and together they made their way to the river.

XXV.

THE WHISPERS FOLLOWED them. They were the whispers of the dead. Of the lost. Of the forgotten. Of the stolen during the night. The whispers of slaves murdered by those who once owned them. Their blood had been spilled on this land, soaking into the fertile soil, enriching the crops that other men bartered and sold. Everything after came from the exploitation of their bodies.

This was what Mira saw. All she could see. The ways in which they'd been harmed. When she looked at the trees, she saw all the bodies hanged from them. Round and round the rope had been tied to the base of the tree. The loop tightened across the neck as someone pulled them up. Fists clenched from their fury. Shouts and cheers as the men hanged. These are the men who would later cloak themselves in white, hide behind white as they crept through the dark. In gangs they came, breaking windows, stealing through doors to steal bodies, taking them away to disappear. Always bodies.

So many had been taken. So many lost. The men and women who'd died on these fields, falling from the work that broke them, only to later be thrown in unmarked graves or sold one last time to the medical hospitals. All that was left of them were these whispers, a cacophony of hushed voices building with every step Mira and Jesse took as they headed across the fields toward the river.

Far off in the distance, Mr. Tatum led a crowd of men. Wild-eyed in search of his justice, followed by the lynching mob in search of blood, all of them in search of Jesse.

"Are they still behind us?" Jesse asked Mira when they reached the tobacco fields. They crouched down low, attempting to hide in the stalks while they caught their breath. Mira stood up slowly.

"They are," she said, as her head hovered over the tops of the stalks. "Although they're moving slower. I guess they figure they have the time."

"We need to get to the river."

"They're too close. There's not enough distance between us and them. I think they'll catch up to us before we get there."

"What should we do?"

"Let's just wait here a little bit more. If we're lucky maybe they'll turn back around."

They both collapsed in the stalks to wait. Mira sat on the ground, her legs splayed out in front of her. Her calves burned, and she massaged the muscles and tendons, hoping the pressure would relieve some of the ache. She briefly stretched, pulling her arms in front of her body and turning her neck from side to side.

After a few minutes, Jesse grew restless and got up to look. "It's dark," he said as he peered a little more above the tobacco stalks to get a better view. "They must have stopped for some reason, maybe figuring out what direction to take? Wait, no—I see Phillip. He's gone into the woods."

Movement in the brush. A glimpse of white. Mira straightened, her attention drawn to what lay before her. Jesse hadn't noticed. It was the woman in white. This time she was close enough that Mira could see her face. Her dark hair fell past her shoulders. She was dressed in a white nightgown that flowed past her knees. The fabric was worn, sheer, but it hadn't been dirtied from the woods. There was something familiar about her. Mira could see it in her eyes, the round shape of them, and in the contours of her face. She knew this woman, felt a kinship with her, and believed she would help them get to safety.

"You're Marceline, aren't you?" Mira asked the woman. She didn't answer. "I know you are. I see my eyes in yours. Can you help us? There are men after us. We're trapped."

"I don't know how we're going to get to the river," Jesse said, not hearing Mira. "Phillip seems to be heading our way—"

The woman retreated farther into the brush. She motioned for Mira to follow. Mira crawled toward her but hesitated, realizing she was about to leave without Jesse.

"Jesse—" Mira began, but the woman stopped her, quickly put a finger to her mouth to let Mira know to be quiet. "We need him to come too," Mira explained, but the woman shook her head.

Following the woman meant she would have to leave Jesse. She didn't want to, but what if this was the way to save both of them? Fear told her to stay, but she had to know what the woman needed to show her. Jesse would understand, and she would find him again.

The woman grew impatient. Seeing Mira would not follow her, she left for the woods. This was Mira's last chance; she had to go now or live with the regret of her inaction. Mira looked at Jesse one last time, waited until his back was turned, and slipped into the brush.

XXVI.

T HE WOMAN DISAPPEARED as soon as Mira left Jesse. Mira called after her as she wandered through the woods, her voice barely above a whisper, too afraid the other men would hear.

She was alone, sweating, tired, and lost once again. She circled around, trying to find the path back to Jesse, but behind her was only darkness.

Above, the moon shone amidst the cloudless night sky, a moon that had once cast its light on the backs of her ancestors as they escaped for home, and she found a comfort in the thought. The same moon that had guided them would see her through.

She pushed the branches away from her face to find her way. The distant warbling hoots of barn owls echoed in the hollows of the trees. A subtle breeze came along, chilling the sweat on her skin. Mira continued, losing her sense of time the longer she went. She feared if she stopped she would give up altogether, collapsing on the ground and hiding until morning, but she'd hid her entire life. Enough now. Enough. She had to keep going, to find what the woman hoped to show her. She would not look away, whatever horror awaited. This time, she would not look away.

A fly buzzed in front of her face and she swatted at it. Another came. Another. The low buzz of their wings filled her ears. Another crawled on the back of her neck. She shook her head and waved her arms. The buzzing grew louder and Mira had to put her hands to her ears to block out the noise. The flies multiplied as Mira walked. She hurried, desperate to get away, moving fast until, at long last, the buzzing suddenly stopped.

Shadows moved in the distance. Jesse. She must be close to where she'd left him. Maybe he'd seen she'd gone and had started to look for her. She walked closer and the glow of a light appeared. Mira went toward it, and as her eyes adjusted she saw that the man wasn't Jesse, but someone else, and Mira immediately ducked down in the grass.

Whoever it was, he had paused to wipe the front of his brow with his shirt. He heard Mira's rustling and stopped, flashed in her direction, but Mira hid her head between her arms and crouched into a ball to keep from being seen. When she looked up again, she saw the back of the man as he searched the brush, hunting.

"Celine? You out here?" someone whispered, their voice low but scratchy. "I know you're there. I saw you. I'm going to find you sooner or later so come on out. Celine?"

A fox pattered through the woods. As it moved it made a series of barking noises followed by a howl. The man stopped. He followed the sound, jerking his body in one direction and then another. Soon enough, he turned around and she saw that the man was Phillip.

"Mira, what are you doing down there? Come on, get up."

She hadn't seen the gun at first, but as soon as he'd faced her she saw it in his hand. Mira stood up slowly. She was cautious of her movements, not wanting to startle him. He had the expression of a wild animal trapped in terror, and the cagey behavior of a man being hunted. His eyes, wide and bloodshot, twitched as he kept shifting his attention from her to the woods.

"I heard you calling for Celine," Mira sputtered out, a reflexive response in the moment. Phillip's eyes darted at her before turning to another sound he heard in the woods. He twitched again, his hands shaking as he held the gun.

"I saw her. Or, I thought I did. She had on her dress. She

looked beautiful. All dressed in white. Glowing almost. I don't understand. I had to make sure."

"Phillip, Celine is dead."

"No, she's not. I *saw* her. Who did I see if it wasn't her? She's tormenting me. That's what this is. She said she changed her mind about the wedding, didn't want to marry me after all. She said she was leaving me. Said she wasn't happy. Wasn't *happy*." He sputtered out the word, refusing to hide his contempt. "After all I'd done for her. I'd given her everything she wanted and she still wasn't happy."

"You're the one who killed her," Mira whispered, backing away in the shock of the realization. She would have screamed it if she could. Called him the monster that he was. Because of his money, Phillip had fashioned himself to believe he was a man unlike the rest, but he was just the same as them, ready to taste the blood of any who dared to believe they were better than him.

Phillip shook his head at her. "No, I— It was an accident, and she's just hurt. She's alive—I saw her. She's out here somewhere. Playing a trick on me. She's not— No, I saw her."

"No one's here, Phillip. Celine's dead. You killed her," Mira repeated.

"It was an accident," Phillip shrieked. He quickly attempted to regain his composure but it was no use. Beads of sweat fell down his face, soaked his shirt collar. He wiped his face. "It's not what you think. You have to know. Last night she came to visit me and said it was over. Said she'd tell people in the morning, but after she left she didn't go back to her room. She came out to the woods. I followed her, wanting to see where she would go. I thought she was meeting someone. Maybe that boy. That had to be the reason. It was the only thing that made sense. I wanted to see who she would leave me for. When I found her, we argued. That's all it was at first. I grabbed her arm and she tried pulling away, but I wanted to know where she was going. I asked her to tell me and she laughed again, and I hit her. Just once, but she—

---

jerked back, tripped, fell. It was an accident, and I thought she was dead but she's not. I saw her. She's hiding in these woods. I'm going to find her. I couldn't let her leave. Not without her telling me why I wasn't enough. Why giving her everything wasn't enough."

"You killed Celine and you're letting everyone think Jesse did it. You can't do this. I won't let you."

"Let me?" Phillip said, raising his eyebrows, and Mira understood her mistake. He gripped the gun. "You're not going to let me do anything."

Phillip's fingers locked on the gun, his muscles tense. Mira saw his reddened knuckles. "Maybe you're right," she said slowly, emphatically. "Celine's out here somewhere." She knew there was no other way out of this, not anymore. Why wouldn't Phillip shoot her and leave her for dead? What had she known of Phillip, after all, to make her think otherwise? She knew nothing of the man he was or was supposed to be, knew nothing of whatever terror he was capable of. All she knew was that she was alone in the woods, too afraid to scream because who knew what the mob would do if they found her.

"Let's look for her," Mira said soothingly.

She braced herself, ready to bolt the second he was distracted enough. She would run to whatever she was meant to find, but until that moment she stood frozen, her heart racing, her eyes refusing to blink lest it be a catalyst for Phillip to direct his rage. She counted—one, two, three, four—in the hope the counting would keep her steady.

The whispers returned, a slow build cresting into a cacophonous harmony. "Do you hear that?" Mira asked.

"Of course I hear it. The whispering—it won't stop."

Mira called to Phillip but he had stopped listening. His hands swatted at the air around him. "Get away from me! Get away! I can't see!" he howled, but Mira couldn't see anything, only Phillip as he scratched and clawed at his skin. His nails dug deep into his flesh, hard enough to draw blood, but he didn't stop. He scratched at his eyes, pulled on his clothes, ripping the fabric, revealing his pale skin underneath. He scratched until reddened streaks marked his chest and arms, but still he wouldn't stop.

In horror, Mira watched as Phillip continued to damage his body. Nothing he did seemed to be enough to stop whatever he believed was attacking him. He shouted again, but this time the words came out in a garbled gasp. Worn out from his efforts, Phillip fell to his knees, succumbing. He loosened the grip of his gun and it fired as it hit the ground.

Blood pooled around Phillip's body as he lay silent and still. Far off, Mira heard the rumble of men as they gathered together and headed toward the sound of the shot.

XXVII.

J ESSE FOUND MIRA shortly after he heard the shot. He stumbled to her from the brush and froze when he saw Phillip's body. He turned his head when he first saw it, horrified, but looked again, as if to be sure of what his eyes showed him. Mira thought he was going to vomit as he leaned forward, but he put both hands on his knees. "What happened? I turned around and you were gone."

The whispering had long since faded, ending as soon as Phillip hit the ground. The ghosts had come for him because he'd refused to see how his history, and his life, were just as entangled in the roots of this place as their own.

Mira thought of the woman. Marceline, her ancestor. Without her, she would never have known her story, the way in which she was tethered to this land. Also, without her she might never have known what Phillip had done to Celine.

"Marceline led me here."

As Mira said her name, she felt the relief of a sigh as she called her into being. Speaking her name meant she was more than a specter, to say it meant she had existed, that like all of them she had been real. "Marceline wanted to show me," Mira repeated, pointing to Phillip. "Phillip killed Celine."

A splatter of Phillip's blood had gotten on the front of her clothes. A drip of it fell down the side of her face and neck and she wiped it off in a panic.

"He did it. That's why she went missing. He came out to the woods because Marceline let him see her, and he thought she was Celine. He was trying to finish what he started. He'd hoped to blame her murder on you."

"Why?" Jesse asked, and his question hurt her heart. *Why* is the question we always ask, she thought, when we know what the answer is. They both knew why. Phillip understood the power his whiteness held and Jesse had been the easy target. Blame Jesse and everyone would believe it. Saying the lie would be enough to make it true. Phillip had done it for no other reason than he knew he could.

Both Jesse and Mira had spent their lives asking why, but it was a waste of a question. Instead of why, they needed to ask themselves what they should do.

"If they find us here they'll think we both had something to do with this," Jesse said weakly.

"There's nowhere left to go. Maybe if we could get to the river—"

"Nothing's at the river, Mira," Jesse said in a mix of anger and desperation. "They're coming, and once they find Phillip they're going to think we murdered them both. All they'll need to do is see it and be convinced. It doesn't matter if it's a lie. They'll believe it and it'll be enough. We can't get out of this."

Mira pictured the men joined together. The pounding of their footsteps grew. They licked their lips in anticipation, spittle dripping from their mouths as they jeered. They moved in lockstep, aligned with a sole interest. Their heavy steps thundered. Their hunt had been the end all along, the culmination of what was always meant to be, but Mira held to the belief that there was another possibility. She could see the lights flashing bright between the trees, growing larger as the men closed in on them. These men had a reason for their violence now. Celine was gone. Dead. In the end that's all that mattered. All it took. A white woman dead and gone. Her body lying host to the insects of the woods. These men would want justice, or revenge, and they wanted to be the ones to inflict it.

The men came closer, close enough for Mira to hear their calls.

"This won't end," Jesse said softly. "I've got to meet them."

"What? No. They'll kill you. That's how it'll end. They'll string you up."

"I know."

"We need to find a way to lead them to the river. It's the only way."

"There is no other way. Never has been. I'm tired, Mira. Aren't you? I'm tired of all this. I can't do this anymore."

Weariness had aged him, but it had also changed who he was. Gone was the boy, bashful and sincere over the things he loved. The one who was self-conscious, yet daring when he needed to be, like how he'd been the one to stick up for Celine and Mira when they were kids. He was someone who knew what he deserved, and what he deserved was a better world than this.

The boy Mira had known was still there underneath, and he'd come back to her; they just had to survive the night. Not only this one but every one after, and maybe in the midst of that, they could find a way to live.

Mira reached for his hand and clasped it. His skin felt hot. She wanted him to hold on to her for just a little longer. A little longer and maybe they would be saved.

"We just have to keep going. We have a chance."

"No, Mira. We don't."

"We have to try," she said.

"Even if we get out, even if we make it somehow, they'll come for me anyway. They already think I killed Celine, and this is their proof. It'll be like with Mr. Loomis. They'll lock me up. I can't go through it again. I can't. They're never going to stop. No matter what I do they're never going to stop. At least if I meet them it'll be my choice. That's got to count for something."

"You're giving up."

"It's not giving up. I'm the one they want, so at least if I go, then maybe I can distract them and you can get out of here. Get out of this place and never come back. Promise me you'll do that. Go and don't look back."

"No, I won't do it. I won't. We're together now, don't you see? It won't be like before."

"It's not your fault what happened, or mine. It's just—I don't know. It's the world. You got to let me go, Mira. Who knows, maybe I'll make it," he said, and he released her hand.

He smiled one last time, content in his decision, and his face showed the glimmer of the boy she'd once known—confident and optimistic, someone who believed in what could be instead of what was.

"Jesse," Mira whispered, but before she could say anything else, could plead with him to wait a little longer, he bolted.

"I'm here," he shouted at the air before veering in the direction of the river. He ran, screaming, hoping the noise would get their attention and they'd start after him, making way for Mira to get out of the fields and off the property for good.

"I see him! There he is!"

The mob followed Jesse. They chased after him in their wild fury, their anger fueling them onward. It looked to be a crowd of fifty, if not more. Many carried rifles, their hands raising them high in the air as they trampled through the grass. Others held a hand on their hip as they ran, ready at any moment to aim their gun and shoot. They carried stolen lanterns taken from the plantation to light their way.

As they ran toward Jesse, one managed to get ahead of the rest, and when he'd gained enough speed, when at any moment he'd have finally caught up to Jesse, he stopped in his tracks. His hand pulled the pistol from his hip's holster. He fired a series of reckless shots, not even trying to aim, believing he'd get his target.

The others behind him suddenly stopped too, each of them aiming and firing.

Bullets rattled in the air, one after the other. *Pop, pop, pop.* Like firecrackers Mira couldn't see. Jesse ran faster, hoping with speed he'd escape the bullets, but there were too many. *Pop, pop, pop,* they continued, and down Jesse went, falling, falling, and as his body collided with the dirt, Mira heard their clamoring cheers.

XXVIII.

THEY WERE LIKE dogs. All grunt and growl. A pack of wolves ready for the take. Yellow-teeth-filled grins as they hollered. They jumped and raised their rifles and pistols in the air, arms stretched high like a praise toward a god they believed would one day welcome them, but there was no god here, not for this. They shouted *yes* and *woo-boy* and even *hallelujah*, some of them, grateful they could stop their chase.

These were the men Mira had feared her whole life. They were what her mother had tried to warn her of, to keep her away from. They were the dangerous ones, the ones who would slip into your room at night to inflict their terror. They were the cross burners, the ones who turned the magnolias and the oaks Mira loved into lynching trees. They were the ones who haunted her nightmares. She watched as they gathered, this mob of men full of ecstatic anger, as they came for Jesse.

"We got him!"

"Is this the one who did it? We need the one who did it."

"There was another one, wasn't there?"

"Must have went toward the river. Maybe we can catch them before they get to the swamps."

"Let's deal with this one first!"

The men stretched their necks and cracked their knuckles for what was next. One held a rope, his fingers stroking the fibers that had been twisted together. His hands were at the ready, and at the first signal the rope would be tied into a noose, tied around a neck, and tied around the base of a tree.

"What'll we do with this one? Take him back?"

"Not yet, I say we should do what we like."

They soon would perform what'd been done hundreds of times. Thousands. The ritual this country perfected. They would take this body apart, limb from limb, each of them marking their own pieces to keep.

Twenty-five cents for a fragment of bone. Ten cents for the bit of liver. *How much for the heart? How much?* they would cry, their greedy hands grabbing, each of them wanting their choice. They would touch and fondle the flesh as it was bartered and sold. They would yank the teeth from the jaw, laughing at the crack of bones. They would take. They wanted to devour. They wanted to consume. When they were done, they would set what remained on fire.

No need to count the ways a body had fallen, how many contorted expressions appeared on the face of a body whose soul had passed. No need to count the number of crows that circled a burning carcass after the flames had smoldered, ready to peck on what these men had left. No need to count because Mira knew, the number haunting her bones like it did so many, like it did all who'd lived on.

Somewhere was a bridge where bodies were hung. Somewhere a tree, its branches twisted in the form of an ache. Somewhere grass grew from land soiled with death. Somewhere was a house built from blood, its prominent columns once a sign of wealth, of prominence, now become an altar. Oh, how beautiful. Oh, how lovely.

Somewhere were other men just like these.

A rumbling came that none of the men recognized. Slack-jawed, their bodies frozen, they stared out toward the darkness ahead, leaning to see the shadows stir. Beyond the trees something lurked for them, whispered just for them.

"What are you waiting for? Quit pussyfooting around. Let's get this over with."

"Wait—did you hear that?"

"Do you see something? Something's moving in the woods."

One man stepped forward, going ahead of the others. He was tall and lumbering. Arrogance made him unafraid, or maybe it was impatience, but after a few steps, even he stopped. He heard a sound that made him pause. "Who's there?" he shouted, voice hoarse but booming. Hidden in the loudness was a slight tremble of unease because he too recognized that just beyond their reach was something lurking in the dark, a threat, one worthy of their attention. "Show yourself," he dared, and he raised his rifle toward the unseen, ready to fire.

He would count to three before firing his shot, and shoot he would. He wouldn't be the only one; his fellow men would soon follow. Together, they would blast ammunition into the night, not caring who they maimed or murdered. They stood waiting in hungry anticipation for their moment, their thick fingers grazing the triggers as he called out each number.

"One! Two! Three!"

A shot bristled through the trees. Everyone listened for the sound of pain, for a howl or a moan, but nothing could be heard.

"Jimmy, let's just take him and go."

"No!" Jimmy shouted back, his face reddened from fury. He wouldn't be made a fool of, not this night, and not wanting any more seconds to pass for them all to change their minds, he ventured in the direction of his shot. The others watched him as he went into the dark.

"Is he coming back?"

"How long we going to wait here for him to come back?"

"He's got to come back, right?"

"Who's going after him?"

"We can't leave him, can we?"

"Well, what are we going to do?"

The minutes passed by as the men decided what to do, hoping he'd return, their decision made for them, and they could continue. Fear made them shift their weight from foot to foot, some of them paced, some of them spit out the watery gobs that had accumulated in their mouths from their chew. *Pfff,* they each went, taking turns moistening the ground with their tobacco-flecked saliva.

"What was that?"

"Was that him?"

"Could have been an animal."

"Sounded human to me. Sounded like Jimmy."

"What do you think happened?"

"You want to be the one to go and find out?"

Would they do it? Would they go after one of their own? The men stood uneasy. They kept their focus on the darkness before them, listening for another sound that would help guide them in what to do, but they were surrounded by the quiet stillness of the night. They were afraid, somehow knowing if they followed, they would not come back.

"To hell with it."

"This ain't worth dying over."

"Let's get out of here."

One after the other they turned in the opposite direction, leaving it all behind. Each and every one disappeared into the darkness. Mira watched until they faded from view.

When they were caught, punishment was swift and severe in its execution. Judge and jury called for their heads to be spiked onto poles and placed for miles all along the roads, a premonition for others to see that this would be the future for any who tried to do the same. Laws were created to silence the rumblings. Any who carried the look of insurrection were beaten. They were wounded and maimed. For decades after, the histories were told of those who had rebelled. Of Southampton. Of the German Coast. Of Stono. They told of what happened to their forefathers—how they were either burned to ash or cut into pieces and bartered off to the bidder with the most expensive want. Fingers chopped and sold like carnival souvenirs. Some men believed if the bones of their dead slaves were consumed you could have their powers. Their bodies a Sunday prayer. Their bodies a communion as the bones were milled to a fine powder. Organs torn from flesh, saved in jars to keep.

Those who remained continued on with their work. Fear made them forget, and so each day they suffered themselves closer to death. They longed to let go, to cast down their tools, to hear the clank of metal as it crashed to the ground and let the fields rot from neglect. They dreamed of the tide turning but knew it would never come, and with this knowledge they watched as their brothers and sisters continued to fall, watched their arms flail and knees buckle as they fell to the ground. They watched, saying nothing, as they hid their faces and closed their eyes. Every day loosening further to the reality before them.

At night before they slumbered off, they remembered the stories once told. As they held them in their minds, they swore they could hear whispers—indistinct at first, always saying their names, a susurration, asking for them to hear.

XXIX.

AFTER THE MEN were gone, Mira ran to Jesse. When Mira got to him she saw his face was pressed down in the grass, his body unmoving. He was so still that she was hesitant to touch him at first, not wanting to feel if his skin was cold and have her fear be confirmed. She didn't see any blood, no pool of it around him, and, taking a breath, she touched his back, felt for the holes, but there was nothing. She searched harder, reaching under his shirt, feeling his sweaty skin, but she couldn't find any wounds, no mark anywhere.

Mira put her hand in front of his face and waited. His breath was sparse but there, and the wash of relief that suddenly overcame her took her aback. At least he was alive, she thought.

"You shouldn't have left," Mira told Jesse, shouting it, too tired and frustrated to hold back any longer. "We could have made it. We could have made it together."

She looked around her, trying to gauge how far they were from the house, but she had no idea where they were. If she were to leave without Jesse, she didn't trust she'd be able to find help soon enough. Looking out onto the expanse before her, she wasn't sure if she'd be able to find her way at all, not without sunlight, not without anything for her to see the path.

Her arms weren't strong enough to carry him. Unconscious, he was nothing but deadweight. She pulled, was able to drag him a few feet, but fatigue set in and she had to stop. She kneeled back on the ground. "Jesse, can you hear me? You've got to wake up. Are you hurt? Are you shot? If you're shot, tell me where."

Jesse didn't answer. Not knowing what else to do, she lifted his body so that he was lying on his back, wanting to check the front of him for signs he'd been hit. It took her a couple of times to do it, and when she got him over she was out of breath between that and attempting to pull him. She settled down to rest. After a moment she leaned over him and tucked her hand under the front of his shirt, feeling once again for a wound.

"Trying to cop a feel?" Jesse whispered. He gave a choked cough and tried to stand. Mira reached to help. The right side of his face had a streak of mud from where he'd hit the ground. He touched his cheek and winced as he wiped the mud away, revealing a bloody patch of skin underneath. "Jesus," he said, wincing again from the pain.

"No, I—" Mira blushed, jerked her hands away from Jesse's body.

Jesse saw her embarrassment and smiled. "I was just joking."

"I don't understand. You fell," Mira said, feeling glad and astonished he was okay. She'd seen it all so clearly, heard the thundercrack of the shots, saw him as he leapt toward the ground, and yet Jesse sat before her, only slightly hurt but alive.

"No kidding." Jesse touched his face again. His fingers lightly tapped the skin, trying to inspect if his face was swollen. "I'm still feeling the pain of it."

"I thought— Are you sure you're okay? You weren't shot?"

"I tripped. That's why I fell. Otherwise I would have kept running. I would have run and never stopped until I got to the river, but I tripped and hit my head. Why would you think I got shot?"

"The men chasing you—" Mira said, but Jesse stared at her blankly. "They fired shots. You didn't hear them? You didn't see?" Jesse's silence answered her question. "You haven't seen any of it, have you?" she asked, and Jesse turned away, unable to look her in the face.

"I thought I did," Jesse confessed. "You were so sure that I believed you, and then with the mob I got so scared at the thought it was happening again—that I'd be blamed again, but no. I never saw anything. Or, I don't think I did, but it doesn't make sense. I don't understand why I couldn't see any of it and you could."

"You said we all had to reckon with our past. I had to too."

Mira pieced together the story of what had been shown to her. The Woodsmans and all the horrors done to his slaves. The night of the failed revolt. The mob of men, ones she'd mistakenly thought were after Jesse, had been hunting the slaves who escaped. They'd given up their search out of the fear of what may have happened to one of their own.

Mira looked in the direction from where Jimmy disappeared, out toward the river. The men had not wanted to follow him there. The river held one final piece that she needed to know. She got up from the ground, wiped the dirt off the front of her jeans. "It's not over. We still need to get to the river," she said, and Jesse nodded.

They hiked in the direction of the sound of the rustling water. Mira made her breath as sparse as she could, worried that if she exhaled too hard she'd disrupt whatever vision the ghosts might have wanted to show her. She led the way, Jesse not far behind her, each of them cautious of their steps as they walked through the woods.

"I think I hear it," she said after they'd gone about another mile. Jesse was silent, listening. The sound of the river was there, slightly hidden among the chorus of other inhabitants of the woods—the crickets' chirps, the movement of deer or raccoons as their bodies snuck through the brush—but underneath was the rustling of water as it flowed, making its way east toward the swamps.

With the rise of dawn approaching, they continued along,

Mira hurrying in the hope of getting there before light, and after walking a few more feet they came upon it. "We made it," Jesse said once they'd reached the edge of the riverbank.

"Yeah, we did." Mira watched in anticipation the ripples in the water, waiting to see what else might be shown to her, but nothing else came. She trod closer to the riverbank, fighting the urge to sink her feet into the soft earth as she stepped farther in, to lower herself into the water and be hit with its shocking coldness as she let it cover her body, her face, as she sank farther down, but she would not be cleansed of this night. No salvation existed in this water but in what lay ahead.

"Hey, Mira, you see that floating? I can't make it out, but it looks like— Do you see? What is that?"

Jesse pointed to a few feet away. Mira's eyes followed, and there, floating along the edge, was Mr. Tatum's body. Mira tensed, watching, waiting, not knowing what to do as Mr. Tatum bobbed in the water. As if the river knew, the current picked up, and before either of them could speak, it was carrying Mr. Tatum's body down into the water, carrying it on, until it had disappeared.

"Do you think—" Jesse stopped.

I do," Mira said. "We don't have to worry about Mr. Tatum anymore. Not Mr. Tatum or Phillip. The ghosts aren't coming back either. At least, not for me. They've shown me what I needed to see."

They made their way back to the main part of the plantation. By the time they'd left the woods, it was almost morning. Around them, the grounds were empty. All the guests had long since gone. What remained were remnants from their day's revelry. Leftover food smooshed in dirt. Drained bottles of champagne tucked among the grass. Flowers wilted, their petals blowing in the humid breeze. Broken bits of glass crunched beneath Mira's feet as she stopped to catch her breath. A few feet away a copy of the wedding program lay crumpled on the ground. Mira reached down to pick it up and that's when she noticed the trampled grass leading back from where they came. She flashed back to the crowd of guests who'd ventured off in search of Celine. How they'd laughed while holding their phones, taking photos with each other as they gallivanted off into the woods. She wondered if they'd met the same fate as Phillip and Mr. Tatum.

Mira dropped the program. "Let's go. When the police come they're going to see all this for what it was—a dispute between Phillip, Celine, and her father. We can leave and forget about all of it."

"Not all of it," Jesse said. His hand wrapped around hers and it was almost as before, back when they were young. Honeysuckle days, the air fragrant and heady. Jesse having gathered bunches of the wild flowers from the edge of the woods. Him in his T-shirt and cutoff jeans holding the bouquet to give her. The frizz of his Afro. His toothy grin. The two of them eating peaches, freshly bought. The sticky juice as it ran down her fingers, glistening her lips, and the taste of its sweet tang long after the twilight hour of their day's end.

But Jesse had been right. He was not the boy she'd once known, not anymore. He was different and so was she, the past having haunted the arc of their lives, shaping who they had become. They needed to learn how to love not who they once thought each other to be, but who they were now. Before any of that could be possible though, she needed to finally tell him everything, all she'd seen, and she would begin with that first day they'd come here.

Up ahead, the gate waited for them, the metal glinting from the burgeoning morning light. As the sun crested along the horizon, its heat warmed her back. She turned to witness its gold glow filtering through the trees, ready to make the world anew.

Soon it would be morning, and those left behind would pre-
pare for another day. Soon they'd gather together, readying
themselves to begin. With the clang of the bell they'd move
through the grounds to take each of their positions. We will
say their names now—there's Tom the butcher as he drains a
hog, his hands bloody as he prepares meat for the smokehouse.
Patty, as she launders the sheets. The slap, slap, slap *her hands*
make as she grips the battling blocks and sticks and beats them
against the fabrics to clean. See Rufus as he tends to the horses
in the barn. He brushes their coats to a smooth shine. See Susan
as she cares for the garden, her hands clawing into the earth
as she pulls vegetables out to be cooked. See Sam as he builds
spinning wheels and parts of looms, his hands rugged and
worn from the wooden splinters his arthritic fingers can never
pick out. See the blacksmith. See the cook. See the younger
girls as they churn milk into butter. Despite the soreness in
their arms they keep their motions consistent, never stopping
or slowing until they see the creamy froth. See the field hands
as they toil with the crops, their thin cotton shirts and trousers
already sweated through from the early rising heat. They get
in a rhythm as they sing their work songs, their voices a build-
ing hum. See them as they work. They repeat their motions,
ones they've done hundreds of times, and on this day, like all
those that have been before, they will begin again, performing
their roles for all who've come to see.

ACKNOWLEDGMENTS

To those who knew before I ever could believe—

First and foremost, to my agent, Monika Woods, who has had such an unwavering faith in this book and in me. You told me during our first phone call that I was worth investing in. Thank you for everything you've done.

To my editor Amber Oliver, who has been the biggest advocate, who managed to see what I was trying to do and knew how to push me to make the book better.

To my editor Mary Gaule for your support and enthusiasm.

To the entire team at Harper Perennial who have put such care into the production of this book.

To my friends, colleagues, and teachers: Brandi Wells, A. D. Carson, Lance Morosini, A. A. Balaskovits, Michael Nye, Gordy Sauer, Nick Potter, Erin Potter, Joe Aguilar, Kate McIntyre, Stevie Devine, Brandon Hobson, Alex Marzano-Lesnevich, Nick White, Scott Garson, Elissa Gabbert, Hairee Lee, Myfanwy Collins, Megan Giddings, Rion Scott, Matt Salesses, Marc Conquest, Nicole Conquest, Gina Hauskenecht, Melissa Sodeman, Amber Shaw, Kate Aspengren, Margaret LeMay, Rick Reiken, Pamela Painter, Maria Flook, Anand Prahlad, and Trudy Lewis.

Lastly, to my family for all their love.

—This book is for all of you.

ABOUT THE AUTHOR

LaTanya McQueen has an MFA from Emerson College, a PhD from the University of Missouri, and was the Robert P. Dana Emerging Writer Fellow at Cornell College. She is an assistant professor of English and creative writing at Coe College in Iowa.